The Rock and Roll Brontë Series

by Tracy Neis

🎵 🎵 🎵

Mr. R - A Rock and Roll Romance

A modern reimagining of *Jane Eyre*

🎵 🎵 🎵

Restless Spirits

An Alternate Take on

Wuthering Heights and *Agnes Grey*

🎵 🎵 🎵

Wildfell Summer

A magical mystery trip through the pages of

The Tenant of Wildfell Hall

🎵 🎵 🎵

Nowhere Girl

Inspired by an unfinished novel fragment

by Charlotte Brontë

Praise for *Mr. R*

Looking for a great summer read? I loved *Mr. R – A Rock & Roll Romance* by Tracy Neis. This modern retelling of *Jane Eyre* surprised and delighted me. For me, I know a book is great when I don't want it to end, and can't stop thinking about it after I've finished. That's what happened when I read *Mr. R*.

—*Syrie James, bestselling author of "The Secret Diaries of Charlotte Brontë"*

I really enjoyed *Mr. R*. Many of the tales of life on the road rang true. I laughed at times, I cried a couple of times, and I really wanted to find out how it ended. I also enjoyed the sly Beatles and contemporary music references that popped up from time to time.

—*Tim Neely, author and editor of 30+ books on record collecting, including "The Goldmine British Invasion Record Price Guide" and "Warman's Beatles Field Guide"*

Mr. R was a page-turner for me. I was so invested in the story and wanted to know how all of the conflicts would resolve. And everything was wrapped up in a believable and emotional way. I thought this was a wonderful retelling—especially for its focus on the character of Rochester.

—*The Eyre Guide Blog*

Praise for *Restless Spirits*

Restless Spirits is an engaging and enjoyable read with plenty of nods to the Brontës and their lives and works...there are some serious Stephen King vibes going on initially [too]...I loved the merging of two very different storylines and the spin Neis puts on it. Reader, I really enjoyed this one, and I actually think it's better than *Mr. R.*

—Nicola Friar, author of
The Brontë Babe Blog

First and foremost, *Restless Spirits* is fun. There are many in-jokes for Brontë fans, but one doesn't have to be a devotee to get the humor...And then there's music. I enjoyed this fun read.

—Denise Longrie, author of
"By Firelight - A Guide to Speculative Fiction before 1900"

WILDFELL SUMMER

By Tracy Neis

A magical mystery trip into the pages of
Anne Brontë's
The Tenant of Wildfell Hall

Wildfell Summer
by Tracy Neis

Published by the author
All rights reserved.
Copyright © 2021 Tracy Neis
The characters in this book are fictitious. Any similarity to actual persons, living or dead, is purely coincidental and not intended by the author.

This book is protected under the copyright laws of the United States of America. Any reproduction or other unauthorized use of the material or artwork herein is prohibited without the express written permission of the publisher and author.

Cover and author illustrations by:
Karen Neis

Summary: A member of a mythical 1960's-era British Invasion pop band travels into the pages of Anne Brontë's classic novel "The Tenant of Wildfell Hall."

Library of Congress Cataloging-in-Publishing Data
Library of Congress Control Number: 2021905177
Neis, Tracy
Wildfell Summer / Tracy Neis

Neis Family Publications
Paperback Book ISBN: 978-1-7343600-4-2

*To all of my friends
who have raised a glass with me,*

*and to Ron Cree
who lives on in the pages of his book.*

Cast of Characters

The Pilots:

Gerry Enis, drummer
Eddie Rochester, rhythm guitarist and lyricist
Jim McCudden, pianist and Eddie's songwriting partner
Tony Wright, lead singer and lead guitarist
Pete Cooper, bassist (a newcomer to the band)
Emmett Poole, the Pilots' manager
Alan Poole, Emmett's younger brother and the band's errand boy

Tenant of Wildfell Hall Characters:

Gilbert Markham, a gentleman farmer from Yorkshire
Mrs. Markham and Rose, Gilbert's mother and sister
Eliza Millward, Gilbert's beautiful neighbor; clergyman's daughter
Frederick Lawrence, Gilbert's irritable neighbor
Helen Graham (Helen Huntington), the tenant of Wildwood Hall
Arthur Huntington, an alcoholic aristocrat
Ralph Hattersley, one of Arthur's drinking buddies
Walter Hargrave, one of Arthur's drinking buddies
Milicent Hargrave, Walter's sister; Helen's friend; later Ralph's wife
Lord Lowborough, one of Arthur's drinking buddies
Anabella Lowborough, a high society flirt
Mr. Grimsby, one of Arthur's drinking buddies
Young Arthur, the son and heir of Arthur Huntington

Available for Sale:

Pilots 1967 Tour Program

Box of 34 historic rock-and-roll tour programs.
Found at Vernon Manor during renovations to remodel the
former luxury hotel into an apartment building.
Near mint condition.
Front and back pictures of the program follow.
All bids considered for both individual programs and the lot.
Interested parties should contact:

Jack Halford
The Belvedere Corporation
400 Oak Street
Cincinnati, OH 45219

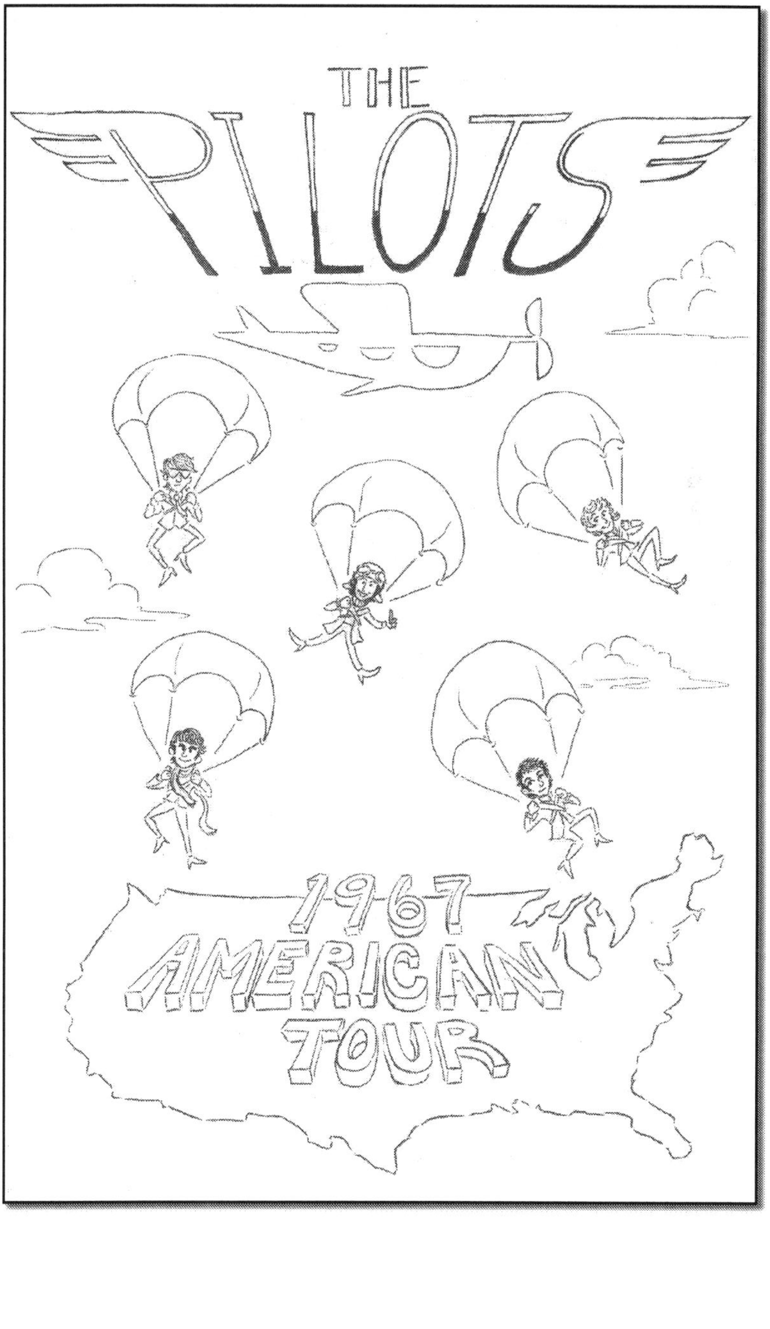
THE
PILOTS
1967
AMERICAN
TOUR

THE PILOTS

Boston, Mass.
New York City, N.Y.
Philadelphia, Pa.
Baltimore, Md.
Atlanta, Ga.
New Orleans, La.
Houston, Tex.
Austin, Tex.
Dallas, Tex.
Kansas City, Mo.
St. Louis, Mo.
Cincinnati, Ohio
Cleveland, Ohio
Toledo, Ohio
Detroit, Mich.
Chicago, Ill.
Milwaukee, Wis.
Minneapolis, Minn.
Denver, Colo.
Phoenix, Ariz.
Tucson, Ariz.
San Diego, Calif.
Los Angeles, Calif.
San Francisco, Calif.
Seattle, Wash.

*A crowd of people turned away.
But I just had to look,
Having read the book.
I'd love to turn you on.*

— *John Lennon and Paul McCartney
"A Day in the Life"*

Chapter One

New Orleans, Louisiana — June, 1967

"That's very good, son. Now cough once more, if you please."

The physician moved his stethoscope to the right and pressed it firmly against his patient's back.

Gerry Enis coughed as directed, then lowered his head and released a rasping sigh.

Dr. Harlan Berger slipped his stethoscope off his ears, positioned himself in front of the ailing pop star, and crossed his arms.

"You're suff'rin' from a case of acute bron-*chah*-tis," he informed Gerry. "Antibiotics prob'ly won't help much, since as like as not your ailment is *vah*-ral in origin. But I can give you something to ease the inflammation in your lungs. And some pow'rful cough syrup too. I reckon you'll be needin' some relief."

Gerry's manager Emmett Poole nodded. "How much longer do you suppose he'll be under the weather?" he asked the doctor, his crisp English accent contrasting sharply with the physician's soft Southern drawl. "My drummer's been ill for some time now already."

The doctor furrowed his brow. "Just how long has he been showin' symptoms?"

Emmett frowned. "Well, he picked up a cough right after our first gig on this tour. In Boston, that was, about a week-and-a-half ago. I gave him some menthol sweets to suck on when he performed on *The Ed Sullivan Show* the next evening—I didn't want him coughing on the telly. He seemed a bit better at our stops in Philadelphia and Baltimore, but he took a turn for the worse after our concert in Atlanta on Wednesday, and he's been coughing ever since."

"That's an awful lot of travelin'," Dr. Berger noted. "No wonder this boy can't recover his strength. He needs some rest."

Emmett sighed theatrically. "Well, he has tonight off. Though he's scheduled to perform tomorrow evening with his bandmates at the 'Big Easy Boogie and Blues Fest'."

"One *naht* is hardly enough time to fight off an infection this strong," Harlan Berger replied with a shake of his head. He pulled a notepad and pen out of the pocket of his white lab coat and started scribbling.

"I'm writin' your boy some prescriptions," he informed Emmett. "The pharmacy downstairs can fill them for you on your way out. I'm givin' him *two* kinds of cough syrup. One's for ev'ryday use. The other'll come in a small vial for this young man to drink right before he goes on-stage tomorrow *naht*. It's laced with a high dose of codeine and should suppress his cough completely for an hour or so. But I don't want him usin' it under any other circumstances. And I'm givin' him some pills to ease the pain and inflammation in his chest. But heed my warnin'. Don't mix *any* of these medicines with alcohol. 'Specially not the pills."

Gerry lifted his damp, bloodshot eyes and glared at the doctor. "Are you trying to tell me I can't drink?" he asked in a raspy voice.

"I'm not *trah*-in' to tell you," the doctor replied, fixing a steely gaze at his patient. "I'm tellin' you straight up. *Do not drink!* There have been sev'ral documented cases of patients sufferin' dangerous hallucinations when they mixed these pills with booze. You can't afford to take that kind of risk with your health, young man. Not with your big concert comin' up."

Gerry opened his mouth to argue but was overcome by a fit of coughing. After he caught his breath, he gripped the edge of the metal examining table for support. The sheet of stiff paper he was sitting on made a sharp, crinkling sound as he clutched it with his fingers. He hung his head even lower than before and released a hoarse sigh.

Emmett clapped his protégé on the shoulder and coaxed him off the table. "Don't worry, Dr. Berger," he assured the physician. "I'll make sure my boy follows your instructions to the tee. He has to be in top shape if he's going to perform at tomorrow night's fête. We can't have him coughing and sneezing throughout the show."

Gerry lifted his head back up and glowered at both men. "But I'm in New Orleans!" he protested. "This is a party town! I am *not* gonna spend my whole time here in bed!"

The doctor made a tut-tutting noise as he shook his head once more. "Listen to your manager, Mr. Enis," he directed Gerry. "He knows what's good for you. Now, you go back to your hotel room and get some rest."

Gerry's face flushed red with anger. "But I don't *wanna* sit in my hotel room and rest," he groused. "I wanna—"

His desire remained unspoken as his shoulders convulsed and his whole body shook with another fit of coughs.

Emmett rolled his eyes. "Yes, yes, we all know what you want, son." He nodded politely at the physician, then called over his shoulder as he guided Gerry to the door, "Thank you, Dr. Berger. You're a lifesaver!"

"Just doin' my job," the doctor called back to him.

A young nurse shouted, "Oh my stars!" and dropped the metal tray she was carrying as Gerry stepped into the corridor. A stack of empty specimen cups flew off the tray as it hit the linoleum floor with a loud clang. One cup rolled into the examining room and came to a stop just in front of the toe of Dr. Berger's polished black shoe.

Gerry let loose a theatrical growl and cried, "Mercy!" in a croaking imitation of Roy Orbison's tag line. Then he cleared his throat and started coughing once more.

Harlan Berger rolled his eyes, then added under the din of Gerry's hacking, "And I suspect my job's a damn sight easier than yours'll be, Mr. Poole, keepin' that boy of yours off the hootch for the next coupla' days."

* * *

Emmett led Gerry down the narrow hallway of the DeSoto Hotel's top floor, then pulled out his key to open the door to the Pilots' suite of rooms.

Gerry flashed an imploring look at his manager. "Can't I just nip into my bedroom through a side door, without having everyone see me?"

Emmett smiled at him indulgently. "I'm sure the others will all want to ask about your doctor's visit."

"That's what I'm afraid of," Gerry replied. He hung his head low and stared forlornly at his shoes.

"Then I'll give them the report, while you slip quietly into your room for a nap," Emmett proposed.

Gerry lifted his head and nodded, then coughed. He took a moment to compose himself and ended up falling into another long coughing fit.

Emmett handed him a fresh handkerchief, then opened the door to the hotel suite.

Gerry followed him into the elegantly furnished sitting room and saw his bandmates Jim, Tony and Pete gathered around a table strewn with dirty dishes. Emmett's younger brother Alan was standing to the side of the three musicians, pouring cups of tea.

"Did you save anything for me?" Gerry shouted to them, his gruff voice hoarse from coughing.

"Sorry, mate," replied Tony Wright, the band's lead singer. "Didn't know when you'd be back. You'll have to call room service yourself."

"Bloody hell," Gerry groused. He considered making a dash to his bedroom, but impulsively decided he felt like company and threw himself on top of a beautifully upholstered settee instead. He grabbed an embroidered silk pillow, plopped it against one of the armrests, and lay down across the cushions, resting his feet on top of the opposite armrest.

Jim McCudden, the band's keyboardist and composer, stood up from his chair and approached his ailing friend. "So what's the diagnosis?"

"Bubonic plague," Gerry replied smoothly. "I've got two months to live, so I should make it through the rest of this goddamned tour. But you lot have all been exposed, so you'd best start ringing your loved ones and writing out your wills."

Jim chuckled, then turned towards Emmett. "How contagious is he?"

Emmett shrugged. "No more than he has been since he first picked up this bug in Boston. Our Gerald has acute bronchitis, I'm sorry to report, no doubt brought on by not taking care of himself properly once he felt that first tickle in his throat. The GP whom the concierge recommended prescribed some medications to temper his cough. But the good doctor's other directives have cut our drummer to the quick. Gerry has been ordered to rest *and* stop drinking whilst he's taking his pills."

"Is that even possible?" Tony laughed. He stood up from the table and joined Jim at Gerry's side.

Gerry glowered at his bandmates, then turned his head to the back of the sofa and made a show of ignoring them.

"Don't you worry, Ger," Alan Poole called out from the lunch table. "I'll drink twice as much at the party tonight for your sake. I'll tell the barkeep I'm drinking for two."

Gerry sprang up to a seated position. His red-rimmed eyes grew wide. "Party? What party?"

Jim threw an admonishing look at Alan, then turned back towards Gerry. "We're going to Fats Domino's house this evening. He's hosting a little get-together for all the bands playing at tomorrow night's fête."

"A *big* get-together," Tony corrected him. "The joint is gonna rock!"

Gerry fell back against his pillow. "Bullocks! This is so unfair! Why, I could just—"

A fit of coughing interrupted his complaint.

Emmett reached into the bag of medicines he'd collected at the pharmacist's and pulled out the larger bottle of cough syrup. "Where's a spoon?" he called to his brother. "I think our patient must be due for a dose."

Alan plucked a clean spoon off the table and approached the sofa.

Emmett squinted at the writing on the bottle and read the instructions out loud. "Take two teaspoons every four hours. Do not exceed twelve spoonfuls in a twenty-four hour period."

Tony clucked his tongue. "Better pay attention, Ger. Wouldn't want you trying to get high off a cold remedy."

Gerry frowned at Tony as he grabbed the spoon and bottle from his manager. He made a face as he swallowed the syrup, then flashed a dirty look at Jim. "Where's Eddie? Why isn't he here mocking me with the rest of you lot?"

"He's out shopping," Jim replied. "Scouring the French Quarter's antiquarian bookshops for some rare tomes to add to his growing library."

Tony took a step towards the television set and reached for the *TV Guide*. "God, doesn't he have enough books already?" he asked no one in particular as he paged through the listings. "I could never read half the books Eddie owns in my entire lifetime. Why would he possibly want more?"

"Because Eddie and I constitute the brain trust of this organization," Jim replied. He snatched the magazine away from Tony and thwacked him on the side of his head. "Remember how you dragged the two of us away from our promising academic careers at the University of Manchester to join your little dog-and-pony-show? Our lyricist has a brilliant mind that needs to be fed and nurtured."

"Brain-trust, my arse," Gerry called up from the couch. "What does that make Tony and me?"

"The chick magnets," Tony answered. He flashed a winsome smile at his drummer and grabbed the magazine back from Jim. "Give me that. I wanna see when *American Bandstand* comes on."

"What about me? What am I?" asked Pete Cooper, the band's newest member. He stood up from his seat at the now-empty table and approached the sofa.

Gerry, Jim and Tony all turned their faces towards Pete, but offered no response.

Rolling his eyes at the group's united silent front, Emmett walked over to Pete and clapped him on the back. "You're the bassist. And you're very much a part of the band."

"Glad to hear *some*one thinks so," Pete said in a sour voice.

Tony sucked in a deep breath, then stepped towards Pete and gently punched his shoulder. "Buck up, mate. Tonight we're hitting the Crescent City in style, and you'll be among the guests of honor at a party hosted by one of the Founding Fathers of Rock and Roll."

Jim offered Pete a marginally encouraging smile, then took a seat in a high-backed wing chair and started singing Johnny Cymbal's old novelty hit, *Mr. Bassman*. Tony quickly joined in with the lyric, crooning, *"To you it's easy, when you say one, two, three—"*

"Hey!" Gerry interrupted. "*I* always count in the songs! Don't you be getting any funny ideas in your head, Cooper. *I'm* the one who founded this dog-and-pony show!"

"I co-founded it," Tony reminded him.

Gerry coughed and reached for the box of tissues on the table at his side. He blew his nose loudly, making a noise like a trumpeting elephant.

Tony returned to the television set, but before he could pull out the 'On' knob, the band's lyricist and rhythm guitar player Eddie Rochester stepped through the front door of the suite.

"Heads up, men! I'm back," he called out in a bright voice, expelling the dark mood that had engulfed his bandmates. "Did you save me any lunch?"

"Sorry, mate," Jim replied. "We figured you'd get a bite to eat in the French Quarter."

"Too busy shopping," Eddie said. He held up two paper sacks. "Guess what I bought?"

"Books!" his bandmates shouted in unison.

"Well, yes," Eddie said sheepishly. "Actually, I bought several books. But that's not what I meant. Come, see what I picked up at an Obeah shop."

"Obeah? What's that?" asked Pete.

Eddie pushed some dirty plates to the side of the dining table and rested his bags on top of the stained linen tablecloth. "It's kind of like Voodoo," he explained. "It's part of the cultural heritage of New Orleans. I stumbled upon this queer little shop in the French Quarter and started chatting with the clerk, and ended up buying three magic potions. He must have put a spell on me! Here, take a look." He pulled three intricately carved glass bottles out of the smaller of his two bags and held them up one-by-one for his friends to admire.

"There's a love potion in this rose-colored flask, and an elixir in the green one that's guaranteed to bring me financial success," he boasted.

Emmett cast a dubious look at the bottles. "Eddie, have you gone completely mental?"

Eddie smiled at his manager. "Oh, c'mon Emmett. What do you think? It's just for laughs!"

Tony picked up the yellow bottle and held it to the light. "What's this one supposed to do?"

"I bought that for my little brother, Rod," Eddie replied. "He's having a rough go of it at school. The man in the shop said this potion could help him with his reading. If he sprinkles a few drops from this bottle on his textbooks, then everything inside them will become so clear it will seem like he just stepped inside the pages."

"Wish I'd had something like that when I was in school," Tony said. "I must have been the world's worst student."

"Don't go flattering yourself," Gerry called up from the couch. "You know perfectly well that distinction belongs to me!"

Pete took the yellow flask from Tony and held it up to the window. A ray of sunlight burst through a gap in the drapes and refracted off the intricately cut glass, casting a pattern of rainbows over the white tablecloth. "I didn't know you had a younger brother, Rochester," he said as he twirled the bottle and admired the dancing prismatic effect.

"Rod's my half-brother," Eddie explained. "From my mum's second marriage. He's a lot younger than I am. I don't talk about him much."

Pete handed the bottle back to Eddie and sighed. "Nobody tells me anything."

Eddie offered him a half-smile, then slipped the three bottles back inside their paper sack. "So how'd your doctor visit go?" he asked Gerry.

Tony and Jim answered for him. "He can't drink!"

"You poor baby," Eddie laughed.

"Hey, I don't need your pity," Gerry barked back at him. He made a game effort to stand up from the couch to demonstrate his resilience, but as soon as he shifted his weight to his feet, another fit of coughing overtook him and he collapsed back against the sofa.

"No, but you might need some company if you can't go to the party this evening," Eddie said. He walked over to the couch and sat down beside Gerry. "But that's okay. I probably shouldn't go out drinking tonight either. I'm still recovering from Wednesday night's party."

"But it's Friday already," Tony pointed out.

"Yeah, I know," Eddie replied. "And I spent all of Thursday feeling hungover. I don't need to start that whole process up again already."

"That's not how it's supposed to work, Eddie," Gerry said. He wiped his nose with a fresh Kleenex and cleared his throat. "If you start drinking the morning after the first party, then you can just slide through your hangover on one long, blissed-out buzz."

Eddie chuckled. "Doesn't work that way for me, Ger. I must not have your Herculean constitution."

Gerry stared at Eddie through his bleary, rheumy eyes and coughed once more.

Eddie turned towards Emmett. "I'll stay with our Ger tonight while you lot go to Fats Domino's party. Maybe I can make some headway in one of the books I just bought."

Emmett frowned. "You should go, Eddie. You need to get out more. Enjoy the pop star life. I'll stay here with Gerry."

"Nah, you need to mingle," Eddie countered. "Hob-nob with the other groups' managers and see if you can't make some new connections. Keep our band's name on everyone's lips. We're counting on you."

Emmett sucked in a deep breath and ran his fingers through his hair. "Well, if you insist. I suppose you could do worse for yourself than to spend the night in this luxurious hotel room and order dinner from the magnificent restaurant downstairs."

"That's just what I intend to do," Eddie replied. He stood up from the couch and collected his two bags from the table. "Neither Gerry nor I will be going anywhere tonight."

Chapter Two

Eddie swallowed his last bite of *Andouille jambalaya,* tore a crust off his baguette, and started wiping drops of the spicy sauce from his plate. He looked up and met Gerry's eye.

"Damn, this is good," he said with a smile. "Sure beats the hell out of English cooking."

Gerry lowered his head and ran his fork over the surface of his nearly untouched plate of food. "Wish I could enjoy it. My throat hurts too much to swallow." He lifted his water glass to his mouth and coughed. "Even the water tastes funny."

Eddie reached for the half-empty wine bottle to refill his glass, then stopped himself. "Emmett would love this Cabernet. I should save the rest for him."

Gerry looked up at Eddie with sad puppy dog eyes.

Eddie frowned. "Don't worry, you sod, you'll be back to your old bad habits in no time. No cold lasts forever." He picked up the room service menu and scanned the list of desserts. "You wanna order some pudding? I'm pretty full, but everything looks so good."

Gerry grabbed the menu out of Eddie's hands and read it over. "How about the Bananas Foster? That's got ice cream in it. Might be good for my throat."

Eddie took the card back and read the description. "It's also got rum and liqueur in it," he pointed out.

"But they set it on fire and burn off the alcohol," Gerry protested. "All that's left of the rum is the taste."

"I'm not sure if that would pass the muster with your doctor," Eddie replied. "There might still be some alcohol left in the sauce."

"Just a hint," Gerry pleaded. "Not enough to affect my meds."

Eddie reviewed the menu again. "We could order some *crème brûlée*. That should be easy for you to swallow."

Gerry leaned back in his chair and crossed his arms in front of his chest. "You're like my mum, offering me a goddamned egg-custard when what I want is a big slice of chocolate cake."

Eddie ignored his comment. "I'll order us both some bread pudding," he said, reaching for the telephone. "The card says it's the chef's specialty." He dialed the hotel's restaurant and ordered two servings of dessert, along with a pot of coffee for himself and some tea for Gerry.

Gerry ran his finger in a wide circle over the linen tablecloth and frowned. "Wonder what the other fellows are up to now?" he asked, his hoarseness nearly masking the catch in his voice.

"The usual," Eddie replied, leaning back in his chair. "Jim's found a piano and is showing off for the guests. Tony's chatting up the prettiest girl in the room. Alan and Pete are probably already pissed out of their minds."

Gerry coughed one more, then sighed. "Wish I was too. 'Course my head's so stuffed up right now, I might not even notice if I was blitzed."

"You'd notice if you started having those hallucinations that doctor warned you about," Eddie said, resting his elbows on the table. "Don't be a pillock, Ger. No party is worth getting truly ill over. You've got to fight off your bronchitis so you'll be well enough to play the show tomorrow night. I'd hate to have to borrow another band's drummer for our set."

"You'll do no such thing!" Gerry bellowed, the fire returning to his eyes. "If I can't go on, *no*-one gets to go on! I founded this goddamned group! And no mother-fucking, substitute drummer is going to—"

His tirade dissolved into another fit of coughing.

Eddie waited for Gerry to calm down, then offered him a glass of water. "Think it's time for another dose of cough syrup?"

Gerry lowered his head and nodded.

Eddie stood up, grabbed the bag of medicine that Emmett had left behind, and pulled out the smaller bottle of syrup. "Is this the one you're supposed to take tonight?"

Gerry eyed the small bottle and tried to hide his smile. "Yeah, I think so," he whispered hoarsely.

Eddie handed Gerry the medicine and a clean soup spoon, then sat back down.

Gerry poured himself two-heaping tablespoons of the extra-strength, codeine-laced syrup. "Ahhh," he said after licking the spoon clean. "Tastes like cherry."

Eddie chuckled. "You're hopeless. My kid brother can handle being sick better'n you can." He picked up Gerry's nearly full dinner plate and stacked it on top of his own empty dish.

Gerry started drumming his fingers against the tabletop in a mid-tempo Bo-Diddly rhythm and sniffed along to the syncopated beat.

Eddie tried to mask the irritation in his eyes while he waited for the room service to arrive. When the knock on the door finally came, he jumped out of his chair to let the waiter in.

A balding, middle-aged man stepped into the room, pushing a cart. He made a showy display of cleaning off the old plates and replacing them with new dishes for coffee and dessert. Then he lit a candle in the middle of the table and asked Eddie and Gerry if they would like him to pour the beverages.

Eddie snorted and reached for his wallet. "Don't bother. I think we can handle that ourselves."

"Oh no, sir," the waiter protested in a smooth New Orleans drawl. "You already tipped me when I brought you the main course. But if you wouldn't mind—" He pulled a glossy teen magazine off the bottom shelf of the cart. "I was wondering if you could ask your friend Tony Wright to sign this picture for my daughter. It would mean so much to her." He opened up the magazine to a full-color pin-up photo of the Pilots' lead singer.

Eddie took the magazine and nodded. "Be happy to. Why don't you write down your daughter's name, so Tony can personalize the autograph for her? And write down your own name too, so I can make sure this gets back to you properly."

The waiter found a sheet of hotel stationery and pen, scribbled down the two names, and handed the paper to Eddie. "Thank you so much, sir," he said as he wheeled the cart out of the room. "My little girl sure likes your friend Tony."

"The git!" Gerry spat out the moment the waiter closed the door. "Why didn't he ask for *our* autographs for his daughter?"

Eddie shrugged. "Probably because the two of us put together still aren't half as cute as Tony is by his lonesome." He placed the magazine and sheet of stationery on the edge of the table, then poured himself a cup of coffee. "Can you pour your own tea, or do you need me to be mother?"

"You're acting enough like my mother as it is!" Gerry groused. He poured himself a cup of tea and added several lumps of sugar. "Give me that magazine!" he demanded. "Lemme see what sort of rubbish they're writing about us!"

"I don't imagine there'll be too many articles about us in here," Eddie said as he handed the magazine to Gerry. "Teenage girls are more interested in the Monkees these days."

"Stupid, bloody actors," Gerry cursed. "They don't even play their own instruments!" He grabbed the pen the waiter had left on the table and drew a handlebar mustache on a picture of Davy Jones.

"Stop that!" Eddie said, pulling the magazine out of Gerry's hands. "That doesn't belong to you!"

Gerry scowled. "Well, what am I supposed to doodle on, then?"

Eddie tore the sheet of hotel stationery in two and handed the blank half to Gerry. "How 'bout you draw a nice picture of Tony for our waiter's daughter?"

Gerry sketched a caricature of Tony leering at a group of large-breasted girls.

Eddie laughed, then shook his head. "You can't give her that. We don't want our innocent young fans to find out our doe-eyed lead singer is a dirty letch."

Gerry put down his pen and grabbed a spoon. He swallowed a few bites of bread pudding without coughing, then washed his food down with a large swig of tea.

"Nice of the waiter to light us a taper, eh?" he said, casting a suggestive glance across the table. "Nothing like sharing a romantic, candlelit dinner with my old mate Eddie."

"I'm not even going to dignify that remark with a response," Eddie replied. He put down his coffee cup, stood up from the table, and turned on the television. An image of Don Adams talking into a shoe-phone filled the round-cornered screen.

"How 'bout we use that love potion of yours to conjure us up some more pleasant company for the evening?" Gerry proposed.

"Well, I wouldn't mind summoning Barbara Feldon for a visit," Eddie said as he watched the raven-haired actress join her bumbling co-star on the television screen. "But I'm not sure if Florence Nightingale is available for you."

"You're a prat," Gerry muttered under his breath.

"Right," Eddie agreed. "And on that note, I'm going to leave you and take a shower."

"You can't desert me," Gerry whined. "You're supposed to entertain me!"

"Watch *Get Smart*," Eddie replied.

"I've seen this episode before," Gerry protested.

"Then read a bloody book," Eddie said with a sigh. He turned off the television and brought his larger shopping bag to the table. "What are you in the mood for, poetry or prose?"

Gerry considered the question. "Did you happen to pick up a first edition of *Lady Chatterley's Lover*? I could re-read the dirty bits."

"No," Eddie replied. He started pulling books out of his bag. "I bought an annotated Austen, a collected works of Paul Lawrence Dunbar, and—"

He pulled a third book from his sack and smiled. "Here, this one might appeal to you," he said, offering Gerry a small, leather-bound volume with yellowed, ragged-edged pages.

Gerry shuddered. "Damn, this is like spending a Friday night with both my mother *and* my fifth form English teacher." He picked up the book with his thumb and forefinger and dangled it in front of him at arm's length, as if it were a dead rodent. "What the hell is this?"

"It's called *The Tenant of Wildfell Hall*," Eddie said. "It was on my list of assigned books the semester I dropped out of uni, though I never got around to reading it. When I saw this old copy in the bookshop, I thought I might give it another chance. It's a fiftieth anniversary edition, printed in 1898. It's very valuable."

Gerry puckered up his lips and made a squeamish face. "What class was it for?"

Eddie grinned. *"Debauchery in Victorian Literature.* Right up your alley!"

"Prat," Gerry repeated under his breath. But then he turned his back to his friend and opened the book. Eddie chuckled and stepped into the adjoining bedroom.

Gerry skimmed the first chapter while he waited for the sound of running water to emerge from the other room. Then he put down the book and poured the remaining contents of his china teapot into Eddie's silver coffeepot. He uncorked the dark-green, half-filled bottle of Cabernet and poured its contents into his empty teapot. Then he poured some of the dark solution from the coffee pot back into the wine bottle so that it was once again half-full. Just as he finished corking the bottle, the sound of running water stopped. Gerry picked up the book and started turning the pages while he waited for Eddie to rejoin him.

Eddie ran into the room, clad only in a towel tied at his waist. Rivulets of water dripped from his soapy, wet hair onto his bare chest. He grabbed the wine bottle off the table with an air of urgency. "I almost forgot to hide this," he panted.

"Oh, ye of little faith," Gerry said disdainfully. "Don't you trust me?"

"Not even slightly," Eddie replied.

"You know, if our waiter's daughter could see you in that skimpy little getup, she might just switch her allegiance from Tony to you," Gerry added as he pretended to read. "Go ahead, Mr. Rochester. Hide your bottle of wine. I am not the slightest bit interested in it. I'm just going to sit here and sip my tea and read my Victorian novel like a proper English gentleman."

Eddie threw a dirty look at his drummer, then turned and started walking back to the bathroom. But before he reached the door, Gerry fell into another loud coughing fit. Eddie turned around and faced his friend. "Is it time for your next pill yet? I can fetch you a glass of water."

"Don't bother," Gerry said, keeping his eyes glued to the book. "I'll just wash it down with some tea. Get back in the shower. You're dripping puddles all over the pretty carpet."

Eddie grunted and returned to the bathroom.

Gerry kept his gaze focused on the novel until he heard the sound of water running again. Then he broke into a wide smile. He rested the book on the tablecloth and filled his teacup with Cabernet. He pulled his bottle of pills from the bag of medicine and took one out. Then he threw the tablet into his mouth and chased it down with a large gulp of wine.

"Ahhhh," he said aloud. "Now that's more like it." He picked the book back up again, opened it to the first page, and started to read in earnest.

* * *

"God, this is tedious," Gerry mumbled under his breath. He closed the book with a loud thump and pushed his chair away from the table so he could turn the television set back on. But as soon as he stood up, he felt light-headed. He grabbed the edge of the table, sat back down, and finished his cup of wine instead. He started reaching for the teapot to pour himself another serving, but stopped when Eddie returned to the room, dressed in pajamas and slippers.

"So how's the book?" Eddie asked, rubbing his wet hair with a dry towel.

"Bloody awful," Gerry answered with a scowl. "I'm twenty pages into it, and there's not even a *hint* of debauchery."

"Twenty pages already?" Eddie replied with a dubious look. He slung his towel over an empty chair and sat down at the table. "I didn't know you could read that fast. Maybe you're not paying enough attention."

"Do you want me to diagram the sentences for you?" Gerry scoffed. "I'm telling you, *nothing* is happening. It starts off with some bloke named Gilbert Markham promising to tell a long and leisurely story. Then he goes hunting outside a mansion called Wildfell Hall and rescues a little boy from falling out of a tree. He has a row with the kid's mum—some woman named Mrs. Graham. Then he goes home and chats up some bird named Eliza."

Eddie shrugged. "Well, it sounds like you've got the makings of a love triangle there—Gilbert might start romancing both birds at the same time. Debauchery is bound to ensue."

"Not bloody likely," Gerry replied. He opened the book back up and found the scene describing Gilbert and Eliza's *tête-à-tête*.

"Get a load of this," he said with a sneer. He raised his voice to a high mocking tone and recited a few lines from the text: '*I tenderly squeezed her little hand at parting, and she repaid me with one of her softest smiles and most bewitching glances. I went home very happy, with a heart brimful of complacency for myself, and overflowing with love for Eliza.*'

Gerry tossed the book at Eddie. "You promised me debauchery, not complacency!"

Eddie shrugged and started paging through the opening chapters of the novel. "Well, I don't know, Ger, here's how Gilbert describes Mrs. Graham in that other scene you mentioned. She's '*pale, breathless, and quivering with agitation.*' I imagine she'll stir up some trouble as the book progresses. Keep reading." He slid the novel back over the tablecloth towards Gerry.

"But I'm not used to reading such big words," Gerry protested, his voice scratchy and hoarse. "I think that teen magazine the waiter left behind is more at my level."

"But this is *good* for you," Eddie insisted. He grabbed his small paper sack off the side table and pulled out the yellow bottle he'd purchased at the Obeah shop. "What the hell—why don't we sprinkle some of this magic potion on the book? Then maybe you could understand the old-fashioned writing style better."

Gerry blew his nose into a napkin, then sighed. "I thought that was a present for your kid brother."

"I'm sure Rod won't mind if we used a little bit," Eddie replied. He popped the top off the bottle and sprinkled a few drops of scented oil onto the book's leather cover.

Gerry stared at the novel intently, hoping it might now vanish into thin air, then threw a disappointed look at Eddie. "Maybe you're supposed to say some magic words."

Eddie bit back a laugh, wiggled his fingers over the book, and said, *"Abracadabra!"* in a deep, sonorous voice.

Gerry glanced back at the novel and coughed once more. "I don't think it worked," he said after he caught his breath.

Eddie shrugged and put the lid back on the bottle. "You'll never know until you start reading it again."

Gerry looked up at Eddie once more and blanched. Instead of seeing a brown-eyed, dark-haired, broad-shouldered man dressed in pajamas, he saw a blue-eyed, sandy-haired, thin man wearing an old-fashioned black frock coat with a ruffled shirt.

He squeezed his eyes shut and cursed. Then he slowly opened one eye and looked back at Eddie. The familiar face of his rhythm guitarist stared back at him.

"You all right, Ger?" Eddie asked.

"Yeah," Gerry fibbed. "I'm fine." He grabbed the edge of the table for support and started to stand once more. "But I think I should probably turn in for the night."

"Good idea," Eddie agreed. "You need a shoulder to lean on?"

"Nah, I can make it," Gerry insisted. He tucked the book under his arm, picked up his teapot and cup, and started shuffling towards his bedroom. "I'll just finish this tea and try to read myself to sleep. With a book this boring, it shouldn't take long."

"Good night then," Eddie called back to him. "Sweet dreams."

Gerry stepped into his bedroom, closed the door behind him, and put the tea things and book on his nightstand. He changed into his striped pajamas and poured himself another cup of Cabernet. He gulped down the wine, slipped under his covers, and stared dumbly at the book.

"Oh, what the hell," he grumbled. "That'll knock me out faster than any bloody sleeping pill could." He opened the novel and re-read the first line, *"You must go back with me to the autumn of 1827."* His eyelids started growing heavy...

Chapter Three

The tawny owl swooped through the air and shrieked as she approached her nest.

Gerry flinched at the sound. He opened his eyes and saw a large, wide-eyed bird perched on a branch above him. She looked down at him and repeated her call: "Ke-*wick!* Ke-*wick!*"

"Holy crap," Gerry muttered under his breath. "Where the fuck am I?" His heart started pounding in his chest.

He looked to his right and saw a tall, dark building silhouetted against a starry night sky. He looked to his left and saw a small expanse of lawn dotted with frosty, fallen leaves that shimmered in the moonlight. He wriggled his toes and felt traces of ice on the blades of grass that tickled his bare feet. His warm and cozy hotel bed was nowhere to be seen.

"Eddie?" he called out nervously. "Are you still there?"

A chorus of voices arose to his right. He turned his head and saw a group of people exiting the building. A soft yellow glow spilled out of the house's opened front door, bathing the speakers in the dimmest of light as they stepped outside.

"My sincerest thanks, Mrs. Markham!" exclaimed a man in a top hat and long frock coat. He started walking towards a waiting horse-drawn carriage that Gerry hadn't noticed before. "You are a most gracious hostess!" he called back to her.

Feeling inexplicably out of place, Gerry jumped to his feet and slipped behind the broad trunk of the tree he had been lying beneath, hoping to mask his presence.

The tawny owl screeched at him once more. He flashed her the evil eye, then looked back at the small crowd of people departing the building.

"You are most welcome, Mr. Lawrence!" called a plump woman standing on the raised front doorstep. She waved to the man in the top hat, then nodded to the small, slim woman and two tall men who flanked her.

A slender woman in a long, full-skirted gown stepped out of the house. Her fringed shawl fluttered in the breeze. She took a few steps towards a second buggy, then turned back to the assembly at the door. "Mr. Markham, would you be so kind as to help me into my carriage?"

"It would be my pleasure, Miss Millward!" replied the shorter of the two men on the doorstep. He hastened to her side.

A man with stooped shoulders stepped out of the building and started scolding the woman in the fringed shawl. "Eliza, that is most unnecessary, and unseemly as well. We must not impose upon our hosts. Take my arm."

Gerry focused his gaze on the stoop-shouldered man and noticed a pair of white mutton chop whiskers sprouting from his cheeks.

Dirty old geezer, he thought. *Stealing that pretty lolly bird from the nice young bloke!*

The young woman placed her hand in the crook of the old man's arm and murmured, "Yes, Papa." Then she looked up at her rebuffed suitor and held his gaze.

"I shall see you in church this Sunday," the young man said to her.

"I shall look forward to it!" she replied in an excited voice before turning and letting her father lead her into the second buggy.

She waved to the young man through her carriage window as she departed. He waved back at her and smiled. Then he lingered by the edge of the cobblestone path and shook hands with each of his other departing guests. When the final carriage pulled away, he remained on the edge of the lawn.

"Gilbert!" exclaimed the plump woman on the doorstep. "Do come back in. This cold night air is most unhealthful."

"One minute, Mama," he called back to her. "I require a few moments of quiet solitude after the excitement of the party. I shall be in shortly, I promise."

The older woman retreated into the house, escorted by the second young man. The young woman remained on the doorstep for a moment and called out in a sly voice, "Gilbert needs a few moments of quiet solitude after his disappointment at being slighted by Eliza's father!" She giggled, then stepped into the house and shut the door behind her.

The young man sighed and stared blankly at the moon.

Gerry watched him in silence for several seconds. Then he felt a sore tickle in the back of his throat, and before he could stop himself, he coughed.

The young man turned towards the tree. "Who's there?" he called out in a wary voice.

Gerry put his hands to his mouth in an attempt to silence his next cough.

The tawny owl spread her wings and leaped from her branch, dive-bombing Gerry and crying "Ke-*wick!* Ke-*wick!*"

He coughed up a clump of phlegm and spat it at the bird, then stepped away from the tree and raised his hands in the air, like a thief caught in the act. His pajama top rode up his chest and exposed his soft belly. He shivered as the cold night air brushed his bare skin, then focused his gaze on the young man. "Don't get your knickers in a twist!" he exclaimed. "It's just me, Gerry."

"Step out of the darkness and reveal yourself, you deceitful spy!" the man replied.

Gerry rolled his eyes and started walking towards the cobblestone path. "It's just me, Gerry," he repeated. "So don't go soiling yourself now, alright? I'm not gonna hurt you."

"Who are you? What are you doing on my property? And why are you wearing your nightshirt?" the young man demanded of him.

Gerry looked down at his pajama pants and bare feet, then lifted his head and started to laugh. "I am Gerald Albrecht Enis," he stated slowly, as if he were speaking to a non-English-speaking foreigner. "But you can call me Gerry. I'm wearing my pajamas because I was just turning in for the night. And I have no idea what I'm doing on your property, or how I even got here." He took another step towards his inquisitor and was overcome by a long fit of coughing.

"Good God, sir, you sound dreadful," the young man declared once Gerry fell silent.

"I feel dreadful too," Gerry agreed. He wiped his mouth with the sleeve of his shirt and added, "I think that medicine the doctor gave me must have wiped me out completely. The last thing I remember was getting into bed. And now I'm standing out here in the middle of the night in my pajamas. Hell, I don't know. Maybe I'm hallucinating from the drugs."

The young man examined Gerry for a few seconds, then spoke in a voice tinged with pity. "You poor, unfortunate soul." He took a step towards Gerry and held out his hand in greeting. "Allow me to introduce myself. My name is Gilbert Markham, and this is my home. You don't look familiar. You must be new to the neighborhood. Where are you staying?"

Gerry wiped his right palm on his pajama bottoms before extending it for a handshake. "I'm staying at the hotel," he replied.

Gilbert frowned at him. "The hotel? Do you mean the inn?"

"Yeah, right, the inn," Gerry agreed. "I'm staying there with my friend Eddie."

"Eddie?" Gilbert replied in a confused voice. "You're staying with a child?"

"Nah, Eddie's my age, or thereabouts anyway," Gerry assured him.

"And yet you call him by a child's name?" Gilbert challenged.

"Err, umm, yeah," Gerry said. "We go way back, so I call him by his nickname."

"Ah, I see," Gilbert said, nodding his head. "But his Christian name must be Edgar. Or Edmund."

"Edgar," Gerry agreed, wondering as he spoke what Eddie's Christian name actually was.

"And you said your name was Gerald. Gerald Enis?"

"Yeah, that's right."

Gilbert smiled at long last. "Are you perchance related to Lord Douglas Enis of Cornwall?"

Christ, Gerry cursed in his head. *How the hell should I know?*

"Well, umm, yeah, I am," he answered, matching Gilbert's friendly grin with a sly smirk. "But only distantly. We're not exactly tight."

Gilbert cocked his head to the side and examined Gerry a little more closely. "I shouldn't have thought you were an immediate member of his family," he added after a moment's consideration. "You don't sound like a Cornish man."

"Hell no, I'm from Manchester!" Gerry replied indignantly.

Gilbert nodded once more. "So what brings a man of the city to these country idylls?"

"Why, *The Tenant of Wildfell Hall*, of course," Gerry answered. And as he recited the novel's name, he realized at long last how he had found himself in this peculiar circumstance.

That bloody potion worked! he marveled. *I've got to get back to the hotel and tell Eddie!*

"I see. So you're a friend of Mrs. Graham," Gilbert said, interrupting Gerry's train of thought.

Gerry stared dumbly at Gilbert for several seconds while he tried to frame his reply. "Well, I wouldn't say we were *friends*," he offered at length. "I mean, I know *some* things about her, but we're not on close terms."

"Alas," Gilbert said with a sigh. He lowered his head and shuffled his boot back and forth over a cobblestone. "I was hoping to find someone who knew her well and could set my mind at ease. Such terrible stories have been circulating about her, but I'm sure they can't be true."

"What are they saying?" Gerry asked, his lips curling into a devilish grin. *So here's that debauchery Eddie promised me!* he thought with a flurry of excitement.

"Oh, I shouldn't like to repeat a rumor," Gilbert protested. "It's so ungentlemanly."

"Oh, right. Yeah. Of course," Gerry agreed with a sigh of his own. He coughed again—softly at first, but then with more force as another violent fit overtook him.

"Good Lord, where are my manners?" Gilbert said. "You are ill. I must take you inside." He took off his overcoat and draped it over Gerry's shoulders. "You aren't even wearing any slippers! You'll catch your death of cold."

Gerry slipped his arms into the sleeves of the coat and followed Gilbert across the lawn.

Gilbert hesitated for a moment at the doorstep. "Wait here," he instructed Gerry. "I shall take you to my library, but I wouldn't want to offend your modesty by allowing Mama or Rose to see you in your nightshirt. Allow me to step inside first to make certain no one is in the foyer."

Gerry nodded and waited at the doorstep while his host entered the house. When Gilbert returned, Gerry smiled at him and whispered, "Is the coast clear?"

Gilbert cast him another perplexed look but ushered him into his house nevertheless.

"Welcome to Linden-Car, my humble home," Gilbert said as he led Gerry into a wood-paneled library. "Come sit by the fire and warm yourself. I shall fetch you a rug." He grabbed a thick woolen blanket off a settee in the back of the room and placed it over Gerry's knees. Then he sat down in a wing-backed chair beside his guest. "So, you suspect you have been hallucinating? Sleepwalking perchance? You mentioned a medicine that a doctor had given you."

"Yeah," Gerry replied. "He warned me that the drug might have that effect."

Gilbert nodded thoughtfully. "Was it laudanum?"

Gerry blanched. "Excuse me?" he replied, his eyes popping with surprise.

"Laudanum," Gilbert repeated. "Tincture of opium. It's what my doctor always prescribes for a bad cough. Though I find it sometimes affects my breathing and heartbeat in a most distressing way."

"Damn, you are one lucky man!" Gerry exclaimed, staring at his host in envious disbelief. "My doctor just gave me some pills."

Gilbert tilted his head at a curious angle. "Do you mean lozenges?"

"Um, yeah, I guess you could call them that," Gerry replied. He coughed a few more times.

Gilbert stood up from his chair and walked to a side table. He opened a decanter and poured a large splash of an amber-colored liquid into a cut-glass tumbler, then returned to Gerry's side and presented it to him. "This brandy should help. My mother always says it's the best remedy for everything."

"Wise woman, your mum," Gerry said as he sniffed the drink's heady aroma. He took a large sip and smiled as the alcohol warmed his throat. "There's nothing like a good brandy to cure whatever ails ya!"

"I'm afraid Mr. Lawrence might disagree with you," Gilbert said as he reclaimed his seat by the fire. "The last two times I've seen him, he spoke at length about the dangers of drinking alcohol. And tonight at dinner, the Reverend Millward took his part as well. Though our parson has often complimented my mother on her home-brewed ale in the past, even if he makes a point of eschewing wine and stronger spirits."

"Your mum brews her own ale?" Gerry asked, his eyes twinkling with delight.

"Well, of course she does," Gilbert replied, casting another perplexed look at his guest. "I should think every woman who manages a home of this size brews ale for her family and servants on a regular basis." He offered Gerry a wan smile, then frowned. "No. I stand corrected. I imagine *Mrs. Graham* might not indulge in such an activity. When last I spoke to her, she was quite insistent that she would never allow her son to drink alcohol of *any* kind. I have never heard a person speak so emphatically against drinking."

Bullocks, Gerry cursed in his head. *For a book about debauchery, there sure seems to be a lot of teetotaling going on around here!* He took another sip of brandy and savored the warm sensation it left in his throat, then decided to shift the conversation back to a topic that interested him more. "So tell me, Mr. Markham, do you find laudanum helpful in fighting off a cough?"

"Of course it is!" Gilbert exclaimed. "There's nothing like it. Don't you ever use it?"

Gerry shook his head and attempted to mimic Gilbert's old-fashioned style of address. "Alas. My doctor gives me naught but lozenges."

"Well, it's no wonder you're coughing like a consumptive," Gilbert replied. "I should think you could use a good dose. Perhaps I could try to find you some."

Gerry grinned. "You just keep it lying around your house?"

Gilbert settled back in his chair with a sheepish expression. "Not always," he insisted. "But last year my brother Fergus fell off his horse when he went badger-baiting with the dogs, so we bought a large supply from the chemist to see him through his recovery. And my sister Rose likes to use it as well." He fell momentarily silent before finishing his thought. "For her female complaints."

Gerry let loose a loud snort of laughter. "Damn, that poor bint must get *wicked* cramps!"

Gilbert's face froze. "I am afraid the lozenge your doctor gave you not only made you sleepwalk and hallucinate. It also loosened your tongue most shamelessly," he stated in a haughty tone.

"Sorry," Gerry apologized. He sat up a little straighter in his chair. "You're right. I really don't feel like myself at all tonight." He finished off his brandy and looked up at his host. "Tell you what, my dear Mr. Markham—do you suppose I could try some of that laudanum of yours and see if it helps with my cough? I'd be much obliged." He feigned a few coughs in a bid to win sympathy, then ended up convulsed in a genuine fit of hacking.

"Of course," Gilbert replied. "I should have offered you a dose earlier. Let me go fetch you some. My mother keeps it in the larder, along with our stock of Jalap Powder, Turner's Cerate, and Spirit of Hartshorn."

"Cor! She's a regular Girl Guide," Gerry replied with a smile. "Prepared for all emergencies!"

Gilbert threw Gerry another confused look, then stood up to fetch the medicine.

As soon as Gilbert left the room, Gerry rested his empty glass on the small table at his side. Then he noticed a small, golden object lying on the floor by his feet. The light from the fire reflected off its surface, making it glitter and shine.

He picked it up and examined it. The object was octagonal and embedded with jewels. He flipped it back and forth between his fingers a few times. Then he heard Gilbert open the library's door. He slipped the mysterious object into the breast pocket of his pajama shirt and turned to his host with an innocent smile.

Gilbert walked up to Gerry's side and handed him a silver demitasse spoon, then opened a small glass bottle filled with clear liquid. "I dare say, this should have a calming effect," he said as he poured a few drops onto the spoon's concave surface.

Gerry downed the laudanum. Almost immediately, a warm, blissful sensation started spreading through his body.

"Damn! I think you're right about this dope, mate!" Gerry exclaimed with a loopy grin. "I'm gonna have to ask my doctor to prescribe me some of this junk the next time I get sick." He rested the spoon beside his empty brandy glass and looked back up at his host. "So who are you in love with anyway? Eliza Millward or Mrs. Graham?"

"Wh-wh-what an impertinent question!" Gilbert stammered. "I daresay, if I didn't already know that you were under the influence of some strange sort of tongue-loosening lozenge, I would throw you out of my home!"

"Sorry," Gerry apologized, walking back his question. "Didn't mean to give offense. I was just curious."

Gilbert focused a steely gaze at Gerry. "You said you knew Mrs. Graham. How is it that you made her acquaintance?"

"Oh, well, um—" Gerry stammered. He tried to remember what he had read about her in the book, and recalled a brief passage that mentioned she was an artist. "I commissioned her to do a painting for me," he replied at length. "I came to the area to see if she was done with it yet."

Gilbert's wary expression grew softer. "I had no idea she was a painter."

"Yeah, well, you'll probably find that out in a later chapter," Gerry replied.

Gilbert started to scowl, but Gerry hardly noticed. The buzz from the laudanum was quickly spreading from his body to his mind, and he was starting to feel deliriously happy. His head began to spin. He threw another loopy grin at his host.

"So what was the special occasion tonight?" he asked with a twinkle in his eye. "Seems like you and your family were hosting quite a big shindig there."

"A shindig?" Gilbert repeated.

"Yeah, you know, a gathering," Gerry replied. "A happening. A love-in. A, um—."

"A party," Gilbert interjected.

"Right, *that's* the word I was looking for," Gerry agreed. His smile dipped into a frown. "Did you know yours was the *second* party I missed out on tonight?"

"Well, I'm hardly surprised at the flurry of social activity," Gilbert replied. "It *is* the Fifth of November, after all. Rather a common night for celebrations, I dare say."

"Goddammit!" Gerry cursed. "I love Guy Fawkes Day parties! Did you light a bonfire?"

"No, we just had dinner and a little dancing."

Gerry sucked in a deep breath and released it with a sigh. "I'm gonna have to go back and re-read these pages. I think I must have missed a good part."

Gilbert furrowed his brow. "I don't understand you."

Gerry gazed into Gilbert's eyes and tried to think of an appropriate response, but he felt unaccountably tongue-tied. He was growing woozy. The closer he examined Gilbert's face, the more it started to look like Eddie's. Gilbert asked Gerry if he was feeling well, but his voice also sounded remarkably like Eddie's.

"Listen, Gil," Gerry stated abruptly. He stood up from his chair, dropped the blanket to the floor and let the overcoat slip from his shoulders. "It's been lovely meeting you, and you've been a really great host and all that, but I've gotta go now."

He started walking towards the set of French doors in the back of the library. His feet felt sluggish and unsteady beneath him. But just when he thought he was going to stumble, he sensed himself flying over the floor…

* * *

"Gerry!" exclaimed a loud voice. It landed on Gerry's eardrums as hard and fast as a thunderclap. "Gerry!"

Gerry opened his eyes and saw Eddie looking back at him with a vexed expression.

"Christ, Gerry, you nearly scared me to death!" Eddie shouted. "It almost seemed like you stopped breathing there for a minute! I could barely feel your pulse!"

Gerry stared back at Eddie and scrutinized his face. "Yeah, I've heard that laudanum can have that effect on some people."

Eddie scowled at him. "What the hell are you talking about?"

Gerry suddenly felt more clear-headed than he had in days. "Tincture of opium," he stated in a calm voice. "Gilbert gave me some. And a little brandy as well. His mother and chemist swear by them both."

Eddie ignored his remark. "You poured what was left of my wine into your teapot," he said reproachfully. "I smelled the dregs in your cup. You are such a fucking idiot. You could've killed yourself!"

Gerry sat up straight and propped his back against the headboard of his bed. "Stop being such a mother hen. I am ab-so-fucking-lute-ly fine."

"You've been hallucinating, just like that doctor said you would if you mixed your pills with alcohol," Eddie retorted.

"Was not," Gerry insisted. "I was just visiting the characters in that book you gave me."

"Bullocks!" Eddie spat back at him. "You're full of shit!"

Gerry fell silent for a long moment while he tried to think of a way to convince Eddie that his visit with Gilbert had been real. Then he smiled in triumph and pulled the eight-sided golden object out of his pajama pocket.

"Think again, Mr. Literary Scholar," he crowed. "Look what I just brought back from Wildfell Hall!"

Chapter Four

Eddie grabbed the jeweled trinket away from Gerry and examined it closely. He wriggled a knob protruding from the middle of one edge. A hinge on the opposite side sprang open.

"This is a snuffbox," he announced in a curious voice. "A very nice snuffbox. Where did you find it?"

"I told you, at Wildfell Hall, by the—" Gerry started to answer. Then he fell silent for a moment and corrected himself. "No, that's wrong. I found it at Linden-Car. That's what Gilbert calls his pad."

Eddie snapped the snuffbox shut and scowled at Gerry. "What the hell are you talking about?"

"I'm *telling* you, you're just not *listening*," Gerry replied in an exasperated voice. "I went there. To the inside of your bloody book. I met the characters. I drank their brandy. I sat by their fireplace—"

"And you pinched their snuffbox," Eddie interrupted.

"Yeah, apparently I did," Gerry chuckled. "But that was an accident. Honestly. I didn't mean to nick it. I just popped it in my pocket when Gilbert returned to the library, so he wouldn't catch me checking out his shit. I must have somehow carried it back with me. I'm not sure how."

Eddie frowned at him. "You're talking nonsense. You're losing your fuckin' mind."

"Like hell I am," Gerry retorted, his face flushing. "*You're* the one who bought that magic potion. And *you're* the one who gave me that bloody book. If I was magically transported into its pages, then *you're* the one to blame. It's not my fault."

"Gerry," Eddie said with a small, sad sigh, "there *is* no magic potion. I just bought that bottle of crap as a gag gift for my brother. And I sprinkled it on the book as a joke, 'cause you said you were having a hard time understanding the old-fashioned language. You can't *really* lose yourself in a book—not like you're describing it. Believe me, I've read a lot more than you have. I should know! You just had a very vivid dream. A nightmare, maybe even."

Gerry opened his mouth to argue, but started coughing instead.

Eddie waited for his friend to calm down, then started speaking in a softer and more sympathetic voice. "Emmett told me that doctor warned you about mixing alcohol with those pills. He said it could cause hallucinations. That's what you've been doing these past couple of hours—having one big, long, vivid hallucination. Shit, man, you've tripped on acid before. You should know a hallucination when you experience one."

Gerry straightened his back and folded his arms in front of his chest. "This was *nothing* like an acid trip," he stated indignantly. "There were no funky colors or blurred sounds. Nothing freaky happened. This was a *real* place, filled with *real* people. Gilbert gave me a brandy—a *real* brandy. I smelled it and tasted it. It even burned my throat a little. I sat by the fire in his library, and the flames felt warm. Really and truly warm! And then he gave me some laudanum to drink, and it made me feel—God, it made me feel *glorious!*"

Eddie sighed once more. "You dreamt about taking drugs. You are *so* pathetic."

"Then how do you explain this?" Gerry demanded, grabbing the snuffbox away from Eddie and waving it in front of his face. "Did I just dream this too?"

Eddie stared at the golden box for a few seconds, then shrugged. "Someone must have left that in this room—a previous guest, I suppose—and you found it last night when you were getting ready for bed. Or maybe the maid accidentally dropped it in the sheets when she was changing the linens earlier today. I don't know. There must be some sort of logical explanation."

He took the snuffbox away from Gerry again and showed him how it opened. "Look at this antique spring hinge. It opens so easily—someone must have just oiled it! And check out the jewels. I'm no expert, but if these gems are real, then I'd say this is one very valuable snuffbox. We should try to find its owner and return it to him."

"That's what I intend to do, you git," Gerry insisted. He grabbed the snuffbox back and slipped it inside his pajama shirt pocket. "I know it's an antique, 'cause it came from 1827. And I know the owner too. His name is Gilbert Markham. He gave me some laudanum, and it made me feel better than I've ever felt in my entire life. I'm going back inside that bloody book at the next possible opportunity to get myself another dose!"

Eddie rolled his eyes. "You're talking rubbish. You took a pill and some wine and some codeine-laced cough syrup before you went to bed. And somehow those three substances joined forces and gave you this crazy nightmare."

"It wasn't a nightmare!" Gerry protested. "It wasn't scary—it was great! And I'm gonna go back there as soon as I possibly can. I'm gonna—"

Another fit of coughing overtook him. He hacked and gagged for almost a full minute. When the spasm finally passed, he leaned back against his headboard and released a soft moan. "Apparently, one dose of Gilbert's laudanum was not enough to cure me," he added with a sigh.

Eddie sat down on the edge of Gerry's mattress and offered him a sympathetic smile. "Listen, mate. I know that dream seemed real to you. And maybe—maybe it *wasn't* just the medicine and the wine playing tricks with your mind. Maybe there was something in the power of suggestion when I sprinkled that potion on the book that made everything seem more real too. I suppose that could happen. If you let yourself believe that something is real, then it can become so real in your mind that you can't be argued out of it. That's how illusionists and hypnotists work their magic."

He patted Gerry's knee. "Maybe if you feel up to it this afternoon, we can go back to that Obeah shop before the concert. Just you and me. I'll let you see for yourself what a rinky-dink operation that place is, and *then* you'll believe me. And while we're in the French Quarter, maybe we can find a jeweler and get the snuffbox appraised. And if you don't want to turn it in to the hotel, that's okay. No one will know but me. Finders keepers, right? Who knows, maybe it's worth a fortune, and it'll make this whole crazy night you just passed seem worthwhile."

Gerry coughed once more, then managed a weak smile. "You really don't believe me, do you?"

"Nope," Eddie assured him. "And no one else is going to either, so don't even try to convince the rest of the band that you went tripping into a Victorian novel while they were out partying with Fats Domino."

Eddie stood up and walked to the bedroom door, then turned and faced Gerry once more. "Let's make a deal—I won't tell Emmett you snuck into the wine I was saving for him, if you don't tell him what a bad babysitter I was."

"I don't need a babysitter," Gerry scoffed. "I'm a responsible adult."

Eddie laughed at him. "Well, you're an adult anyway. I'll fetch you a fresh glass of water. You need to drink some fluids. I threw away the wine in your teapot." He stepped out of Gerry's bedroom and closed the door behind him.

"Prat," Gerry mumbled under his breath. He slipped back under his covers and closed his eyes so he could pretend to be asleep when Eddie returned with his water.

* * *

Eddie checked his map against the sign hanging from the ornamental lamppost. "I think the shop is this way," he said. He started leading Gerry down a narrow road lined with colorfully painted buildings, each decked with multi-tiered balconies.

"How come we never get attacked by our fans in the streets like the Beatles did in *A Hard Day's Night?*" Gerry complained as he followed Eddie through a small pack of tourists.

"We might, if we brought Tony along," Eddie replied.

"I'm not that desperate," Gerry scoffed. He started whistling the melody to *We're In The Money* for a few seconds, then started to laugh. "Can you believe what that jeweler told us? That little snuffbox of mine is gonna be my retirement fund. I've got a pocket full of rubies!" He patted the breast pocket of his shirt contentedly.

Eddie frowned at him. "Maybe we ought to report it to the hotel management after all. If the snuffbox is as valuable as the appraiser said it was, someone is bound to come looking for it. I'm sure the previous occupant must have left it in your room by accident."

"Oh, ye of little faith," Gerry replied. He patted his pocket again, then noticed a vintage clothing shop on the side of the road. He grabbed Eddie's elbow and pulled him to a stop.

"Check out that suit!" he exclaimed, pointing to a tailor's dummy dressed in a wide-collared, tight-waisted, woolen frock coat and a pair of dove grey, snug-fitting pants. A printed silk vest, tall top hat, and elaborately tied cravat completed the mannequin's old-fashioned, foppish look. "I should wear something like that the next time I go visit Gilbert. I'll fit in better with the *mise-en-scène*."

Eddie laughed. "Let's hope the shop's tailor can let out the seams for you in time for your next trip."

Gerry stuck out his tongue in reply.

"Ick," Eddie groused. "Your tongue looks all manky. Maybe we should go back to the hotel now so you can squeeze in a nap before tonight's show."

"Not until you show me that Obeah shop where you bought your magic potion," Gerry countered. He turned away from the shop window and gave Eddie a small push.

"Are you planning to purchase a bottle of your own?" Eddie asked.

"'Course I am," Gerry replied. "I wouldn't want to steal your little brother's stash. He'll need it to get through school this coming term."

Eddie sighed. "Gerry, you do know that these charms and potions are all just codswallop, don't you? There is no such thing as magic."

"Like hell there isn't," Gerry scoffed. "I've always been a firm believer in charms and superstitions. Remember how I wore the same pair of socks every day on our first American tour without washing them once? And we sold out every show? I'm thinking I should maybe try that again this summer. I saw a lot of empty seats in the stands at our last couple of gigs."

"God help us all," Eddie mumbled under his breath. He noticed a small street sign hanging beside a narrow alleyway and pointed to a building. "There it is. Just past that *parfumerie* with the pink canopy. It's the 'Shop-and-Save Discount Obeah Warehouse'."

"*That's* not what's painted on the sign," Gerry corrected him. "It says 'Madame Francesca's Emporium of Charms'."

"Well, I didn't see any fancy-looking madam working there yesterday," Eddie scoffed. "Just some middle-aged bloke wearing a musty-smelling suit." He led Gerry down the alley, opened the shop's door, and set off a small tinkling chime.

Gerry followed Eddie into the store. "Helloooo!" he called out. "Is anybody home?"

"I shall attend you in a moment!" replied a deep voice from a back room.

Gerry started running his eyes over the shop's merchandise displays. A large assortment of odd-shaped candles, sparkling trinkets and glass bottles dotted the oblong tables scattered throughout the showroom. Racks of shelves lined the walls, filled with books, pamphlets, and more bottles and trinkets. A small glass display case sat beside an antique cash register on a long mahogany counter. Inside the case stood a painted statue of a man dressed in a medieval jester's costume. An oversized deck of Tarot cards rested at the base of the figurine, with the Fool's card upturned at the jester's feet.

Gerry turned towards Eddie. "Do you suppose they sell shrunken heads here?"

"Of course. There's some right over there, behind the Voodoo dolls," Eddie answered.

Gerry's eyes brightened. "Really?"

"No," Eddie said, rolling his eyes.

"May I help you?" asked a dour-looking, balding man standing behind the counter.

Gerry flinched, then nudged Eddie in the ribs. "Where do you suppose he came from? No, wait, I know—he magicked himself here out of thin air!"

Eddie ignored Gerry's remark and approached the counter. "Hello again. I don't know if you remember me, but I was here yesterday. I bought a few of your potions."

"Ah, yes," the man replied. "You're the English musician. You bought the love potion, the money potion, and—hmmm—what was in that third bottle you bought?"

"That's what *we* want to know!" Gerry barked back at him.

Eddie squirmed uncomfortably in his shoes. "I bought something to help my little brother with his schoolwork. It came in a yellow bottle. You said it would make the pages of his books come alive."

The bald man nodded. "Ah, yes, of course. The animation potion."

"Come again?" Gerry laughed. "You sold Eddie a bottle of *cartoon* potion?"

"*Animation* potion," the shopkeeper repeated, throwing Gerry a dirty look. "It makes inanimate objects come to life."

"Ahh," Gerry said, nodding in recognition. "Well, I guess that explains everything."

The man stretched his long arms out over the counter and leaned in on his knuckles. "Did you try it already?" he asked, raising one eyebrow in a curious expression.

"*He* did," Eddie said, pointing at Gerry. "He sprinkled some of it on an old book right before he fell asleep. Then he dreamed he became a character in the book."

"Did not," Gerry protested. "*You* sprinkled the damn potion. I just followed through on the spell that *you* cast and walked into the pages of *your* book. Honest to God—my hand on my heart—I truly did step into that novel. I'd swear it on my mum's grave."

"Your mother's still alive," Eddie reminded him.

"Yeah, well, then on my Oma's grave."

"I thought both of your nans were still alive too," Eddie added.

"Shut up," Gerry said.

The shopkeeper smiled at the two men and stood up a little straighter.

Eddie turned away from Gerry and met the balding man's gaze. "We wanted to know what was in that potion."

The shopkeeper folded his arms in front of his chest and assumed a condescending pose. "I'm sorry, I cannot reveal the secrets of the products that I peddle. But even if I could, I do not know the contents of that particular bottle. Madame makes the potions. I simply sell them."

"I see. You're just the snake oil salesman," Eddie replied.

The man arched his left eyebrow once more. "No, my good sir. I am Madame Francesca's business partner, Signor Giuseppe Paglio."

Gerry stepped closer to the counter and examined Giuseppe's forehead. "Damn, how do you raise one eyebrow like that without moving the other even the slightest bit?" He turned towards Eddie. "Do you suppose he could sell us a potion to make our eyebrows work like that? It might be a fun parlor trick."

Giuseppe scowled at Gerry. "I tend to this shop's finances, along with my apprentice. I read fortunes and he conducts séances. Madame Francesca makes the potions."

Gerry broke into a wide smile. "Really? You're a fortune teller? Could you read mine?"

"Are you prepared to pay?" Giuseppe replied.

Gerry puffed out his chest. "Hell, yeah," he answered indignantly. "You're talking to one very rich English musician." He focused an affronted gaze at the shopkeeper but almost immediately had to turn away so he could cough.

"Please step this way," Giuseppe said once Gerry had finished hacking. He walked to the back corner of the shop and pulled back a long, fringed curtain, revealing a round table covered with a dark burgundy cloth.

Gerry's eyes fell on the large glass globe resting atop a gold filigree stand in the middle of the table. "Woah! Is that a real crystal ball?" he gushed.

"Of course it is," Giuseppe said irritably. "Everything in this shop is real." He gestured for Gerry to take a seat, then looked up at Eddie and smiled. "You are welcome to join us."

Eddie sighed, then walked to the back of the shop and stood behind Gerry.

Giuseppe held out his palm.

Gerry reached across the table and shook his hand.

"I require payment in advance of my readings," Giuseppe stated in a droll voice as he slipped his fingers away from Gerry's.

"Ah, right, I forgot," Gerry replied. He pulled a ten dollar bill out of his wallet, offered it to Giuseppe, then held out his own hand. "Read my palm first, why don't you, before you look into your crystal ball. I wanna see if you read my fortune the same way this hunchbacked gypsy woman I once saw in Blackpool did."

"As you wish," Giuseppe replied, barely hiding his growing impatience in his sullen expression. "And might I state, for the record, that I learned the art of fortune telling from my grandmother, who was also Romani." He ran his fingers over the creases in Gerry's skin and made a few curious "hmm" and "ahh" sounds, but said nothing more. Then he turned his face to the glass globe and waved his hands over it with a theatrical flourish. He stared at the crystal ball intently for some time, breaking his gaze only to look up briefly into Gerry's eyes. After a full minute had passed, he rested his hands back on the dark red tablecloth.

"Please excuse me, but I momentarily found myself at a loss for words," Giuseppe announced. "Your palms suggest that you will live a long, happy, successful life. But the crystal ball indicates that you will spend your first fifty years plodding a treacherous, narrow path. One false step will lead you into an abyss of misery and despair. However, I believe your hands speak the greater truth. I foretell that you will manage to navigate your precarious way to safety."

Gerry broke into a wide grin. "That's just what that gypsy woman told me five years ago!" he laughed. He stood up from his chair and clapped Giuseppe on the shoulder. "Now do Eddie."

"No," Eddie protested.

"Oh, c'mon, it's just a lark," Gerry insisted. "You said so yourself." He pulled another ten dollar bill from his wallet and handed it to the fortune teller. "My treat."

Eddie still refused to move, so Gerry walked behind him and pushed him towards the chair. "It was *your* idea to come in here," he reminded his friend. "Now sit down and let this nice bloke with the funny eyebrows see your grubby little hands."

Eddie reluctantly took a seat. Giuseppe examined both of his palms. Then he waved his hands over the crystal ball and looked back and forth between the glass and Eddie's face. He closed his eyes and drew in a long breath, then released it with a sad-sounding sigh.

"Your fortune is even harder to decipher than your friend's," Giuseppe informed Eddie. "According to the fate written in your hands, you will have a long and happy marriage. But the crystal ball tells me that no woman yet born will bring you true love and joy."

"Thanks a lot," Eddie groused. He slipped out of the chair. "That's just what I wanted to hear."

Gerry clapped Eddie on the back. "Don't worry, mate. I think he just means you won't settle down for a while yet, but when you do, it'll be with some sweet young thing who'll be born after 1967."

"So I'll end up a dirty old goat, marrying a girl half my age when I'm in my forties or fifties," Eddie surmised.

"Sounds like a good plan to me," Gerry laughed. "She'll keep you feeling young." He smiled at his friend, then looked back at Giuseppe. "Thanks for the fortunes, mate. Now if you'll just sell me one of those magic cartoon potions, we'll be on our way."

"As you wish," stated the shopkeeper. He led his two customers back to the counter and found another yellow bottle of animation potion for Gerry.

Gerry attempted to move his right and left eyebrows independently as he completed the transaction, then gave up, disappointed.

Eddie opened the shop door, setting the chimes tinkling once more, and ushered Gerry back into the alley.

"See, I told you," he stated smugly once they had left the store. "That shopkeeper is nothing but a charlatan."

"Oh, I don't know," Gerry replied. He coughed a few times, then smiled. "He seemed like a perfectly respectable chap to me. And I liked my fortune too. I'll have some ups and downs, but everything will turn out alright in the end."

"Fine, sure," Eddie agreed. "Now let's head back to the hotel. We don't want to be late for the sound check."

"Not so fast," Gerry protested. He stopped in front of the vintage clothing shop and smiled at the top-hatted mannequin. "I've got some more shopping to do before I go visit my mate Gilbert again."

Chapter Five

Eddie, Tony and Pete set down their guitars and walked to the front of the stage for their final bow. Jim stepped away from his keyboard and jogged to Eddie's side. Gerry rested his sticks on the skin of his snare drum, then leaped off his platform and crashed into one of the microphone stands. The mic fell back onto a large VOX amplifier. An ear-piercing jolt of feedback surged through the speaker, like a screaming chorus of tone-deaf banshees.

Gerry made a great show of covering his ears and twisting his body in pain as a black-clad roadie ran onto the stage to silence the buzz. Then he joined his bandmates at the front of the stage. Applause swelled as the five musicians draped their arms around each other's shoulders and dipped into a nearly simultaneous group bow. Tony blew a kiss to the crowd, setting off a burst of high-pitched shrieks from his teenage fans that drowned out all memories of the feedback debacle. The Pilots exited stage left and ran to one of the trailers parked behind Tad Gormley Stadium as the emcee introduced the festival's final act.

"Great show, boys!" Emmett Poole exclaimed as the band members filed into their crowded dressing room. "You did me proud!"

"We had 'em dancing in the aisles!" replied Pete. He peeled off his shiny blue jacket and handed it to Emmett's brother Alan.

"Well, let's keep 'em dancing," Gerry proposed. He handed his matching suit jacket to Alan and smirked. "How many girls have you got lined up for tonight's party?"

A small hush fell over the group. Gerry coughed to clear his throat, then turned to face his bandmates. "Why so glum, mates? The night is young! You all had your chance to chat up the local birds last night. Now it's my turn!"

Jim stepped forward and clapped Gerry on the shoulder. "Sorry, Ger, but we decided not to throw a party after tonight's show. Our flight leaves tomorrow morning at ten, and we're all still a bit tired from last night's bash. We figured we should maybe take it easy this evening."

"'Cept for me," Tony piped in. He handed his jacket to Alan and threw Gerry a knowing smile. "I've got a date with a girl I met at the hotel restaurant this afternoon. She was running the crêpe station at lunch, and she promised to show me what else she can do with a flick of her wrist tonight. I'll rest on the plane tomorrow."

Gerry glowered at Tony, then turned to his other bandmates with a frustrated look. "What is wrong with you lot? Are you turning into a bunch of middle-aged geezers? You are all perfectly capable of partying two nights in a row and still catching a morning flight!"

"Gerry," Emmett said softly. He wrapped his arm around Gerry's shoulder and led him to the back corner of the trailer. "You still haven't taken all your pills yet. Dr. Berger wanted you to finish the entire prescription. And you know you can't drink while you're taking that medicine.

"Listen," he added in a whisper once he was safely out of earshot of the other band members. "The lads are doing this for you. They didn't want to go to another party that you couldn't attend. You've got twenty-four more hours to use up your medicine. And then—*if* you feel up to it—you can start living the pop star life again."

"Fuck you!" Gerry spat back at him. He threw off his manager's arm and stormed into the trailer's small bathroom, shouting, "I don't need your pity!" He slammed the door shut with a loud bang.

Emmett shrugged and returned to the front of the trailer.

"Well, that went well," Eddie noted.

"He'll get over it," Emmett replied, though his voice sounded doubtful. "His cough is almost gone, and he doesn't seem to be running a fever anymore." He turned his head and yelled towards the bathroom, "Gerry, Alan needs your trousers! He has to get these suits to the dry cleaner's straight away. They're staying open late just for us."

An awkward minute passed in silence as the band members changed into their street clothes. Then the toilet flushed and the bathroom door slammed against the trailer's wall with a loud crash. Gerry stormed into the circle of men, wearing nothing but his undershorts, and handed his trousers and shirt to Alan.

"So tell me, Mr. Poole," he asked his manager, his voice dripping with sarcasm, "however did you convince the dry cleaner to agree to that arrangement? It seems to me that you're wasting your powers of persuasion on a Louisiana launderer, when you ought to be using them with the Grand Poohbahs at EMI and getting us a better contract! The label isn't promoting our records anymore. They've practically written us off!"

"They're promoting you," Emmett insisted. "They still believe in you. They just want you lads to record something a little more—well—*commercial* sounding."

Gerry turned towards Eddie and Jim. "Well, brain trust, did you hear that?" he bellowed. "The toffs at EMI want you to write us something *commercial sounding*. So what are you waiting for? Hop to it! You have an entire free night ahead of you, with nothing else to do!"

"Well, actually," Jim said sheepishly, "I asked a girl I met at last night's party to stop by the hotel tonight, so we could spend a little more time together before I leave town."

"Right," Gerry said, acknowledging Jim's remark with a sneer. He grabbed a pack of Lucky Strikes that was lying on a table and pulled out a cigarette. "So I guess that leaves Eddie and me to spend the night reading Victorian novels once more."

"You could hang out with Alan and me," Pete offered. "We're gonna chat up chicks at the hotel bar."

"But you forget—our manager won't let me to go to a bar," Gerry retorted. He lit his cigarette and inhaled. "I'm on fucking bed rest. No goddamned alcohol for the likes of me!"

Emmett took a seat at the table and sighed. "Doctor's orders, Ger, not mine. And you probably shouldn't be smoking either. I can't imagine that's good for your lungs, with all the coughing you've been doing lately."

Gerry took another deep drag on his cigarette and glowered at his manager. He blew a long stream of smoke in Emmett's direction, then slammed the tip of the cigarette into a cut glass ashtray and angrily crushed out the flame.

"Don't worry, mate," Eddie said encouragingly, offering Gerry a half smile. "It's only one more night. And anyway, you said you wanted to re-read those chapters that you just skimmed yesterday. Who knows? Maybe the story might actually start to get interesting."

Gerry threw Eddie a skeptical look, but then he curled his lips into a sly smile and attempted to cock his left eyebrow. "We'll just have to see about that, won't we?"

He reached for a pair of jeans hanging over a wooden chair and slipped them on. "Well, come on, lads. Let's head back to the inn. I've got me a bloody book to read."

* * *

Gerry rested his china teacup in its gold-rimmed saucer, then stood up from the table and started walking towards his bedroom.

"You sure you want to turn in already?" Eddie called up from the sofa. "We can watch a movie. One of the local stations is playing *The Time Machine* on its late show. I just saw a commercial for it on TV."

"You just saw an *advert* for it on the *telly*," Gerry corrected him. "Honestly, Eddie, why is it that every time we cross the pond, you start slipping back into your American accent?"

"Because I'm half Yank and proud of it," Eddie answered. He turned his gaze back to the television set. Footage of soldiers boarding a plane for Vietnam flashed across the screen.

"At least I am sometimes," he added in a sad voice. He stood up from the couch to change the channel, then looked back at

Gerry. "We'll be in Cincinnati for the Fourth of July. My grandparents invited us all to their farm for a cook-out."

"Sounds great," Gerry said unenthusiastically. "But right now, I just want to turn in and read my book. See if maybe that chapter about Gilbert's party was more exciting than I gave it credit for. There must be *some* debauchery going on in this story *some*where."

"No alcohol tonight," Eddie reminded Gerry as he reached for his doorknob. "Emmett made me promise to stand sentry."

"Don't worry," Gerry called back to him. "I'll be a good boy."

He closed the door behind him, stripped out of his street clothes, and changed into the costume he had purchased in the French Quarter. He struggled with the cravat, but managed to tie it into an elaborate knot with some effort. Then he grabbed the bottle of animation potion he had bought at the Obeah shop and placed it on his nightstand beside Eddie's leather-bound copy of *The Tenant of Wildfell Hall*.

He stepped into his bathroom, grabbed his toiletry bag, and removed a bottle of Listerine and his vial of prescription pills. He washed down a tablet with a large swig of mouthwash, shuddered briefly, and made a sour face at his reflection in the mirror. Then he gulped down the remaining contents of his small bottle of codeine-laced cough syrup. He kicked back another large gulp of Listerine, then returned to his bed and sprinkled a few drops of potion on top of the book's cover. He lay down, opened the novel, and read until his eyelids grew heavy...

* * *

The loud bark of a dog roused Gerry from his slumber. The animal's toenails clicked and clacked as it bounded down a wooden floor in the not too far off distance.

Gerry opened his eyes and surveyed his surroundings. He was lying on a bed, though it wasn't as comfortable as the one he had fallen asleep on earlier. He turned his face to the side and saw a silver comb-and-brush set and lace doily lying on top of an antique-looking table. A high-backed wooden chair stood in front of the table, with a woman's nightgown draped over it.

I'm in a lady's bedroom, he realized with a rush of excitement.

He smiled to himself, imagining what sort of fun awaited him this evening. But then the bedroom door opened, and a pretty young woman rushed inside. The hem of her long, green skirt made a soft rustling noise as she hurried across the floor to her dressing table. She pulled a brass clasp out of the back of her hair and threw it on the table top, releasing her long, chestnut-colored curls in a cascade of tresses over her shoulders. A plainer looking woman wearing a long, dark maid's uniform followed the young woman into the room and closed the door behind her.

Gerry sucked in a deep breath and tried to think of a polite way to explain his presence to the ladies. But they paid him no mind.

"Just undo my laces and my corset, if you please," the young woman directed her servant. "I'll brush my hair myself."

"As you wish, Miss Rose," the maid replied.

Gerry sat up and watched the maid unlace the back of her mistress's snug-fitting silk bodice, then untie the top knot on her corset. The young woman sucked in a deep breath, then released it with a loud sigh of relief as the servant loosened the strings on her undergarment.

Gerry considered lingering in the room, since the women didn't seem to notice him. But then his conscience kicked in. *I came for the drugs, not the sex,* he reminded himself. He slid off the mattress, walked across the floor, and opened the door. He saw a plump, middle-aged woman marching down the hallway towards him with a cross look on her face.

Christ, it's Gilbert and Rose's mum! he panicked. *What if she sees me in her daughter's boudoir?*

He ducked back inside the room.

Mrs. Markham stopped in front of Rose's door. "Darling, you left your door open. You should be more careful. I wouldn't want your brothers' manservant to see you undressing."

Rose turned on her heels and frowned at her maid.

The maid lowered her head. "I'm sorry, miss, I was certain I had closed it."

"Oh, never mind," Mrs. Markham said. She stepped into the bedroom and gave her daughter a quick goodnight kiss, then returned to the hallway, closing the door behind her.

Hell, she didn't see me either, Gerry realized. *Something fishy is going on in here.*

He threw a quick glance at Rose. She was leaning against the table while her servant undid the final loops on the back of her corset. He savored the view for a brief moment, then put his hand to the doorknob and slipped out of the bedroom, making certain to close the door in his wake. He proceeded down a long hallway towards a grand staircase. He stood at the top of the steps for a brief moment, admiring the crystal chandelier that hung over the foyer, then started walking down the stairs.

When he reached the bottom step, he saw Gilbert rush in front of him, open the door to the house, and bid welcome to a man wearing pajamas and an overcoat.

Bloody hell, that's me! Gerry marveled as he stared at his pajama-clad twin. He bit back a laugh. *I'm revisiting the scene I was in last night!*

He followed Gilbert and his other self into the building's spacious library. He listened to their conversation, smiling as he recalled each person's words before they were spoken. After a few moments of hovering in the back of the room, he decided to step out of the shadows. He puffed out his chest and walked to the fireplace, passing directly between the room's two occupants. Neither man paid him any mind.

Bullocks! That Listerine must not have been strong enough to do the job right, he thought with a wave of remorse. *I'll have to stick with proper booze next time.*

He watched Gilbert leave the room to fetch the laudanum, then saw his other self pick up the golden snuffbox and slip it inside his pocket. After Gilbert returned to the room with the medicine and spoon, Gerry watched himself sample the tincture of opium. He paid careful attention to the expression on his face as the laudanum took effect.

Damn, I look so fucking happy! he marveled.

Then he watched himself fling off Gilbert's coat and blanket and run to the French doors. Gilbert followed at his heels, calling, "Gerald! Gerald! What are you doing, my good man?"

"I'm helping myself to another taste of your laudanum," Gerry replied, reaching for the bottle and spoon.

Gilbert paid him no heed.

Gerry snuck a quick dose of the drug, then rested the spoon and bottle back on the small table just as Gilbert returned to the fireside. Gilbert collected the medicine and left the room.

A small but powerful sensation of warmth started spreading through Gerry's body. He felt lightheaded and wonderfully soft inside, though the rush was not as potent as the one he'd experienced the previous night. He walked across the library and lay down on the settee in the back corner of the room.

Gilbert returned to the scene a few moments later, followed by a large, black dog. He picked up the blanket the pajama-clad Gerry had left by the fireplace and flung it at the settee. It smacked Gerry squarely across his face.

"Excuse me!" Gerry shouted at him. "You just hit me!"

Gilbert ignored him. He grabbed his coat off the floor and started walking out of the room. The dog ran up to Gerry and started sniffing him.

"Come, Keeper!" Gilbert called to the animal. "Come! Now!"

The dog lingered for a few moments by Gerry's side, sniffing furiously at his crotch, then turned and followed his master out of the library.

Gerry closed his eyes and let the laudanum lull him back to sleep...

* * *

A sharp rapping noise called him back to reality.

Eddie stopped knocking on Gerry's bedroom door and called through the wood. "Time to wake up, Ger! We leave for the airport in an hour. I ordered breakfast for you."

Gerry yawned and stretched, then stood up from his bed and examined himself in the floor-length mirror hanging from his closet door. His new jacket was rumpled and his silk vest was creased.

But it's nothing I can't straighten out with an iron, he decided as he ran his fingers over the fabric of his suit. He threw a loopy smile at his comically dressed reflection, then stripped off his costume, draped it over his bed, and put on the jeans and shirt he had left on the floor. He stepped into the next room and approached the breakfast table.

"Did you leave me any coffee?" he asked as he pulled back a chair.

"Half a pot," Eddie answered without looking at him.

Gerry poured himself a cup, then grabbed a slice of bacon off Eddie's plate.

Eddie looked up at last and frowned. "There's rashers on your own plate."

"Yeah, but it's more fun to steal yours," Gerry replied.

Eddie rolled his eyes, then started buttering his toast. "So, did you read ahead in the book last night?"

"Nah, I just went back to the same scene I visited earlier," Gerry said with a smile.

Eddie bore his eyes into his drummer. "You don't mean what I think you mean, do you?"

Gerry chuckled. "Yeah, I do. But don't worry. I didn't sneak any wine or whiskey into my bedroom on your watch. I just washed back my meds with a couple shots of Listerine. Tasted bloody awful, but it sent me back to Gilbert's pad all the same. Though it was different this time. Nobody recognized me."

"Uh-huh," Eddie said doubtfully. He brought his toast to his mouth and crunched into it.

"Honestly, it was a very strange experience," Gerry continued. "I felt like a ghost or something, just floating through the pages. I even saw myself as I appeared the day before, dressed in my jammies and sitting by Gilbert's fireplace. Mind you, that was pretty damn weird! But I drank another spoonful of laudanum while I was there, so it was worth the trip."

He brought his coffee cup to his lips and took a sip.

Eddie rolled his eyes. "Right. If you say so, Ger. You dreamt you were a ghost, and you drank some more imaginary laudanum."

"No, the laudanum was real. It's just me that wasn't," Gerry countered. "Nobody recognized me. Not even my other self." He took another sip of coffee, then stared thoughtfully at Eddie. "I take that back. The dog saw me. His name was Keeper. He kept trying to sniff me."

Eddie chuckled and reached for his coffee cup. "Maybe Keeper noticed you were wearing the same pair of smelly socks that you wore the night before."

Gerry plucked a slice of bacon off his own plate. "No, I was barefoot the first night I went there. And I didn't meet the dog that time."

"Right," Eddie mumbled. He rested his elbows on the table and offered Gerry a weak smile. "Well, I suppose your return trip into the novel was harmless enough. It can't be good for you to drink mouthwash like that, but I don't suppose it'll kill you."

"Nah, I feel great," Gerry insisted. "Honestly. I've never felt better."

"And are you done with your pills yet?"

"I've got three left."

"Good," Eddie replied. "You can take one this morning, one this afternoon, and one at teatime. And then maybe tonight you can switch back to your old twentieth-century bad habits."

"Yeah," Gerry agreed. "Maybe tonight." He finished his cup of coffee and stood up from the table. "I'm going back to my room to pack up my new suit. I'm gonna need to have it pressed when we get to Houston. I think I might be wearing it again before long."

Chapter Six

Houston, Texas

Eddie rolled to the far edge of his mattress and pressed his pillow against his ear to drown out the sound of Gerry's snores. His head was reeling from drinking too many shots of tequila at the after-show party, and his mood was decidedly out-of-sorts.

He closed his eyes and tried to will himself to sleep. Then the couple in the next room started grunting and groaning, providing an unwelcome counterpoint to Gerry's low-pitched snuffles. He cursed under his breath and folded his pillow over itself in a futile attempt to double its muffling power.

Then Gerry released a thundering snore and bolted upright in his bed, shouting, "Fuck me, *that's* where it came from!"

Against his better judgment, Eddie rolled to his other side and called to his roommate through the darkness, "That's where *what* came from?"

"The snuffbox!" Gerry exclaimed. "I just saw Frederick Lawrence pull it out of his pocket and lob it at the fireplace!"

Eddie rolled over again and pushed his folded pillow back against his ear.

Gerry switched on the lamp between the two beds and flooded the room with a shock of bright light.

"Dammit!" Eddie cursed. "Turn that off! I'm trying to sleep!"

Gerry cast a worried look at his friend. "Then take that pillow off your face. You shouldn't sleep with your head all covered up. You might suffocate yourself."

Eddie threw the pillow at Gerry, then covered his eyes with his hands to block out the lamplight. "I can't sleep with you snoring like a rutting pig either."

"Well, good then," Gerry said. "If you can't sleep, then I can tell you all about my latest adventure. I just found out who my snuffbox belongs to."

"You just told me," Eddie said crossly. He sat up against his headboard, but continued covering his eyes with his hands. "Some wanker named Lawrence Frederick."

"No," Gerry corrected him. "Some wanker named Frederick Lawrence. He was one of the guests at Gilbert's Guy Fawkes Day party."

"Right," Eddie sighed. "So you went back to Wildfell Hall, then, did you?"

"No, I went back to Linden-Car," Gerry replied. "I've told you already. That's what Gilbert calls his pad. Wildfell Hall is the name of the house that Mrs. Graham is renting. She's the tenant in the book's title."

"Fine," Eddie groused. He lowered his hands and blinked, then threw a bleary-eyed gaze at Gerry. "So how'd you get back there? I thought you finished your pills at dinner."

"Nah, I've still got two left. I'm saving them for my literary jaunts."

The couple in the next room started shouting in ecstasy.

Gerry frowned. "Damn, is that Tony having a mister-and-missus?"

"Nah, Pete's in the next room," Eddie mumbled. "I saw him leaving the party with a very fit ginger."

"Hhmm," Gerry sighed. "So how come you didn't score tonight?"

"I almost did," Eddie answered in an irritated voice. "But when I brought her up here, she saw you sprawled across your bed, dressed like some extra from a low-budget Edgar Allen Poe horror film and rumbling like a Formula One motor car, and she bailed on me. I walked her back to the lobby and called her a cab."

"Hhmm," Gerry repeated. "Pity, that."

Eddie rubbed his eyes and shrugged. "Yeah, well, I suppose bad luck comes in threes. The lights blinked out in the middle of our concert. The Sheridan screwed up our reservations so we had to shack up at this crap Howard Johnsons for the night. And now you've scared off my date, but I still have to listen to Pete Cooper shagging some bird in the next room."

Gerry threw a glance at the half-empty bottle of whiskey sitting on his bedside table. "Want a shot? Maybe it'll get your mind off things."

"No," Eddie whined. "I just want to sleep."

"Well, let me tell you about my trip first," Gerry insisted. He slid off his bed, sat down on the edge of Eddie's mattress, and handed him back his pillow.

"So I went to Linden-Car again, but this time, I was fully present, just like I was the first night," he began. "The dog caught my scent and started barking at me. Then one of the footmen spotted me and started asking who I was. So I dodged him and made a dash for the library. I hid behind the settee and tried to figure out what I should do next. Then Frederick Lawrence barged into the room, all hot and bothered. He pulled my snuffbox out of his vest pocket and hurled it at the fireplace, shouting, 'Damn you, Arthur Huntington!' Then he stormed out of the room. But he was too upset to aim properly, so the snuffbox bounced off the grate and landed on the floor by the chair where I'm supposed to sit later in the scene."

Eddie rubbed his throbbing temples. "So I take it you read some more of the book? You can confirm that all of this nonsense happened in the actual text?"

"Nah, none of this happened in the book," Gerry replied. "But since I was there in the house the night of the party, I could see some of the bits and pieces that the author left out of the novel. You know, like deleted scenes from a movie that end up on the cutting room floor."

Eddie slid back under his covers and arranged his pillow behind his head. "Sounds great, Gerry. But who is Arthur Huntington?"

"Haven't a clue," Gerry replied. "I suppose maybe I should read ahead a few chapters. I've been to Gilbert's dinner party three times now, and it's gettin' to be kind of a drag."

"Except for the imaginary laudanum you keep quaffing," Eddie noted.

"Yeah," Gerry said with a wistful smile. Then he frowned. "Bullocks! I didn't get to take a dose tonight! I woke up as soon as I found out who that damned snuffbox belonged to!"

"Pity, that," Eddie replied.

Gerry sighed. He switched his gaze to the leather-bound novel sitting on the end table, then picked it up and returned to his bed. "Mind if I keep the light on for a while? I think I'll do some reading, as long as I'm up."

"Be my guest," Eddie replied. He rolled back to the far edge of his bed.

"So where are we playing tomorrow?" Gerry asked as he opened the book. "Dallas?"

"No, Austin tomorrow, Dallas the day after that," Eddie grumbled.

"Sounds good," Gerry said indifferently. He found his place in the novel and started to read. Then his eyes widened and he dropped the book in his lap. "The Thirteenth Floor Elevators come from Austin, Texas! You suppose we could catch them at a club while we're in town?"

Eddie rolled back over and faced Gerry once more. "*We're* giving a concert in Austin tomorrow night, you pillock. Remember? We can't just run off and see some other band play!"

"Oh, yeah," Gerry agreed. "I suppose you're right." He fell silent for a long moment before continuing his thought. "But maybe we could send the Elevators some passes to our show and throw them a little party afterwards." He started singing the lyrics to the band's hit single, *You're Gonna Miss Me*, then brought his hands to his lap and pounded the rhythm to the tune on the book's leather cover.

Eddie watched him in irritated silence for several seconds, then reached for the half-empty bottle of whiskey and poured himself a glass.

Chapter Seven

Austin, Texas

Eddie paid the taxi driver his fare, then helped his bandmate Jim McCudden out of the cab. They stepped into a brightly lit hotel lobby, trailing a cloud of sweet smelling smoke behind them, and turned into a side corridor to summon an elevator. Jim pushed the "Up" button, then looked at his songwriting partner with a curious expression.

"What is wrong with this picture?" he asked, trying but not quite succeeding in focusing his gaze at Eddie.

Eddie glanced over his shoulder at the framed sketch of a bowlegged cowboy that hung behind him. "Are you mocking that cowpoke? Or do you mean why are we shacking up in a cheap hotel for the second night in a row?"

Jim giggled and leaned against the wall for support.

Eddie threw him a lopsided smile. "The perspective is off on the drawing. That's why the cowboy looks wonky. And I'm gonna guess we're staying at this crap hotel because Emmett wasted half the tour's budget on that posh suite of rooms in New Orleans."

The elevator doors opened. Eddie guided Jim into the car.

Jim rested one hand on Eddie's shoulder to steady himself, then pushed a button for the third floor. "No, I meant something else entirely," he said, smiling dreamily. "Though you're right, those digs in New Orleans were sweet. I meant why were *we* the last two Pilots to leave our party with the Thirteenth Floor Elevators? Emmett sent those invites to Roky Erikson and Tommy Hall at *Gerry's* request, but he barely shook hands with them before he skipped back to the hotel. He didn't even stay to smoke a toke. What gives?"

The elevator doors opened. Jim stumbled out of the car.

Eddie reached out his hand to steady Jim, then started leading him down the corridor to his room. "Gerry has found a new preoccupation," he explained. "Victorian literature."

Jim stopped walking and giggled once more. "You're having me on!"

"No, I'm quite serious," Eddie insisted. "I lent him one of the books I bought in the French Quarter, and he's taken a quite a shine to it."

"I didn't know our Ger even knew how to read," Jim said.

"Well, he's not exactly *reading* it," Eddie replied. He threw Jim an exasperated look, then pointed to an alcove in the middle of the hallway that housed the floor's vending machines. "Sit with me for a minute and I'll try to explain."

Jim plopped himself down on a red vinyl couch that stood beside a tall ice machine. The torn plastic cushion made a farting noise as he landed on the seat. He giggled again.

Eddie rolled his eyes, then sat down on a metal folding chair across from his songwriting partner. "Remember how Gerry's doctor in New Orleans gave him those pills for his cough and warned him not to mix them with booze or they'd cause hallucinations?" he began.

Jim smiled. "Right, yeah, that sounds familiar. So let me guess—he mixed them with booze and had a hallucination."

Eddie nodded. "Brilliant deduction. But on a lark, Gerry and I also sprinkled some of that magic potion I bought for my brother on a book, to 'make it come alive.' Then Gerry fell asleep and dreamt that he traveled into the story and met the characters."

Jim snorted, then stood up and leaned against a vending machine. "I need some nibbles. I'm gonna buy a packet of crisps." He pulled a few coins out of his wallet and fed them to the machine, then examined the offerings for sale. "What the hell are corn nuggets?"

"I'm not sure," Eddie replied. "Try the pork rinds. They're like pork scratchings back home, only Texan."

"Right," Jim agreed. He pulled a knob to release a packet of snacks from a top slot of the machine and collected his food. "So this book of yours must be pretty compelling, if it lured our Ger away from a night with the band that coined the term 'psychedelic rock'."

"Actually, it's rather staid," Eddie retorted. "At least the first couple of chapters are. That's all I managed to read when I pried the book out of Gerry's hands this morning. Some bloke named Gilbert meets a mysterious widow named Helen Graham, but another bloke named Frederick tries to steer him away from her. And then this bird named Eliza, who's got a thing for Gilbert, starts spreading nasty rumors about Helen to scare Gilbert off."

"Sounds like an episode of *Coronation Street*," Jim scoffed. He opened his packet of snacks and bit into a pork rind. His eyes grew wide and his cheeks flushed red. "Holy crap, these are spicy!"

Eddie grabbed the bag away from him and read the label. "Of course they are. You bought the jalapeño flavored brand, you pillock!"

Jim turned to the neighboring soda machine and bought himself a can of Fresca. "I think my crisps are hotter than that novel of yours."

"Maybe so," Eddie agreed. "But Gerry claims he's traveling into the scenes that the author left out—the scenes in which Gilbert offers him doses of laudanum to help with his cough. So the book has a certain addictive appeal."

Jim giggled again. "That's the daftest thing I've ever heard." He pulled the tab off his drink and sat back down on the torn couch, releasing another farting noise. He shrugged, swallowed a sip of Fresca, then looked back at Eddie. "So that's why he hurried back to the hotel right after our gig? So he could hallucinate himself into this book?"

"He's gone there the past three nights," Eddie replied. "Or rather, he's washed down his pills with booze the past three nights, then fallen asleep and dreamt about going there."

"Right," Jim said. He chomped on another pork rind and washed it down with a swig of Fresca, then stood up from the couch. "Well, to each his own. I'm gonna turn in now. My head's reeling, but I want to make a phone call before I go to sleep. Good night."

Eddie stood up and walked Jim down the corridor.

Jim put his ear to his bedroom door. "Sounds like Tony's done with that bird he picked up at the party." He found his room key in his trouser pocket and jabbed it into the lock.

Eddie leaned against his own bedroom door. The drone of Gerry's snores rumbled through the wood.

"Gerry sounds like he's out for the night too," Eddie replied. "Though I imagine his fun is only just beginning." He bid Jim goodnight, then unlocked his door and stepped inside his room. He found Gerry sprawled across one of the two beds, dressed in his old-fashioned suit.

Eddie turned his attention to the nightstand that stood between the two beds. Cluttering its surface were an open flask of whiskey, an empty shot glass, Gerry's prescription pill bottle and flask of animation potion, and the seventy-year-old copy of *The Tenant of Wildfell Hall,* splayed open with its spine facing the ceiling. He picked up the book and noticed that its pages were damp with a scented liquid. His face flushed red with irritation, and he threw an angry look at his roommate. "You poured your goddamned potion on the paper, you wanker!" he swore. "You were just supposed to sprinkle the bloody cover!"

Gerry's eyes fluttered beneath his closed lids. His lips curled into a contented smile.

Eddie kicked off his shoes and flopped down on his mattress. His hair and clothes stank of weed. He considered taking a shower but felt too tired to move. He lay in silence for a long moment, then rolled his head over his pillow and looked back and forth between Gerry and the novel.

"If you're gonna ruin the pages of my book, then you'd better let me join you for your final trip inside," he told his somnolent drummer.

He sat up, opened the prescription bottle, and tossed back Gerry's last pill with a shot of whiskey. Then he grabbed the book, sprinkled a few more drops of animation potion on top of the page that Gerry had left splayed open, and lay back down to read himself to sleep…

* * *

The inside of Eddie's eyelids glowed bright red. He opened them briefly, then immediately shut them again to blink back the blinding sunlight that was beating down upon him. He turned his head to the right, opened his eyes once more, and examined his surroundings. He was lying in a meadow. A cool breeze drifted through the tall blades of grass, tickling his face and sending a slight chill through his body.

Where the fuck am I? he cursed in his head. Then a powerful realization dawned upon him and he smiled to himself. *That pill worked! I'm inside the bloody book!*

He rubbed his fingers through the damp grass beneath him, then lifted his hands back to his chest and felt a small object resting on top of him. He picked it up and inspected it. It was his leather-bound copy of *The Tenant of Wildfell Hall*.

He chuckled to himself, then felt a sudden tug of panic. "Gerry?" he called out, hoping he'd dropped into the same chapter as his drummer.

"Bugger! Is that you, Rochester?" came a loud voice from behind a large elm tree.

Eddie stood up, tucked the book into the front pocket of his jeans, and started walking towards the tree. "Damn, I shouldn't have taken off my shoes back at the hotel!" he shouted to Gerry. "My socks are all wet now!"

Gerry stepped out from his hiding spot and adjusted his top hat. "Christ! How the hell did *you* get here?" he shouted back.

"I followed you," Eddie replied. "So where are we?"

"We're standing outside Wildfell Hall, you git!" Gerry barked. "And what do you mean, you followed me?"

"I did exactly what you did," Eddie stated matter-of-factly. "I took one of your pills with a chaser of whiskey and sprinkled some magic potion onto the page of the book where you'd left off reading. Then I started to read too."

Gerry's face flushed. "You took my last pill? Shit, you wanker, those were *mine!*"

Eddie shrugged. "Yeah, well, it's *my* book." He took another step towards his drummer and tripped over a rock. "Bullocks!" he cursed as he hit the damp ground again. "That hurt!"

"Well, of course it hurt, you pillock," Gerry said. "You just fell on your face."

Eddie looked up at Gerry and frowned. "No, I meant, that *really hurt!* I'm dreaming, but I just felt a jolt of real pain, right here." He lifted his throbbing hand to his eyes and watched a trickle of blood run down his index finger. "I'm bleeding! I'm bloody bleeding!"

"Right, fine, you're bleeding," Gerry agreed. "Now shut up, would ya? I don't want Gilbert to hear you."

Eddie plucked a violet off the ground and brought it to his nose. "Christ, I can smell this flower! It smells just like the violets that grow behind my grandparents' farmhouse in Ohio!" He broke into a big smile.

Gerry sighed loudly and asked Eddie once more to be quiet.

Eddie stood back up and walked to Gerry's side. "This place is amazing!" he gushed. "It's so fucking real. It's mind-blowing!"

"Yeah, well, wait till you try the laudanum," Gerry replied. "That'll keep you coming back for more."

Eddie opened his mouth to speak again, but Gerry clamped a hand over his face. "Shut up, already, Rochester," he hissed. "Gilbert's right over there!"

Eddie cut his eyes to the spot where Gerry was pointing and saw a man in an old-fashioned coat standing in the shadows of a dilapidated mansion.

"He's spying on Helen Graham," Gerry explained in a low voice. "He was trying to chat her up, but she sent him away. She asked him to meet her on the moors tomorrow and promised to tell him then why they couldn't be together. But Helen was sobbing when she gave him the brush, so he stuck around to make sure she was okay. And now she's gonna step out of her house with Frederick Lawrence. Look—there they are! Frederick's got his arm around her, and she's just about to nestle up against his shoulder. Yup. There she goes. Quite the nestler, our Helen."

"Wow, this is so cool!" Eddie marveled. He glanced back and forth between Gilbert and the strolling couple, then looked back at Gerry. "I didn't get this far in the chapter. What's Gilbert gonna do now?"

"He gonna throw himself over that fence," Gerry replied. "Watch, here he comes."

As soon as Gerry spoke, the man standing in the shadows hurled himself over the fence that Gerry was pointing to and started rolling on the ground, his body wracked with sobs, his limbs flailing in despair.

"Damn, would you look at that?" Gerry said dismissively. "And to think, you called *me* pathetic earlier."

"Well, the poor bloke's heart is broken," Eddie noted as he watched the pitiful spectacle unfold. After a full minute had passed, he looked back at Gerry. "So how long do you suppose he's gonna keep up at that—thrashing against the cruel blows of fate?"

"I'm not sure," Gerry replied. "It was a little unclear in the book. A while, I think."

Eddie reached into the pocket of his jeans and pulled out his copy of *The Tenant of Wildfell Hall*. "I'll check in here," he said. "Damn, I lost the page!"

Gerry scowled at him. "Fuck it, Rochester, you brought the *book* with you?"

"Apparently," Eddie said with a shrug as he leafed through the novel. "Don't you usually bring it along too?"

"I never have before," Gerry replied with a frown. "Do you suppose that'll make a difference? The characters might find it and start reading about themselves and discover they're not really real."

"Will it matter?" Eddie asked as he continued thumbing through the book. "They're only fictional." He found the page he was looking for and started reciting the text out loud:

I saw him put his arm round her waist, while she lovingly rested her hand on his shoulder; —and then, a tremulous darkness obscured my sight, my heart sickened and my head burned like fire: I half rushed, half staggered from the spot, where horror had kept me rooted, and leaped or tumbled over the wall—I hardly know which—but I know that, afterwards, like a passionate child, I dashed myself on the ground and lay there in a paroxysm of anger and despair—how long, I cannot undertake to say; but it must have been a considerable time...

"Yeah, well, let's hope he doesn't take too much *more* time," Gerry interrupted. "I haven't got all day. Emmett's gonna wake me up soon, and put me on a plane to Dallas."

"Why did you want to visit *this* chapter?" Eddie asked as he watched Gilbert continue his wild gyrations.

"Read on, my friend," Gerry replied. "No—I take that back. Let me summarize. Gilbert's gonna go home in a few minutes and lock himself in his room. His family will be concerned, but he'll just ignore them. And he won't go to the moors tomorrow to hear Helen's explanation either. His mother is going to say at the beginning of the next chapter that Gilbert's been out of sorts for *days*."

"So?" Eddie asked. "I still don't see why you'd want to visit this part of the book."

Gerry tapped his top hat and straightened his cravat. "So what do you suppose Gilbert is going to do to drown his sorrows for the duration of this chapter? Don't guess—I'll tell you—he's going to pass away the hours with his very sympathetic new friend Gerald, the long-lost nephew of Lord Douglas Enis of Cornwall. *That's* what he's gonna do. Believe you me, Eddie, I know *just* how to get that poor bloke's mind off his troubles."

He turned away from Eddie and stared at Gilbert. "Just look at that poor sod. Give us a minute—yes—now—all *right* then! He's starting to calm down. This is my chance." Gerry started walking towards the fence.

"Wait, Ger, what about me?" Eddie called after him. "What am *I* supposed to do?"

"How the hell should I know? I hadn't planned on your tagging along!" Gerry called back to him. "You're not dressed properly and you reek of Maryjane. You'd just confuse the poor bugger if you showed up next to me, looking and smelling like that."

He fell silent for a brief moment, then shrugged his shoulders. "Tell you what, mate—why don't you just sit there by the tree and read for a while? You dig books, right?"

"But how am I supposed to get back to the hotel?" Eddie cried out as Gerry turned and started walking away.

Gerry spun around again and offered him a sympathetic smile. "Don't worry. When the drug wears off, you'll find yourself back in bed. At least I always have. Now, if you don't mind, I have a friend who needs a little touch of my own particular brand of tea and sympathy."

He turned back towards the fence and started walking across the meadow at a brisk pace. When he reached Gilbert's side, he exclaimed in a voice loud enough for Eddie to hear, "Good gracious, Mr. Markham! Imagine my meeting you here! I've just come from Wildfell Hall to check on my painting, but Mrs. Graham was not available to talk. My word, you look peaky. Why don't you let me walk you home? You look like you could use a spot of brandy. I remember your once telling me that a brandy makes *every*thing seem better."

Eddie watched the two men in silence, then sighed aloud in frustration. He found a large tree stump to sit on and opened his book to the place where he had left off reading. Then he looked up again and saw Gerry and Gilbert walking away from Wildfell Hall.

Chapter Eight

Dallas, Texas

Tony Wright motioned for the band to stop playing and glowered at his drummer. "Bullocks, Gerry, what the hell is wrong with you? That's the third song you've messed up this afternoon! When did you stop remembering when to come in on *Too Much Trouble?*"

Gerry tossed a bleary-eyed gaze at his lead singer. "Calm down, you wanker. It's just a bloody sound check. I'll get it right at the show tonight."

Tony rolled his eyes, then looked back at the engineer working the boards at the Dallas Memorial Auditorium. "Alright then, Mark—let's try this one more time." He turned his head and nodded at Jim McCudden.

Jim put his fingers to the piano keys and played the intro to the band's second biggest hit once more. Tony and Eddie joined in with their guitars, then Gerry did a quick drumroll. Just as Pete started coming in with the rollicking bassline, Alan Poole ran up to the stage.

"Christ, guys, I need your help! I am in such deep shit!" he shouted over the music.

Tony called the song to a second halt and leaned into his microphone. "Drop everything, lads, our dogsbody needs help. Ooh, that didn't sound right, Mark. Could you bring it up a few notches? Thanks. Testing—one, two, three—*Alan's in deep shit!*"

Alan scowled at Tony. "Stop it, you tosser. I'm not kidding. I picked up the dry-cleaning this morning before we left Austin, but I forgot to count the clothes. We're missing Eddie's jacket and Gerry's trousers. How are you five supposed to go on stage tonight?"

Pete and Jim started to snicker, then the rest of the band joined them in laughing at their manager's younger brother.

"Don't worry, Alan," Eddie said once he managed to compose himself. "I'll just wear a bright blue shirt this evening. And Gerry can go pants-less. The drum-kit should shield his furry legs from the fans. At least until he jumps down to the front of the stage for his bow."

"No problem," Gerry assured Alan in a dead-pan voice. "I promise to wear my cleanest knickers."

"This isn't a bloody joke!" Alan swore. "You five *have* to wear matching clothes."

Jim sighed theatrically. "No, we don't. A lot of groups have stopped wearing matching suits. And I, for one, am all in favor of ditching those ridiculous blue jackets we've been wearing all summer. Who picked those out, anyway?"

Tony turned towards Jim. "I did. And they're not blue. They're cerulean."

"Excuse *me*, Mr. Carnaby Street," Jim replied, looking back at his keyboard.

"Cool down, everyone," Gerry urged his bandmates. "Eddie can wear my jacket tonight, since he'll be standing up front, and I'll just dress in black. It won't make much difference since I'll be sitting behind my kit."

"But I couldn't fit in your jacket," Eddie protested. "My shoulders are too big."

"Maybe Eddie can wear my jacket and I can trade off with Tony," Pete suggested.

"Then what am I supposed to wear?" Tony challenged.

"Gerry's knickers!" Jim proposed.

The band members fell into another fit of laughter.

"Shut up, will ya?" Alan shouted at them. "This is serious! What are you blokes gonna wear at tonight's show?"

"Fear not, Master Poole," Tony proclaimed once he had composed himself. "After the sound check, I'll zip over to Neiman Marcus with your brother and buy five new suits for tonight's gig, while you lot have your tea at the hotel. Emmett should know everyone's size. And our style-conscious pianist can tag along and offer suggestions, if he'd like."

"That's all right, mate," Jim chuckled. He put his hands to the keys and started playing the melody to the Kinks' recent hit *Dedicated Follower of Fashion* while he threw Tony a lop-sided grin. "I'll bow to your judgment. Just please don't buy anything else in that hideous shade of blue."

"I like green," Pete piped in.

"Nobody asked you," Tony replied curtly.

Pete rolled his eyes at Tony. "Damn, you sure know how to make the new guy feel welcome, don't you?"

A short silence followed his remark. Then Eddie worked his way over some loose electrical cords and clapped Pete on the back. "Don't mind him. He's just having you on."

"Yeah, right," Pete said. He turned away from his bandmates and shared a knowing look with a roadie who was sitting in the first row of the empty arena.

"Enough, already," Tony said testily. "Let's finish this bloody sound-check. Otherwise, I'll only have time to pick out something nice for myself at Neiman's, and the rest of you lot will have to wear cast-offs from one of those cowboy outlet shops we saw near the airport."

"Ooh, I want a ten-gallon hat!" Gerry squealed. "Could you find me one in orange?"

Tony flipped off his drummer, then leaned into his mic. "Testing, one, two, three." He turned his head and nodded at Jim to play the intro to *Too Much Trouble* one more time.

* * *

"Now *that's* what I call a groovy coat," Jim laughed. He slipped on the satin, paisley-patterned, wide-collared suit jacket that Tony offered him and buttoned it at his waist. "Bit of a low cut at the neck, though, in'it? What are we supposed to wear underneath this?"

"A ruffled shirt," Tony replied. He started distributing coats and shirts to his bandmates. "We'll all match on top, but I bought different colored trousers for each of us." He reached into another shopping bag and pulled out five pairs of pants.

"Purple for you, Jim, since you complained about the cerulean," Tony added as he tossed him the pants. "Orange for Gerry and green for Pete, at their own special requests. Gold for me, 'cause I'm the band's golden boy, and coral for our rosy-cheeked lyricist."

Eddie groaned. "Seriously? You expect me to wear pink satin pants on stage?"

"They're coral," Tony repeated.

"I'd call them salmon-colored," Emmett Poole said with an encouraging smile. "Or maybe even peach."

Eddie rolled his eyes at his manager. "I am *not* going to wear this ensemble in Cincinnati for my grandparents to see."

"I'd trade with you, Eddie," Gerry offered. "'Cept you already pointed out that we're not the same size."

Emmett examined Gerry's physique. "Actually, Ger, it looks like you've lost some weight since the tour began. Are you still feeling under the weather?"

Gerry winked at him. "Nah, I'm fit as a fiddle. I just haven't been drinking as much lately." He slapped his belly and smiled.

"Right," Emmett replied. He scrutinized Gerry's appearance for a more few seconds, then turned towards the rest of the band. "Now suit up, lads. You're entertainers, and these new outfits that Tony selected are—*entertaining*—to say the least. Be grateful that I didn't let him buy the matching hats he was eyeing. Now, about tonight—"

He glanced at his watch, then looked back at his protégés. "The limo should be here in half an hour to take you to the auditorium. And our hotel has agreed to let us use one of their ballrooms for a small party after the show. Some blokes from a local radio station helped me organize it."

He turned back towards Gerry and frowned. "I assume you'll be joining us?"

Gerry buttoned his new ruffled shirt and sighed. "Yeah, I suppose I will. Got naff all else to do this evening." He threw a brief, irritated look at Eddie, then turned back towards his manager. "I might as well rejoin the twentieth century again."

* * *

"Hey, hold the lift!" Eddie shouted at Gerry. He worked his way unsteadily down the hotel corridor and threw a loopy grin at his drummer.

"Going up?" Gerry asked as he reached for the elevator button.

"Sure," Eddie replied. "'Less you'd like to go to the basement with me and—play cards with the janitor." He leaned against the elevator wall and flinched when the car started moving.

"Might as well," Gerry said. "Not much happening at that party Emmett threw for us."

Eddie shrugged. "He didn't—he didn't know the radio station had given out—so many passes to our—younger fans."

Gerry shook his head. "Yeah, they're cute little bints, but I wouldn't be caught dead taking one of them back to my room."

"Right," Eddie agreed. He belched loudly, then smiled in relief. "That felt good."

Gerry laughed at him.

The elevator came to a halt, and the doors opened. Eddie stepped out of the car and immediately bumped into the tall cylindrical receptacle that stood beside the doors. A smattering of sand flew out of the can.

"Shit," Eddie cursed as he wiped specks of white ash off his shirt and jeans.

Gerry squared his eyes at him. "How much did you drink at the party?"

Eddie swayed back and forth on his feet. "Too much, I suspect. How 'bout you?"

Gerry pulled a metal flask from the back pocket of his trousers and waved it at Eddie with a sly smile. "I just had a few wee drams downstairs. But the kindly barkeep filled this with whiskey for me so I could drink it tonight on my lonesome."

Eddie frowned at him, then started searching his pockets for his room key. "Bullocks, I must have left my fob in my room."

Gerry made a tut-tutting sound, then chuckled. "Come to my room, you souse. You can ring the front desk and ask them to send up a bellhop to rescue you."

"Thanks," Eddie replied. He followed Gerry into his room and called the lobby, then lay down on Gerry's bed while he waited for someone to bring him a spare key. He noticed Gerry was changing from his jeans and polo shirt into the costume he'd purchased in New Orleans.

"Christ, Ger, you can't be thinking of—of going back into that bloody book again," he stammered between hiccoughs. "I thought you were out of—magic pills."

"Thanks to you, prat," Gerry replied. He buttoned his silk vest, then walked to the mirror hanging over his chest of drawers and checked his reflection as he tied his cravat. "I've got another idea of how I might get back inside. But I'll need the book. Once that bellhop comes with your key, you can fetch it for me."

Eddie shot him a confused look. "But I don't have it. I lent it—to you."

Gerry stopped tying his knot and scowled at Eddie. "You had it last. You were reading it in the meadow outside Wildfell Hall!"

"Yeah, but I didn't have it with me when I—woke up this morning," Eddie insisted. He belched once more and put his hand to his rumbling gut. "I figured you must have—taken it and thrown it in your bag."

Gerry's face flushed. "I did no such thing! Dammit, Rochester, if you left that book behind in Wildfell Hall, then I'll—"

A knock on the door interrupted him.

Eddie stood up from the bed and started swaying on his feet. He reached his hand towards the wall to steady himself.

"Lie back down, you tosspot," Gerry groused. "I'll get the bloody door."

Eddie collapsed back on Gerry's bed and closed his eyes.

Gerry opened the door and took the spare key from the bellhop, then turned back towards Eddie. "Alright, *now* you can stand. We're going across the hall to search your room."

Eddie stood up slowly, then staggered after Gerry down the hall and into his own room. "You can check my—suitcases," he directed his friend as he sat down on his bed. "I'll look through this crap—on my nightstand."

Gerry scowled at him, then dumped the contents of Eddie's bags onto the floor and started rifling through his clothes. After a few minutes of fruitless searching, he looked back at Eddie and caught him leaning against his pillow, perusing a book. "What the fuck is *that?*"

Eddie put down the book and threw Gerry a loopy grin. "It's the collected works of—Jane Austen. I bought this in—New Orleans too." He squinted at Gerry's costume and frowned. "Maybe you could visit—*Pride and Prejudice* tonight. Your clothes aren't too far off the mark, and Mister—Darcy probably kept some laudanum on hand for—medicinal purposes."

Gerry sat down on the edge of Eddie's mattress and groaned.

Eddie put down his book and scooted closer to his friend. "I can make you a list of—Jane Austen's rogues. You might like to meet—George Wickham."

"Bugger, I don't have the energy to meet a new set of characters," Gerry whined. He fell silent for a long moment, then reached into the pocket of his coat and pulled out his jeweled snuffbox. "Maybe I could sprinkle some cartoon potion on this instead. It might work. This snuffbox actually belongs inside the novel, after all."

Eddie shrugged. "Go ahead and—try. But how are you gonna get there without your—pills?"

Gerry said nothing for several seconds, then turned towards Eddie with a twisted smile and made a concerted effort to raise his left eyebrow for effect. "Come back to my room and I'll show you." He slid off the bed, grabbed Eddie's arm, and led him across the hallway.

As soon as Eddie stepped inside his drummer's room, Gerry locked his door. "I've got me some windowpane. I'm thinking maybe that might work."

Eddie's face fell. "Ah, Christ, Ger, don't—do that. You can't control yourself when you're—tripping on acid."

"It's not the acid I'm craving. It's the laudanum," Gerry insisted. He stepped into his bathroom, then returned with a small vial of tablets. "I got these from Pete. I know we've been giving him a hard time, but he's actually not that bad of a bloke."

Eddie stood frozen on his feet and offered no reply.

"C'mon, Rochester, don't judge me," Gerry said. "It's just LSD. You've tried it before."

"I know I did," Eddie replied. The light returned to his bloodshot eyes, and his drunken stupor and hiccoughs suddenly vanished. "And I *hated* it. I thought I was gonna die."

"Everyone has a bad trip sometimes," Gerry said reassuringly. "The more you take, the more smoothly things go. Believe me, I should know! Now, tell you what—since you already know what it's like inside the book, why don't you tag along with me tonight? I can introduce you to the joys of imaginary opium. Just slip one of these little dots under your tongue, and I'll guide you. It helps if you trip along with someone you trust."

Eddie furrowed his brow. "But I don't trust you."

Gerry threw him an irritated look. "Well, thanks, mate. 'Preciate the vote of confidence."

"I am *not* gonna drop acid with you," Eddie insisted. He turned on his heels and reached for the doorknob.

Gerry grabbed Eddie's arm and pulled him away from the door. "Please, Eddie. You can't stay conscious if you wanna visit Wildfell Hall with me again. You've gotta be dead to the real world, so to speak."

Eddie glowered at Gerry. "I just told you," he said, enunciating each word precisely. "I don't *want* to visit Wildfell Hall with you again. Now let me go!"

"C'mon, Eddie," Gerry pleaded. "You've *gotta* come with me. We have to find your book before the characters do. *You're* the one who left it behind. And if you don't want to visit Gilbert with me, then we can maybe go to a chemist's shop instead and purchase a perfectly legal stash of nineteenth-century laudanum for ourselves."

Eddie held Gerry's gaze. "Brilliant idea, Ger. Just brilliant. Except for one small thing. The chemist might notice that the wrong monarch's face is printed on your pound note."

Gerry swallowed hard. "No matter. I'll just pinch some laudanum then. I've got sticky fingers."

Eddie turned back to the door.

Gerry grabbed his elbow and pulled him further into the room. "C'mon, Eddie. Open your mind to the possibilities! Just think—you read English at uni. I'm giving you the chance to explore literature in a way that your stuffy old professors never even dreamt of! Let go of your conscious inhibitions. Give yourself over to the unconscious. I mean the semi-conscious. The not quite so conscious—"

"I am *not* taking a hit," Eddie insisted. He pushed Gerry away with all his strength.

Gerry landed on the floor with a loud thump. His eyes flashed with anger. He stood back up and curled his right hand into a fist. "Oh, yes, you bloody well are, you prat!" He threw a hard punch at Eddie's face.

Eddie fell backwards, hit his head against the sharp corner of a wooden chest of drawers, and collapsed on the floor in a heap.

Gerry stood over Eddie's limp body and rubbed the sore knuckles of his right hand.

"Bugger," he mumbled under his breath. "Shouldn't have done that."

He stared at his unconscious friend for a long moment and watched a small trickle of blood drip down Eddie's temple to his cheek. Then he shrugged in resignation.

He collected his snuffbox, potion, and LSD, and brought them to Eddie's side. He lifted Eddie's arm off the floor, rested it over his chest, and placed the snuffbox on top of his hand. Then he sprinkled some animation potion on the snuffbox and sat down on the carpet next to his friend. He considered his situation for a brief moment, then sprinkled a few more drops of animation potion on top of Eddie's bleeding forehead. He made a quick sign of the cross for good luck, then placed a tablet of acid under his own tongue and focused his gaze at the snuffbox until the colors of the jewels started melting into each other and the glitter of the gold casing began to leap like a glowing, orange flame…

Chapter Nine

A cool, soft rain caressed Eddie's aching cheek. He opened his eyes slowly but could only see out of his right one; his left was too swollen and painful to be of any use.

Pushing his hands against the ground, he realized he was once again lying in the middle of a grassy field. But this time the grass wasn't just damp—it was soaking wet.

"Bullocks," he cursed under his breath. "Here I go again."

He scanned the field with his good eye, searching for Gerry, then called out his name.

"Who's there? Who's calling me?" came the response.

Eddie turned towards the sound of Gerry's voice and just barely made out the shape of a mid-sized man crouching down in the grass about twenty yards away. He stood up and approached his drummer, clenching his hands in and out of fists as he walked.

"You hit me," Eddie stated in a menacing voice when he reached Gerry's side.

Gerry looked up at him and smiled. "Hey, Eddie! You're here too! Your face is a funny shade of purple. You must be turning into a grape. Isn't this place groovy? Just look at all the raindrops on these blades of grass! Have you ever seen anything so beautiful?"

Eddie stared blankly at Gerry for a long moment, then sighed. "You're flying pretty high right now, aren't you, mate?"

Gerry bent back down to inspect the raindrops. "If you look at this grass at just the right angle, you can see dozens of little rainbows on each drop of water. So many, many rainbows—" His voice drifted off blissfully.

Eddie crouched down so he could meet Gerry's eye. Rain started running over his thick mop of hair and dripping down his neck. "Come with me, Ger," he said, extending his hand towards his friend. "Let's get out of this rain. There's a small grove of trees over there. We could use them for shelter until the sun comes out."

Gerry frowned. "But I haven't finished counting all the rainbows yet!"

Eddie sighed and grabbed Gerry's hand. He tried to pull him up to a standing position but slipped on the wet, muddy grass and fell down instead.

"Shit," Eddie cursed. "How the hell are we going to get out of here?"

A crestfallen expression washed over Gerry's face. "Why would you want to leave, Eddie? This place is so beautiful! I've never seen *any* place as beautiful as this."

"The trees are beautiful too, Gerry," Eddie replied in an irritated voice. "I'll bet there are dozens of raindrops clinging to the bark of those trunks. And even more rainbows on the dripping leaves."

Gerry's eyes lit up. "Let's go see 'em!" he exclaimed. He bolted upright and started running away.

Eddie stood back up and wiped his wet palms against his damp jeans. He fell into pace behind his drummer, keeping his half-blind gaze at the ground to watch for more patches of mud. He noticed a large circle of mushrooms a few yards in front of him.

Gerry ran into it and spread his arms out wide. He lifted his face to the sky and let the rain wash over him as he started spinning. "I'm in a fairy ring, Eddie!" he laughed. "I'm in a fuckin' enchanted fairy ring!"

"Indeed you are," Eddie agreed. He sighed in frustration as he watched Gerry twirl. "C'mon, Ger. The trees are just a few yards away. Let's get out of this rain."

Gerry stopped spinning and smiled at his bandmate. "Look, Eddie! The fairies have come out to say hello! They're dancing with me! Come say hello to the fairies, Eddie!"

"You say hi for me, Ger," Eddie replied with a sigh. "I'm gonna sit this number out." He left Gerry to his new friends and stepped into the shelter of the nearby grove of trees. The rain thumped steadily against the leaves in a dreary rhythm that contrasted sharply with Gerry's ecstatic giggling.

"They're so pretty!" Gerry gushed. He raised his arms over his head and started dancing a jig.

Eddie sat down on a tree stump and buried his head in his hands. He kicked the ground in frustration and knocked a small object out of the pile of damp, dead leaves by his feet. He bent down, picked up a slightly sodden, leather-bound book, and broke into a smile.

"Hey, Gerry!" he called out. "I found the novel! You were right! I must have left it here last night!"

Gerry ignored him and continued dancing as if no one were watching.

Eddie cast another irritated look at his friend. Then he opened the book, found the page he had left off on, and covered his sore eye with his left hand. He read ahead in the novel until the sound of footsteps crunching through the dead leaves broke his train of thought. He looked up and saw Gerry gazing down at him.

"Hey Eddie," Gerry said in a worried voice. "One of the fairies just told me to eat a mushroom. She said it would help me see even more pretty colors. Do you think I should?"

Eddie closed the book with a loud clap. "No! *Never* eat wild mushrooms, Gerry! Never, *ever!* They could be *poisonous!* You could *die!*"

Gerry shook visibly at Eddie's harsh reply and started to cry. "I don't wanna die, Eddie," he sobbed. "I don't wanna die!"

Eddie sighed. He stood back up, rested the book on the tree stump, and placed his hands on Gerry's shoulders. "You're not gonna die, mate," he said gently. "I'm sorry. I didn't mean to scare you just there. I just don't want you to do something stupid while you're under the influence of—the influence of—"

"Of the fairies?" Gerry guessed. "Oh, no, Eddie. They're *good* fairies. They wouldn't try to pull one over on me like that. Can't you see them, Eddie? They're nice fairies. Just look how pretty they are!" He glanced back at the mushroom ring and waved.

Eddie fell silent for a long moment while he chose his next words. Then he squeezed Gerry's shoulders more tightly to hold him in place. "I know they *seem* friendly, Ger, but you don't know this particular group of pixies," he explained, hoping he'd found the right tone of voice to mollify his unpredictable friend.

He released his grip on Gerry's shoulders and folded his arms in front of his chest, assuming a professorial air. "The small folk are a tricky lot, you know? Sometimes they *look* like fairies, but they're really wood sprites or hobgoblins in disguise. Trust me, I've read a few collections of Celtic fables. You have to be *very* careful with fairies."

Gerry gazed at his friend in awestruck wonder. "Wow, you sure are smart, Eddie."

"Right," Eddie agreed. "Now come out of the rain and sit with me."

Gerry glanced at the tree stump. "What's that?" he asked, pointing to the novel.

"I tried to tell you," Eddie replied. "I found the book that we lost. I'm reading the chapters that follow your last meeting with Gilbert Markam. Ever since Gilbert saw Helen embrace Frederick Lawrence, he's become consumed with hatred for his rival. Gilbert's not thinking very clearly anymore."

"Gilbert? Who's Gilbert?" Gerry asked.

Eddie's face fell. He drew in a deep breath to settle his rattled nerves, then briefly summed up the novel's plot and reminded Gerry that it was his obsession with the book that had brought the two of them to this soggy field.

Gerry grinned. "Oh, right, I remember Gilbert now. I sat in a library with him, didn't I? He gave me some really groovy stuff to drink off a shiny silver spoon. That was *great* shit!"

"Yeah, right," Eddie agreed.

"I remember what I said to him now!" Gerry added excitedly. "I told him to stop being such a pansy and start acting like a man. I told him to fight for his woman!"

"Well, I think he must have taken you at your word, my friend," Eddie replied with a roll of his one good eye. "Because this next chapter is entitled 'The Assault'." He opened the book back up, skimmed a few pages, and started summarizing the new plot developments for Gerry.

"Gilbert goes horseback riding on a drizzly day," Eddie began. "He's feeling very angry with Frederick…then Frederick comes riding up behind him…Frederick tries to make polite conversation, but Gilbert ignores him and starts gripping his horse whip in his hand…Frederick notices and starts taking Gilbert to task…"

Eddie cleared his throat and started reading aloud from the text:

'Markham,' said he, in his usual quiet tone, 'why do you quarrel with your friends, because you have been disappointed in one quarter? You have found your hopes defeated; but how am I to blame for it? I warned you beforehand, you know, but you would not—'

He said no more; for, impelled by some fiend at my elbow, I had seized my whip by the small end, and—swift and sudden as a flash of lightning—brought the other down upon his head. It was not without a feeling of savage satisfaction that I beheld the instant, deadly pallor that overspread his face, and the few red drops that trickled down his forehead, while he reeled a moment in his saddle, and then fell backward to the ground—

Eddie looked up from the book and smiled ruefully at Gerry. "Sounds like Gilbert did the same thing to Frederick that you did to me."

Gerry stared back at him, dumbfounded. "What do you mean?"

"Don't you remember?" Eddie replied. "In the hotel room? You smacked me hard across my face. You knocked me unconscious, you wanker!"

"I did?" Gerry's eyes started welling with tears.

Eddie noted Gerry's guilty expression and felt a sudden rush of pity.

"'S'alright, mate," he assured his old friend. "I know you didn't mean it. You were probably 'impelled by some fiend at your elbow,' just like Gilbert was."

Gerry flinched, then started flapping his arms wildly, hurling a small puddle of rain that had collected on the wool of his sleeve directly into Eddie's face.

"Aacckk!" he screamed. "There's a fiend at my elbow! Christ! It's a monster! Help me, Eddie! He's got me! Help!" He flailed his arms and started stomping his feet in the dead leaves.

Eddie tossed the book on the ground and rested his hands back on Gerry's shoulders. "Calm down, Ger. There is no fiend at your elbow. You're just hallucinating. There's nothing there. Honestly. Trust me!"

"Yes, there is!" Gerry sobbed. "It's horrible! It's ghastly! It's—it's one of those goddamned fairies! You were *right,* Eddie! They *were* hobgoblins in disguise! Oh, Christ, it's gonna eat me!"

Eddie stared helplessly at his friend. *Dear God, how the hell am I supposed to help him?* he worried. But then a useful distraction appeared along the dirt path at the edge of the field. A man approached on horseback, trotting slowly towards them. Then a second equestrian galloped up from a few hundred yards behind the first, spraying thick jets of muddy water into the grass as his horse splashed through the puddles that dotted the road. He pulled his animal to a swift halt, deftly keeping it from slipping, and started arguing with the lead rider.

"Look, Gerry, look!" Eddie said excitedly. "It's Gilbert and Frederick! They're right in front of us!"

Gerry turned towards the men and stared at them in wide-eyed wonder, all fears of the imaginary fiend at his elbow swiftly erased from his mind. He stood transfixed in his spot and watched the scene from the novel unfold.

Gilbert struck Frederick with his whip. Frederick fell from his horse and collapsed in the middle of the road. Frederick's hat rolled into a large puddle, and his horse wandered off a short distance. Gilbert surveyed the damage he had done, then started to ride away. Frederick moaned in pain, then crawled to the side of the road and started wiping his head with a handkerchief. His horse wandered further away and started grazing on the damp grass.

Then Gilbert returned to the scene. He dismounted from his horse, plucked the hat off the ground, wiped a clod of mud off its brim, and offered it to Frederick. Frederick flung the hat back into the road. Gilbert took Frederick's horse by the bridle and walked it back to its owner. Frederick refused Gilbert's offer to help him climb back on.

"Let me alone, if you please!" Frederick shouted at him.

"Humph! With all my heart!" Gilbert replied. "You may go to the devil if you choose—and say I sent you!"

Gilbert wrapped the reins of Frederick's horse over the branch of a nearby bush. He offered Frederick a clean handkerchief. Frederick flung it into the mud. Gilbert remounted his horse and rode off at a gallop, once again splashing sprays of mud in his wake. Frederick slowly lifted himself off the ground and attempted to mount his horse. He raised his right foot to a stirrup. His left foot slipped as he repositioned his weight and he collapsed back in the grass.

Eddie's face flushed with excitement. "This is so incredible," he whispered to Gerry. "We really *are* in the middle of this book!"

"I'm telling you, man," Gerry replied with a nod of his head. "I'm telling you, man—I—I'm sorry, man. What was I telling you?"

A few minutes passed in silence, punctuated only by the steady thump of rain pummeling the leaves. Gerry lost interest in the immobile man sitting at the bottom of the hill and started examining the raindrops that had collected on a large spider web.

Eddie continued staring at Frederick. The rain slowly started to peter out. He squared his shoulders and started walking away from the trees. "Stay there, Ger," he called back to his friend. "Don't move from your spot. I'm just gonna make sure that Frederick's okay." He walked down the small hill, minding his step so he wouldn't slip on the grass, and stopped at the edge of the dirt path.

Frederick appeared startled by his sudden appearance and backed away. "I say, who are you? What are you doing, lurking about in those trees? And what are those clothes that you're wearing? You, you—you have a black eye! You seem to be a most disreputable character!"

"No, I'm not a disreputable character," Eddie replied with a faint smile. "Just a very minor one. My name is Edward Rochester. I'm a—ah—I'm a newly ordained Methodist minister visiting these parts, hoping to find some converts for my parish across the moors. I was attacked by a wandering vagrant. But, umm—but God gave me the grace to realize that he meant no harm. He only hit me because he was frightened and confused. So I gave him my coat and hat, as he seemed to need them more than I did. And then—and then I saw you being attacked as well. I watched you fall from your mount."

Eddie stood up a little straighter and cleared his throat. "This patch of land seems fraught with danger today," he added in a more serious tone. "I don't think it wise for an injured man such as yourself to remain here. Please allow me to offer you my humble assistance. Let me help you back onto your horse, my good sir."

He offered his hand to Frederick, who reluctantly took it. Eddie supported Frederick's weight as he stood back up and climbed on his horse. Then Eddie untied the horse's reins from the bush and handed them to Frederick.

"Thank you, Reverend Rochester," Frederick said softly. "I am much indebted to you."

"Think nothing of it," Eddie replied. "Now, if you'll excuse me, I must help that wretched soul whom God has seen fit to place under my care this afternoon. He seems to be in need of further—guidance."

Both men looked up at Gerry, who had returned to the fairy ring and was beating at the air with a pair of imaginary drumsticks. He started singing—quietly at first, then with mounting bravado: "Purple haze! In my—ooh—fuck—what's the next line? Blowin' my mind—something, something—is it tomorrow or the end of time?"

"He seems to be a drunkard," Frederick noted. "What do you suppose he is doing here?"

Eddie sighed theatrically. "He told me he came to this area looking for laudanum."

Frederick shook his head. "You have assumed a mighty burden, Reverend Rochester. You are a Good Samaritan and a credit to your profession as well. May God bless you."

"Yes, I think I may need God's help with this poor lost sheep," Eddie agreed. He started walking back to the mushroom ring.

Gerry lifted his head and started screaming into the soft sprinkle of rain. "'Scuse me, while I kiss the sky! Ooh, Jimi, I love ya!"

Frederick turned his horse around and rode away, leaving his hat and Gilbert's dirty handkerchief behind on the road.

Eddie returned to Gerry's side and deftly led him back to the shelter of the trees. He sat Gerry down on the tree stump and handed him a damp daisy. Gerry started examining it from every angle.

Eddie sat down beside him in the pile of wet leaves. He picked up the novel and started to read. Then Gilbert returned to the scene. Eddie looked up from the book and watched Gilbert dismount, retrieve the incriminating hat and handkerchief, then climb back on his horse and ride away. Eddie paged backwards in the book and re-read the paragraphs that described Gilbert collecting those items. He shook his head in wonder, then resumed reading ahead.

A quarter of an hour passed in silence. Then the sun broke through the clouds and a rainbow started forming in the east. Eddie poked Gerry to call his attention to the sky.

Gerry ignored him. He put down his daisy and climbed off the stump. "I think I need a little lie-down," he said with a yawn. He curled up in the leaves beside Eddie and closed his eyes. Soon he was snoring.

Eddie sighed in relief, then closed his eyes as well. When he opened them again, he was lying on the floor of Gerry's hotel room, soaked to the skin, clutching his damp copy of *The Tenant of Wildfell Hall*. He lifted his aching head from the carpet and saw Gerry sprawled across the floor beside him. The snuffbox glistened innocently in the palm of his hand. A torn, dead leaf poked out of his right sideburn.

Chapter Ten

Tony knocked on the door of Gerry's hotel room. "Wake up, little drummer boy!" he shouted through the wood. "Emmett's calling a morning meeting."

"Shut the fuck up, you twittering twonk!" Gerry barked back at him. "I'm trying to get my beauty rest!"

Tony crossed the hall and knocked on Eddie's door, "Head's up, Rochester. Your presence has been requested by our manager."

Eddie opened his door and stepped into the hotel corridor. "I got his phone message, Tony. You didn't need to collect me."

Tony stared at Eddie's bruised, swollen left eye and swore. "Jesus Christ, Eddie! What the hell happened to you?"

"Gerry slugged me," Eddie replied nonchalantly. He slipped his hands into his trouser pockets and started walking towards Emmett's suite.

Tony ran after him. "He hit you? Why the hell did he do that?"

Gerry emerged from his bedroom and fell into place behind his bandmates. "I had no other choice," he called up to Tony. "Eddie wouldn't take a hit of acid. So what's this meeting about, anyway?"

Eddie glanced back at Gerry. "I'm not sure, but I hope Emmett's ordered breakfast. I'm famished."

"Yeah, I'm feeling a bit peckish myself," agreed Gerry.

Tony grabbed Eddie by the shoulder and pulled him to a halt. "How can you even think about food at a time like this? Gerry attacked you!"

Eddie shrugged. "Well, I suppose I had it coming." He crossed his arms in front of his chest and looked squarely at Tony through his one good eye. "He wouldn't have done it if I hadn't cleared out his stash of pills." He slipped out of Tony's grasp and stepped into his manager's suite.

Emmett stood up to greet him, then blanched. "Good lord, Eddie! What happened to you?"

"Gerry beat him up," Tony butted in. "Because Eddie took away his drugs and refused to join him on an acid trip."

Gerry bounded into the room. "That's not true," he protested. "It was an accident. I was aiming for Tony. Ahh—so you *did* order brekkie! Thank God!" He claimed a seat at the table in the middle of Emmett's sitting room, grabbed a clean plate, and piled it high with sausages.

Emmett ignored Tony and Gerry and focused his gaze on Eddie. "Tell me what happened, son," he commanded his protégé.

Eddie sucked in a deep breath and peered at his manager through his one good eye. "It's a long story. A very long story."

"So long you could practically write a novel about it," Gerry called up from the table.

Emmett cut him off. "I'm talking to Eddie."

Eddie sighed and offered Emmett a sad smile. "I can't explain everything just now. It's rather complicated. But don't worry, it was—well—it was *kind* of an accident. Or at least Gerry didn't mean to hurt me. And I'm fine now—my eye's just a little swollen."

"A *little* swollen?" Tony protested. "Damn, you look like Sonny Liston after Cassius Clay wiped the floor with him!"

Emmett stepped to the side of the room and reached for the telephone. "I'll ring for the hotel doctor. Maybe he can do something quick. We can't have you going out looking like that."

"Where are we going?" Eddie asked, casting a hungry look at the breakfast table.

"To the radio station that sponsored last night's party," Jim called up from the breakfast table. He pushed aside the vase of flowers that blocked his view of Eddie. "Emmett arranged for us to do an on-air interview. That's why he called this meeting."

Eddie squinted over Tony's shoulder and smiled at his songwriting partner. "Oh, morning, Jim! I didn't see you there behind those daisies!"

"I'm surprised you can see anything with that shiner of yours," Jim replied. "Now sit down and grab some food before Gerry eats it all."

Alan Poole stepped out of his bedroom and mumbled a quiet greeting to the band.

His older brother covered the phone's mouthpiece with his hand and put him to work straight away. "Go make up an icepack for our Eddie. See if you can't get that swelling down. We can't have anyone seeing him like this."

Alan threw a curious look at Eddie. He smirked for a brief moment, then returned to his bedroom to fetch his first aid kit.

Eddie claimed a seat at the table and called across the floor to his manager. "Nobody will see me if I'm just doing a radio interview."

Emmett frowned at him. "The disc jockey will," he pointed out. "And the station manager. And the reporter from the *Dallas Morning News*, who'll be interviewing you lot after you do your radio spot. He's writing a series of articles on British Invasion bands that outlived the glory days of Beatlemania." He lifted his hand from the phone's mouthpiece and asked the concierge for the name of a good local doctor.

"The toffs from Capitol Records will see you too," Jim added as he buttered his slice of toast. "One of the V.P.'s lives in Dallas, and he's invited us to his ranch tonight for a barbeque. Some local country bands will be coming too. Should be fun."

Eddie frowned. "I thought this was supposed to be our day off." He grabbed the bowl of butter pats from Jim and picked up a knife. "Where's Pete, by the way?"

Tony shrugged. "Sleeping in, I suppose." He grabbed a banana off the table, then started walking towards the door. "I'll go fetch my make-up kit and see if I can't find some concealer to cover up your bruise."

Gerry finished his cup of tea in one swallow, then stood up from the table as well. "I'll look through my Dopp kit and see if I still have some Vitamin B tablets," he informed the gathering. "I take 'em whenever I'm hungover. They soothe my eyes when they don't want to open and make 'em look less puffy. They work best when you wash 'em down with chocolate milk and sauerkraut." He turned towards his manager. "Call room service, would ya, Emmett, and order some for our Eddie." He walked to the door and stepped out of the suite.

Eddie poured himself a cup of coffee and refused to answer any more questions about his injury.

* * *

Gerry grabbed Eddie's elbow and led him down the narrow aisle of their chartered jet. "I want to talk to you where no one can hear us," he whispered as he passed Emmett and Alan.

His manager threw him an exasperated look, then turned back to the stack of papers he was reviewing with his brother.

Gerry and Eddie sat down in the last row of the plane and buckled their seatbelts. Once the engines roared to life, Gerry leaned towards Eddie and offered him a belated apology.

"Listen, I'm real sorry about decking you," he began. "I didn't mean to hurt you. I'm just feeling out of sorts lately. More short-tempered than I usually am."

"'S'alright, mate," Eddie replied. "It was kind of fun traveling back into that book with you again, so I suppose it was worth it."

Gerry sighed. "For you, maybe. But I hardly recall a damned thing about our last trip. 'Cept for this daft memory of a manky-looking hobgoblin chasing me out of a fairy ring."

Eddie chuckled. "Right. Well, at least you're learning what *not* to take if you want to venture back inside the novel. Acid leaves you too fuddled to enjoy the experience, and mouthwash makes you walk invisible through the pages."

"Yeah," Gerry agreed. "I need to find a new gateway."

"The sock to the jaw worked pretty well for me," Eddie noted. "If you want to try that route, I could probably round up some volunteers to oblige you."

Gerry rolled his eyes, then hung his head.

"Hey, enough with the long face," Eddie chastised him. "My black eye worked like a chick magnet at last night's barbecue. For the first time since I joined the band, I had more birds gathered around me than Tony did! And they all wanted to give me a little 'southern comfort'."

Gerry eyed him curiously. "Did ya get laid?"

Eddie flashed him a knowing grin, then put his hand to his bruised cheek. "Hmm, maybe I ought not to smile so wide. It hurts my face."

"Well, good on you," Gerry said begrudgingly. "I hardly had the chance to chat up any chicks, what with Emmett shooting daggers at me all night. I felt like I was back in fifth form, with the Creepy Catholic Brothers of Perpetual Torment breathing down my neck."

Eddie laughed again. "At least he didn't cane you."

Gerry turned towards the window and watched the clouds pass by. "Nah, *I* get to mete out all the corporal punishment around here." He looked back at Eddie. "So how is your eye, anyway?"

"Better," Eddie assured him. "The bruise looks worse today than it did yesterday, but I can open my eye easier now. If I'm lucky, it should look okay by the time we get to Cincinnati, so my grandma won't make too big a fuss over me."

"When will that be?" Gerry replied. "I've lost all sense of time and space on this tour. I don't even know where we're playing next."

"We'll be in Cincy for the Fourth of July," Eddie reminded him. "My grandparents are hosting us on their farm. We can light sparklers and set off bottle rockets and eat apple pie and hamburgers and pretend we're wholesome young chaps."

A wicked look washed across Gerry's face. "Your granddad lives in a turn-of-the-century farmhouse, if I remember right. Do you suppose he might have a stash of laudanum hidden away in his larder?"

Eddie snorted. "I'm sure Grandpa's never even heard of it. He's drinks nothing stronger than Hudepohl beer from the local brewery."

Gerry shrugged in defeat. "Well, I suppose that'll have to do then. So chart our course for me, my fellow Pilot—is it St. Louis next, then Cincinnati?"

"We'll be in St. Louis in *two* days. This morning we're going to Kansas City."

"Ahh," Gerry sighed. He eyed the stewardess walking down the aisle and grinned. "You know, I've heard they've got some crazy little women there."

"And I'm gonna get me one!" Eddie sang back. He raised his right hand and motioned for the flight attendant to bring them some drinks.

Chapter Eleven

Kansas City — Late June, 1967

Eddie tipped the bellboy and followed Jim into their suite. He cast his gaze about their elegant sitting room and admired the polished tabletops, plush carpets, and brocade curtains. Then he noticed an antique upright piano tucked into the far corner of the room. "I see that Emmett has assigned us a suite with a piano," he noted dryly. "He must really want us to write a new hit."

Jim laughed. "We're going to *have* to write a chart topper if we're ever going to pay the bill for these digs. What gives with our tour budget, anyway? One night we're holing up in a cheap dive, and the next we're living like kings!"

Eddie shrugged and walked over to the piano. He lifted the cover off the keys, struck a few notes, then turned back towards Jim. "I don't know. Nothing else on this tour makes any bloody sense. Why should our accommodations be any different?"

Jim collapsed on a chintz sofa and rested his feet on the teak coffee table. "I could get used to this, you know? Alan told me when we were checking in that the Beatles stayed at this hotel on their first American tour."

"Yeah, and Emmett told me their Kansas City gig was the only show they didn't sell out on that tour," Eddie replied as he walked back to the middle of the room.

Jim shrugged. "Have you heard how our ticket sales are going?"

Eddie made a "so-so" gesture with his right hand, then sat down in a chair opposite the couch. "We've sold out tonight's concert at Memorial Hall. But it's not nearly as big a venue as the Municipal Auditorium, where we played the last time we were in Kansas City."

"Hmm," Jim mumbled. "Well, I'd rather play to a full house than to a half-empty arena. I can feed off the audience's energy better."

"Yeah, me too," Eddie agreed. "So, how do you think Gerry and Tony are getting along? It's been years since Emmett assigned the two of them to the same room."

Jim laughed once more. "Dunno. But I'm guessing they might *both* show up at tonight's sound check with black eyes."

Eddie chuckled. "Well, then at least I won't be stealing Tony's spotlight anymore."

Jim slid his feet off the table and sat up straight. "So what *really* happened in Dallas? Why did Gerry sock you?"

Eddie lowered his head and stared at his shoes for a long moment. "You're not going to believe me," he offered at length.

"Try me," Jim urged him.

Eddie looked back up and met Jim's eyes. "Do you remember what I told you in Austin, about Gerry dreaming that he'd traveled into the pages of a book I bought in New Orleans?"

Jim thought for a bit and frowned. "Vaguely. Was that when we were sitting by a vending machine, and I was eating some scratchings that set my mouth on fire?"

"Yeah. You were kind of stoned."

"But obviously not as stoned as Gerry was, if he thought he could travel inside a novel."

"Well, that's what I thought too," Eddie agreed. He stood up and returned to the piano, keeping his back to Jim. "Until I went there with him later that night. Inside the book."

Jim started to laugh. "Right, Rochester, right."

Eddie turned around and faced his song-writing partner. "No, seriously, I did. I took his last magic pill with a chaser of whiskey and followed him inside the story."

"Mm-hmm," Jim mumbled dismissively, his eyes twinkling.

Eddie held Jim's gaze for a long moment, then turned away once more. "But while I was there, I left the book behind in a field in Yorkshire. So the next night, Gerry insisted we *both* go back there to fetch it before the characters found it. But I refused. So he knocked me out cold with a right hook to my jaw. Then he dropped some acid and joined me there. But he was flying so high he hardly knew where he was. He started chatting up some fairies he found in a mushroom ring. I talked to one of the characters for a bit. Helped him climb on his horse and tried to make excuses for our Ger. Then I sat down in a damp pile of leaves and read ahead in the novel while Gerry slowly came down from his high. And then we woke up on the floor of his hotel room—wet as drowned rats—with the book once again in our possession."

Eddie turned around and saw his songwriting partner smiling at him.

"What a load of rot," Jim said with a laugh. "Gerry must have slipped a tab under your tongue after he knocked you out and guided you on a trip, then thrown you in a shower to help you come to."

"No," Eddie insisted. He walked back to the middle of the room and reclaimed his chair. "He didn't. We *both* traveled inside the pages of that book. I'm not having you on. We really and truly went there."

"Mm-hmm," Jim said dubiously.

Eddie threw his hands in the air in defeat. "Fine, right. Don't believe me. I didn't want to believe Gerry at first either. But I've been inside that goddamned book twice now, and the 'realness' of that place is something I can't explain away. I've never experienced anything even remotely like it before in my life."

Jim leaned forward and offered Eddie a sympathetic smile. "Well, to be honest, mate, you haven't taken that many drugs. Not like our perpetually stoned drummer has. You don't have much to compare this experience with."

"But I didn't *take* a drug that second time I went there!" Eddie insisted. "I was just reeling from getting smacked in the face! And if those two trips were just imaginary, then how is it that Gerry and I both experienced the same hallucination?"

"Bullocks," Jim cursed, "I don't know." He stood up and crossed the room, then sat down at the piano bench and rested his hands on the keyboard. He pressed his fingers softly against the yellowed ivory keys without striking them. A dull hum of harmonics resounded from the back of the instrument. He swiveled around on the bench and looked back at Eddie.

"Your mind can play tricks on you," he said. "Even when you're not under the influence of a drug or unconscious from a head injury. You can drift into a daydream and forget where you are. Or lose yourself in a story that you're reading. Sometimes I've been so caught up in a song that I'm playing that I've lost all sense of the world around me and just gave myself over to the music. For a few minutes, I could swear that I *was* the music, and the music was me."

He squared his eyes at Eddie. "I took a philosophy class back at uni that explored different notions of reality and how our perceptions can alter it. And even though I didn't understand everything the professor said, I could relate to his lecture, based on my experiences playing piano."

Eddie opened his mouth to argue, then lowered his head and looked down at his shoes. "I suppose it doesn't really matter anymore," he replied. "Gerry used up all the funky medicine that doctor gave him in New Orleans, and the acid he dropped in Dallas didn't work very well. So he shouldn't be able to travel back inside that bloody book anymore, and I won't have to worry about him becoming a laudanum addict."

Jim rolled his eyes. "Oh, come off it, Eddie. Gerry's not *really* taking laudanum. He's just dreaming that he is. And that's probably a good thing, you know? This imaginary opium he's been quaffing is no doubt safer than the real drugs he usually indulges in."

Eddie stood up and grabbed his guitar case from the pile of luggage the bellhop had left by the door. "Yeah, you're probably right," he agreed. He pulled out his instrument and strapped it over his shoulder. "I've tried very hard to keep a level head about all of this. But lately, I've been getting just as caught up in the lure of that blasted book as Gerry has. He's tripping into the pages to score drugs, but I'm fascinated by the notion of actually traveling into a work of literature. It's something I've always fantasized about doing."

"Maybe that's how your magic Voodoo potion works," Jim suggested. "It plays on your desires. If you want something badly enough, then you're willing to suspend your disbelief and get caught up in the illusion you think you're conjuring when you sprinkle a few drops on top of something. It's just like going to a magic show. You *let* yourself get taken for a ride."

Eddie started walking towards the piano. "I know. And now that I'm here in this room talking to you, it all seems so ridiculous. But when I'm with Gerry—"

Jim laughed. "Shit, Eddie, Gerry's a consummate showman! He's a master at drawing people into his own personal world. Remember how he talked us both into dropping out of uni to join his band, so we could follow along on his rock-and-roll fantasy?"

"Yeah, but he was right about that, though," Eddie reminded Jim. "Within a year of joining Gerry's band, we had a number one song on both sides of the pond. I've made more money these past three years than I ever would have if I'd stayed in college and taken a job as a high school English teacher or junior editor at a publishing house."

Jim turned back to the piano and rested his hands on the keys once more. "Yeah, it's been quite a ride. And we're still selling out concerts, even if we're playing smaller halls than we used to. Which reminds me—Emmett wanted us to write another hit, didn't he?"

Eddie strummed a few chords on his guitar, then started tuning his E string. "Right. You got any good melodies bouncing around in your head?"

"Just one," Jim replied. "I wrote it for a girl I met in New Orleans. How about you? Have you been keeping up with your journal?"

"Bugger," Eddie cursed. "I've been too busy tripping into old novels to write any new poems. I've lost my muse."

"Hhmm," Jim mumbled. "Well, how about that girl you shagged in Dallas? You could write a song about her. What was her name?"

Eddie chuckled. "Lucy. So John Lennon's already beat me to the punch on that one. There's no way I'll ever write a lyric that'll match 'Lucy in the Sky with Diamonds'."

"Yeah," Jim agreed. "*Sgt. Pepper* is one fucking amazing album. Though it doesn't have a traditional commercial feel to it. None of the songs on that record screams 'hit single' to me."

Eddie formed a G-suspended-4th chord with his left hand and strummed his guitar, producing a dreamy sort of sound. "So let's tell Emmett we've stopped writing hits and we're gonna start working on a concept album instead."

"Sounds good to me," Jim laughed. "What sort of concept have you got in mind?"

Eddie dashed off a quick flamenco flourish on the strings of his instrument. "How about the adventures of a lonely hearts club band that goes tripping into the pages of an obscure Victorian novel?"

Jim started playing the melody to 'Strawberry Fields Forever' on the piano. "Sounds good to me, mate. Nothing is real. And there's nothing to get hung about."

Chapter Twelve

Milcotte, Ohio — July 4th, 1967

"Slow down, would you?" Gerry called up to his friends. "You're leaving me behind!"

Tony, Jim, Eddie, Pete, and Alan ducked under the shade of a tall sycamore tree and waited for their drummer to catch up with them. A pair of whip-poor-wills sang out from the branches above them, their three-note call providing a plaintive counterpoint to the ubiquitous drone of the cicadas burrowing in the fallen leaves beside the hiking path.

Eddie wiped the sweat from his brow and apologized to his bandmates once again for the heat and humidity. As soon as Gerry joined the group, he drew everyone's attention to a patch of dark green foliage growing next to a blossoming trillium plant at the side of the dirt path.

"That's poison ivy," he warned them. "See how the leaves grow in clusters of three? And they're smooth, with no teeth along the edges? Keep an eye out for that plant. It grows like a weed around here, and you'll itch like crazy if you get even a drop of its sap on your skin."

Tony swatted a mosquito away from his bare arm and frowned. "Right. Any other dangers lurking in your grandfather's woods that we need to know about?"

Eddie curled his lips into a sly smile. "Well, since you asked—remember that old farmhouse we passed near the start of this trail? There's a huge stock of the worst kind of poison buried away in its cellar—homemade moonshine!"

Pete laughed. "Are you telling me your sweet old grandpappy used to keep a still on his farm?"

"No, not Grandpa, his neighbor," Eddie assured him. He swatted away a buzzing blue bottle fly and wiped his brow once more. "That house used to belong to a man known as 'Lightning Louie.' He fell on hard times during the Depression, and the bank was gonna foreclose on his property. So Grandpa offered to buy his farm instead and told Louie he could keep living in his house and pay back the debt as he was able. But then Louie lost both his sons in the War and stopped caring about anything else. He brewed his own hooch in a still he kept behind his barn and slowly drank himself to death. Grandpa chopped down his still after Louie passed on, but he kept the house up for his field hands to use as lodging in the summers."

"And just how do you know there's a cellar full of moonshine in there?" Alan asked with a teasing smile.

Eddie chuckled. "One summer when I was about fifteen, my friend Bob Carter and I snuck inside Louie's basement. We found a stash of old bottles behind a spool of rusting chicken wire and helped ourselves to a little. God, it tasted vile!"

Gerry smirked at him. "Glad to know I'm not the worst boozer in this band. My hand to God, when I was a lad of fifteen, I'd never sipped anything stronger than Communion wine."

Tony rolled his eyes. "I thought you told me you were kicked out of the altar boys when you were twelve after a priest caught you sneaking into the sacramental wine."

Gerry placed his palms together, fingers up as if praying, and raised his eyes towards heaven. "I solemnly swear, I only ever helped myself to the unconsecrated variety. I would never have taken the piss with the blessed Blood of Christ. That would have been a mortal sin." He made the sign of the cross to conclude his confession, then winked at his bandmates.

Eddie chuckled and gestured for his friends to follow him on their walk through the woods.

"Damn, this is hilly, Eddie!" Gerry called up from the back of the pack. "I thought the Midwest was supposed to be flat. I feel like I'm hiking in the bloody Peak District!"

"You're in Ohio River Valley," Eddie called over his shoulder. "It's hilly here!"

"And it's hotter than blazes, too," Alan groused. "And so goddamned humid!"

"Right," Eddie agreed. He called his friends to another halt. "Sorry. I grew up with this weather so it seems normal to me. But I guess you lot must feel like you're stuck in a sauna. We can turn back if you'd like, though the path we're on is a loop. It won't make much difference if we go forward or head back to the truck now."

"Then let's keep walking," Jim said. "It's nice being outside again, after all these weeks being holed up in hotel rooms. Even if it does feel like we're in the tropics."

"I'm with you, mate," agreed Tony. "Let's forge ahead. It's good exercise."

Gerry rolled his eyes. "Fine. You lot go ahead, and I'll walk back to the truck. I'll meet you at the trailhead."

"I'll join you, Ger," Alan offered. "The hills ahead look higher than the ones we just climbed."

"Fine," Eddie said. "Just watch out for the poison ivy."

Gerry undid the top few buttons on his shirt and wiped the sweat from his neck while Alan swatted at a mosquito that had pricked his arm. They waved goodbye to their friends, then started retracing their steps.

* * *

Eddie's grandfather stood up from his webbed lawn chair, stretched out his burly arms to loosen his stiff joints, and turned to his grandson. "I think I'll turn in now, son, and join Alma. Make sure you tamp out the fire before you go to bed."

"Of course I will, Grandpa," Eddie replied.

The Pilots and the Poole brothers joined Eddie in bidding their host goodnight. Then they turned back to the bonfire crackling inside a small, stone-lined pit in the lawn beside the old Rochester farmhouse.

Gerry speared another marshmallow with the stick he'd broken off the nearby elm tree and held it over the flames. "Damn, these s'mores are good. Almost makes me want to join the Girl Guides. Someone hand me two more pieces of chocolate, would you?"

Alan grabbed a melamine plate off the wooden picnic table at his side, tore two squares off a Hershey bar, and handed them to Gerry. "Don't you want some graham crackers too?"

"Nah," Gerry replied. "I'm watching my calories." He blew out the small flame that had engulfed the corner of his marshmallow, then squeezed his burnt morsel of goo between the two squares of chocolate to make a sandwich.

"Ah, perfection!" he proclaimed after he gobbled up his sweet.

Emmett chuckled. "Gerry, I suspect you've gained back all the weight you lost at the beginning of this tour. How many pieces of apple pie did you eat tonight at dinner?"

"I stopped counting after two," Gerry replied. He threw a quick glance at Alan. "Toss me another one of those Hudy's, would you?"

Alan grabbed two cans of Hudepohl beer from the ice bucket at his feet and handed one to Gerry, then popped the top off the other for himself.

A firecracker exploded in the distance, setting off a small flash of red light in the northern sky.

"Too bad we used up all our bottle rockets," Pete said with a sigh. "We could answer your neighbor's shot with one of our own."

Eddie started to reply, but Tony cut him off. "We should be quiet now, for Eddie's grandparents' sake. I imagine they'll be getting up a lot earlier than we will tomorrow morning." He stood up from his lawn chair and slipped his acoustic guitar back inside its case.

Eddie nodded in agreement. "A farmer's day begins before the crack of dawn."

The seven men sat in silence for a long moment, listening to the rhythmic chirp of the crickets and stretching out their feet in front of the crackling fire. Eddie threw another log on the flames. A small spray of sparks popped into the air as the shriveled bark started burning.

Emmett pulled a packet of Lucky Strikes from his shirt pocket, removed a cigarette for himself, then passed his pack and lighter to Eddie.

"No thanks," Eddie said as he passed them along to Jim. "I'm trying to give up smoking, remember?" A small cloud of smoke wafted up from the bonfire and hit him squarely in the face. Eddie waved his hands in front of his nose and started coughing.

Jim laughed. "Looks like that bonfire has other ideas!" He lit a cigarette for himself, then passed the packet and lighter along to Gerry.

Alan lowered his can of beer and wiped a frothy mustache of foam off his upper lip. "So what should we do now? Tell ghost stories around the campfire?"

Tony laughed. "Gerry's been telling me a crazy story these past couple of days. No ghosts in it, but there *have* been a lot of supernatural comings and goings."

"Eddie's told me the same tall tale," Jim chimed in.

Gerry's eyes flashed like a cat's in the flickering firelight. "It's *not* a tall tale!" he insisted. "Eddie and I really went there!"

Emmett, Alan and Pete immediately started bombarding Gerry and Eddie with questions.

Eddie threw an irritated look at his drummer, then shared a few details with the assembly about his and Gerry's trips into the pages of *The Tenant of Wildfell Hall*.

Emmett clucked his tongue in disapproval. "I'm surprised at you, Eddie. I can understand *Gerry* believing these adventures were real, but I would have thought you knew better."

"And I thought you promised not to let our Ger mix booze with his meds that night in New Orleans when you babysat him at the hotel," Alan added.

Eddie frowned at Alan. "Yeah, right. *You* try keeping Gerry off the sauce the next time, why don't you?"

Pete leaned in a little closer to Gerry. "Could you really feel that laudanum?" he asked in an incredulous voice. "I mean, did you get genuinely high off it?"

"Better than high," Gerry boasted. "'Cause when I came out of the book, I didn't feel any side-effects. There was no crash.

No hang-over. No headache. No nothin'. And what's more, laudanum is a form of opium, and even *I* know that's addictive. But I'm not hooked."

"Because you never really took it," Jim pointed out. "You just *dreamt* that you did."

Gerry sipped his beer and shrugged. "Well, maybe so," he admitted as he wiped off his own foamy mustache. "But it was a *very* sweet dream."

"Such stuff that dreams are made on," Eddie murmured.

Tony turned towards Eddie. "That's a good line, mate. Has a real musical feel to it. You should write that into a song lyric."

Eddie snorted. "Shakespeare beat me to it. That's what Prospero says at the end of *The Tempest.*"

"I thought that's what Puck said in *A Midsummer Night's Dream*," Jim countered.

Eddie shook his head.

Gerry looked down at his shoes. "It doesn't matter," he said with a sigh. "Though it *is* mid-summer, and it *is* nighttime. And *I*, for one, wouldn't mind going back into that dream."

Pete scooted his lawn chair a little closer to Gerry's. "I'll go with you next time," he offered. "It sounds like a really cool trip."

"But I can't go back," Gerry groused. "My magic medicine's all gone. I've tried tripping into the book with acid, but that didn't work very well."

Emmett flashed a stern look at his drummer. Gerry ignored him and licked a streak of dried marshmallow off his thumb.

"Eddie went there the night you clocked him," Jim piped in.

"Right," Gerry scoffed, turning towards his pianist. "So maybe I should pay some prize fighter to beat me up."

"I'll do it to you for free," Tony offered.

Gerry turned his head and glowered at Tony. "Like hell you will," he retorted.

Emmett cleared his throat to call the band to order, then looked back at Eddie. "So is that how your enchanted story ends? With Gerry's friend Gilbert knocking that Frederick fellow off his horse and riding into a drizzly, English sunset?"

"No, that's hardly even a third of the way into the book," Eddie replied. "I've read ahead a few chapters these last couple of days. Want me to tell you what happens next?"

Gerry finished off his beer, then crushed the can flat with the heel of his shoe. "Why not? We've got naff all else to do."

"Don't worry, Ger," Eddie said reassuringly. "You'll like this part. It's where the debauchery begins!" He poked the dying bonfire with the tip of a long branch and sent another flurry of sparks into the air. Then he settled back in his lawn chair and smiled at his drummer.

The dancing flames cast an eerie glow over his face, basking the remnants of his green and purple bruise with pulses of orange light. A pair of fireflies flitted up to his side for a brief moment, winking flashes of light, then darted away towards the giant elm tree that stood across the lawn.

Eddie crossed his arms in front of his chest and started summarizing the next few chapters of *The Tenant of Wildfell Hall*:

"After Frederick came home injured, Helen confronted Gilbert. He was too embarrassed to speak to her, so she thrust her diary at him and told him to read it. She said it would answer all his questions about her. And at this point, the novel changes direction completely. Gilbert's no longer the narrator of the book—Helen is.

"When her diary begins, she's a young debutante who's just been sent to London for the 'season,' so she can try to snag herself a wealthy husband. Her aunt and uncle keep trying to foist this old sod named Mr. Boarham at her, 'cause he's filthy rich, but she wants nothing to do with him. Then one night at a party, when Boarham starts chatting up Helen, a bloke named Arthur Huntington comes to her rescue. He's everything that Boarham is not. He's young and fun and shares her rude opinions about the stuffy old people they have to keep company with. He flirts with her and asks her to dance. And Helen falls for this chap—hook, line, and sinker."

"Arthur Huntington," Gerry interrupted. "Where have I heard that name before?"

"It's the name you called out in your sleep in Austin," Eddie reminded him. "You told me you saw Frederick Lawrence hurl his snuffbox at a fireplace and shout 'Damn you, Arthur Huntington!'"

"Huh?" Alan asked. "I'm confused. How does a snuffbox fit into all of this?"

"Never mind," Eddie replied, rolling his eyes. "The snuffbox is not actually in the book. But Arthur is, and he has one hell of a reputation. Helen's aunt and uncle try to warn her off him. They claim he's wild, unprincipled, and prone to every vice common to youth."

"He sounds like my kind of bloke!" Gerry laughed.

"Yeah, I figured you'd prefer him to Gilbert," Eddie agreed. "So anyway, Helen starts running into Arthur at parties. Then one night, another drunken old geezer starts hitting on her and Arthur saves her again. Then he makes an improper advance of his own, but Helen doesn't mind too much. And before you can say 'Bob's your uncle,' she marries the bastard."

"And they live happily ever after?" Tony guessed.

"Hardly." Eddie replied. "Helen starts regretting her hasty marriage straight away. Arthur taunts her with dirty stories about his former flames on their wedding night, then cuts short their continental honeymoon. He whisks her back to his country estate in Yorkshire, then abandons her so he can party with his mates in London. When he finally comes home to her, they start fighting, so he goes back to town, claiming he needs to finish up 'a little business'."

"And what sort of 'business' might that be?" Gerry asked in a knowing voice.

"I think you can imagine," Eddie chuckled. "This part of the novel is written from Helen's point of view, so the details aren't spelled out. All the reader knows is that Arthur Huntington is gone for three months, and when he finally comes home, he's weak, sick, and showing all the classic symptoms of withdrawal from alcohol and drugs. It takes him several months to get his strength back. But as soon as he does, he invites his London friends up to his estate for the shooting season—along with their wives. That's where I am in the book now. The moveable feast has just restarted at Arthur's country manor home."

Gerry stared at the smoldering fire for a long moment, then sighed. "I wish I could transport myself into that chapter where Arthur Huntington is hanging out with his mates in London. That sounds like a lot of fun."

"I'll come with you," Pete volunteered.

"Me too," Alan piped in.

Gerry looked up at Alan and started snickering, but Alan stuck to his guns.

"Hey, who's gonna pick up your laundry or hail you a cab while you're there?"

"I hope you can flag down a horse-drawn carriage better than you can summon a taxi," Tony teased him.

Emmett turned towards his brother. "Well, I'm sorry, Alan, but Gerry doesn't have any of his hallucinogenic medicine left. So even if this whole pissed-up wonderland actually does exist, *none* of you can travel there anymore."

"That's right," Tony agreed. "Unless Gerry finds another drug that'll work the same magic."

Gerry stared into the dying bonfire, then put his hand to his mouth to cover his growing smile. The soft golden light of the flames reflected off his eyes and made them shine like beacons from the dark shadows of his face, giving him a devilish air.

He lowered his hand to his lap and threw his manager an enigmatic look. "That's something I might just have to ponder for a while," he said. He stood up from his lawn chair and kicked his crushed, empty beer can into the fire. "But for now, I think I'll just have a little lie-down. I may have drunk one too many cans of Hudy."

Chapter Thirteen

Cincinnati, Ohio

Gerry stood up from his drum kit and banged one last flourish on his cymbals, then threw his sticks to the cheering crowd and jumped down to the stage for a final bow. With the thunder of applause still ringing in his ears, he jogged after his bandmates through the labyrinth of tunnels that led to the Pilots' dressing room in the underbelly of the Cincinnati Gardens.

"Well, it wasn't a sell-out," Jim said once they closed the door behind them. "But the fans were still pretty enthusiastic."

"Pretty *damn* enthusiastic," Tony corrected him. "We've got the best fans in the world!"

"It's almost addicting, isn't it?" Eddie added. "Sometimes I get so sick of touring and sleeping in different hotel rooms every night that I almost want to give it all up and just focus on making records, like the Beatles have. But then I hear a crowd going wild like this one tonight, and I want to keep coming back for more!"

Gerry straddled a metal folding chair from behind and frowned at Eddie. "You never told me you wanted to give up touring."

Eddie's face flushed. "Well, not really," he said, stepping back his remark. "It's just something I think about every now and then." He offered Gerry a weak smile. "C'mon. That shouldn't surprise you. You know I've never gotten into touring like you have. I can only take so much of the party scene that goes hand-in-hand with life on the road."

"Yeah, well, *I'm* still up for a little partying!" Tony exclaimed. He handed his paisley coat to Alan and squared his eyes at Eddie. "You grandparents are great, mate, but let's face it—we just spent a quiet night in an old house with an old man and an old lady on a farm in the middle of outer-bumble-fuck. And I, for one, would like to do something a little more exciting this evening."

Pete tossed Alan his coat as well. "Is your brother throwing us another party where he'll be taking attendance? Or can we just hit a nightclub in Cincinnati and let our hair down?"

Alan laid their coats out flat on a long, wooden table and reached for a clothes brush. "Nah, Emmett doesn't have anything planned for you lot tonight."

Eddie slipped off his coat and rested it on top of Pete's. "You'll probably have better luck hitting the bars in Northern Kentucky, Cooper. What passes for nightlife in Cincinnati might fall short of yours and Tony's standards for excitement."

Gerry stood up from his chair, threw his jacket onto the pile of stage clothes, and clapped his hands to call the room to order. "Gentlemen, I have a proposal. What do you say we head back to our hotel suite and go visit Arthur Huntington for a little Victorian-style debauchery?"

Jim rolled his eyes. "I thought you used up all your magic meds."

"I did, but I found something else that might just do the trick," Gerry boasted.

He turned towards Eddie and bowed his head in an expression of mock contrition. "Bless me, Eddie, for I have sinned. Yesterday when Alan and I cut short our walk, we snuck into Lightning Louie's old farmhouse and pinched a few bottles from his cellar."

Eddie frowned. "No, fucking, way. I am *not* going to drink any more of that manky moonshine. I still remember how awful it felt retching that up when I was a teenager."

"I'm not talking about the bloody moonshine," Gerry replied, curling his lips into a sly grin. "That rubbish was disgusting, even by *my* low standards. But after I spat out the bit that I sampled, I noticed an old wooden case hidden behind a red wheelbarrow. I opened *that* up and found four properly labeled bottles from France. Now I can't say for sure, but I'm gonna guess your old neighbor Louie either picked this case up at a fancy import shop when he was *very* young or purchased it from a high-end smuggler."

Eddie furrowed his brow. "Why would he have had to get it from a smuggler? You can buy French liquor in the States. Even in Butler County, Ohio."

"Not this kind," Gerry replied. "Most countries banned it right before the First World War."

A look of recognition washed over Eddie's face, followed almost immediately by an expression of shock. "You *can't* have found what I *think* you're suggesting. There's no way! My grandpa wouldn't have kept something like that on his property all these years."

"I'm sure he didn't know it was there," Gerry replied smugly. "I couldn't read the labels on the bottles myself at first, they were so covered in dust. But then I saw this little widget in the bottom of the case and figured our lad Louie might just possibly have hidden a few bottles of *la fée verte* amidst his private stock of homemade poison." He pulled a small, tarnished, slotted spoon out of his trouser pocket and held it up for his bandmates to admire.

Pete took the spoon from Gerry and held it up to the buzzing overhead light. "What is this? Some sort of sieve?"

Jim frowned at Gerry. "Your French pronunciation leaves much to be desired, but I think you were trying to say, 'the green fairy'."

"*Très bien,* Monsieur McCudden!" Gerry laughed. "Your French is right on target!"

He flashed a wicked smile at Jim, then turned to face the rest of the band. "But if you lot prefer, we can call this rare French delicacy that I unearthed by its English name—*absinthe!*"

* * *

Gerry gathered his friends around the small table in the middle of the band's private sitting room in the historic Mount

Vernon Hotel. On top of the table stood four bottles of absinthe, six small drinking glasses, a large pitcher of ice water, and a bowl of sugar cubes. Eddie's leather-bound copy of *The Tenant of Wildfell Hall* lay beside the sugar bowl, along with Gerry's yellow flask of animation potion.

"I had a conversation with the hotel barkeep earlier this afternoon," Gerry began. "He'd never drunk any absinthe himself, but he showed me an old book with instructions on how to serve it. First, you pour a shot into the bottom of a glass. Next, you rest your little slotted spoon along the edge of the glass and place a sugar cube on top of that. Then you slowly drizzle some ice water over the sugar, so that the sweetness mixes in as you dilute the spirits."

Tony threw a nervous look at Gerry. "How strong are these spirits, anyway?"

"I tried to translate the label," Jim piped in. "The print's pretty worn, so it was hard to read, but it looks like the absinthe is 150 proof."

"Damn!" Pete exclaimed. "That's one powerful little green fairy!"

Gerry nodded in agreement, then continued with his presentation. "The barkeep's book said the absinthe will turn cloudy as soon as you mix in the sugar water. But that's okay. It just means the ingredients are being released, so you can taste some of the subtler flavors."

Alan eyed the bottles dubiously. "What's it supposed to taste like?"

"I've never had it before, so I can't say for sure," Gerry replied. "But the book said absinthe is made from distilled white grape alcohol, steeped in a mix of herbs. You'll probably recognize the tastes of anise and fennel, but wormwood is what gives the drink its reputation."

Tony flinched. "Its reputation?"

Eddie squared his eyes at his drummer. "Mind if I take over?"

Gerry nodded once more.

"Absinthe is supposed to be a mind-altering substance," Eddie explained. "Capable of causing sudden and powerful hallucinations—kind of like magic mushrooms or peyote. A lot of writers and artists used it in the nineteenth century to spark their imaginations. Oscar Wilde and Samuel Taylor Coleridge drank it. So did Van Gogh and most of the French Impressionists. But ironically, the praise the artists heaped on the drink gave it a bad reputation and led to its ban."

Pete tugged worriedly at his sideburns. "Does it really work? I mean, if we drink this, are we gonna start freaking out like Van Gogh did and cut off our ears?"

"We'll never know until we try," Gerry said, pouring a shot of the green liquor into one of the glasses. "I've only got the one slotted spoon," he apologized, "So this might take a while."

He balanced the tarnished spoon and sugar cube on top of the glass, then used another spoon to drizzle a stream of cold water over the sugar and into the absinthe. The six men stared at the glass and watched the translucent liquid slowly cloud up.

"I'm not so sure about this," Alan fretted. "I mean, if it's been banned, then maybe we shouldn't be drinking it."

"Pot's been banned," Gerry noted as he started preparing a second drink. "That's never stopped you from smoking a spliff."

"Yeah, but pot's just harmless fun," Alan protested. "I don't wanna take something that'll make me want to cut off my ear, or jump through a window, or—"

Eddie cut him off. "Van Gogh was a manic depressive. He was sick *before* he cut off his ear. This won't make you want to commit suicide like he did."

"What makes you so sure?" Pete challenged. "I thought you were the one who didn't like taking drugs."

"This isn't a drug," Eddie insisted. "It's just a spirit. No worse than vodka or scotch." He hesitated a moment, then added, "Well, maybe a *little* worse than those drinks. But not much. A lot of old writers drank absinthe and lived to describe their experiences. Some more contemporary authors tried it too, like Hemingway."

"Didn't he also commit suicide?" Jim asked.

Eddie shrugged. "That wasn't from drinking absinthe. He probably just re-read a couple of his books and got depressed."

Tony clapped Eddie on the back. "Well, if *you're* willing to try it, then I am too."

Gerry finished preparing the last drink. Then he opened *The Tenant of Wildfell Hall* to the page he had marked and sprinkled a few drops of animation potion onto the paper.

"That's it then?" Pete laughed. "You just sprinkle some of that Voodoo juice on the book and—*pop!*—you're inside the pages?"

Gerry frowned at him. "No. You have to get pissed first, then fall asleep."

Jim snorted. "Well, the only way to get legless is to start drinking." He picked up one of the glasses, threw back his head, and swallowed the absinthe in one gulp.

"Hey, don't just down it like a shot!" Gerry chided him. "This shit is rare, and I've only got the four bottles. We should be savoring it!" He lifted his glass, took a small sip, then made a sour face. "Christ. This tastes like licorice that's gone rancid."

"Let's just down 'em," Tony proposed. He led his friends in gulping down their drinks.

Pete grimaced at the taste. "Now what? I don't see any green fairies yet."

"Maybe it takes a little time to kick in," Eddie suggested.

"Oh, shit!" Gerry cursed. "We forgot to put on our Victorian clothes!" He ran over to the chair where Alan had draped the band's paisley coats and ruffled shirts. "We've got to look like we're from the nineteenth century if we want to fit in with Arthur Huntington and his mates."

"These clothes won't fool them," Jim protested. "The cut of the coats might look Victorian, but nobody in that day and age wore colors like these."

Tony scowled at him. "These coats aren't cut to look Victorian. They're *Edwardian*. Don't any of you pillocks know a thing about fashion?"

Eddie cast an exasperated look at his lead singer, then started to laugh. "Apparently not as much as you do, mate. But it doesn't matter. We're still missing the mark on the story's timeline. *The Tenant of Wildfell Hall* takes place in the 1820s, which would put the action in the Georgian period, before Victoria ascended to the throne."

"Fuck all that," Gerry cursed as he passed out the stage clothes. "We'll just have to make do with what we have." He handed his own outfit to Alan, then stepped into his bedroom to put on the costume he'd purchased in New Orleans.

"Should we have another round of shots?" Pete asked. "I'm not feeling anything yet."

"Yes! Start making up more drinks!" Gerry called back from his bedroom.

Jim opened another bottle of absinthe and started preparing a second round of drinks.

Alan looked across the room and noticed two bottles of whiskey sitting on top of the television set, each sealed with hardened drips of red wax. "What's that?"

Gerry returned to the sitting room and buttoned his silk waistcoat. "Maker's Mark—the finest Kentucky bourbon that money can buy. The barkeep sold me those this afternoon."

"Couldn't we drink that instead?" Alan asked. "I think I'd prefer the blue grass of Kentucky to the green fairies of France."

"No!" Gerry barked. He stepped in front of the gilt-edged oval mirror hanging beside the television set and started tying his cravat into a Windsor knot. "We need a drink with magical properties if we want to go on a magic carpet ride."

"And for once, Gerry, I'm in complete agreement with you," Eddie chimed in. He picked up his freshly prepared glass of cloudy absinthe and brought it to his lips.

Alan made a sour face as he downed his next shot, then leaned against the table for support while he waited for Jim to make him a third. "Damn, this stuff is strong. It's going to my head already. How much more do you suppose we'll have to drink before we start time traveling?"

"We're not traveling through time," Gerry reminded him. He downed his own shot, then grabbed Alan's glass and took over the drink-making duties from Jim. "We're traveling into a book."

He opened the next bottle, poured out six large shots, and grabbed the slotted spoon. He rested it on top of the first glass, then cursed in frustration and set the spoon aside. He plopped some sugar cubes directly into the shots and filled the glasses with splashes of cold water.

"Drink up, mates," he encouraged his friends. "Arthur's waiting for us, and we've still got one more bottle to finish off."

Eddie downed his drink, then staggered across the floor and picked up his Alvarez guitar. "So what are your plans for when—for when we get inside the novel?" he asked Gerry. "How are you going to introduce us to—Martha Funtington?"

Gerry eyed Eddie warily, then started to chuckle. "I'm not sure, but I have an idea. Keep playing your guitar. Tony, Pete—fetch your axes too!"

Tony downed his drink, then clapped his left hand on Gerry's shoulder as he slammed his glass back on the table with his right. "Which one—my Martin or my Fender?"

"Your acoustic guitar, you pillock!" Gerry scolded him. "There won't be any electric current where we're going to plug your amp into."

"Oh, right," Tony agreed. "I suppose not." He giggled for a few seconds, then lifted his hand off Gerry's shoulder. He started swaying unsteadily on his feet.

Alan accepted another drink from Gerry, downed it quickly, then threw a bleary-eyed gaze at the table. "Damn, I thought you said we only had one bottle left. But you're holding up two."

Jim stretched his fingers over the edge of the tabletop and started playing an imaginary keyboard. "I count three," he said, his voice slurring. "*Un, deux, trois*—"

Pete grabbed his guitar and started strumming it with such force that he broke his high E string. "Fuck me!" he shouted. "We must be in the book now—Jim's speaking French!"

Gerry rolled his eyes at him. "Everyone speaks English in Wildfell Hall," he assured his bassist. "Now gather round, lads, so I can fill up your glasses with the last of this plonk."

Tony left his guitar case unopened on the floor and stumbled back to the table. He rested his hands on Gerry's shoulders for balance once more and watched him work.

"Step back, you wanker," Gerry warned him. "You're giving me the heebie-jeebies."

Tony staggered away from Gerry and started singing, "Heebie-Jeebies—oh Reebies!" to the tune of Little Richard's old hit *Tutti Frutti.*

Gerry cast him a dirty look, then opened the last bottle of absinthe. He distributed its contents evenly between the six glasses, then threw in sugar cubes and splashes of water.

"The ice is all melted," Tony noted as he watched Gerry work. "Think it'll make a difference if we drink this magic fairy crap warm?"

"Nah," Gerry replied. "But let's have Eddie…*hic*…drink the first one. He looks like he's almost…*hic*…out cold already." He passed a drink down to his bandmate.

Eddie accepted the glass and stared at the cloudy, pale green distillate. "This looks manky," he muttered. He drew in a deep breath and exhaled it loudly. "But if it was good enough for Charles Baudelaire, then it's—good enough for me." He downed his drink and made a sour face. "Oh, the things I do—for literature."

"If only your old English professors could see you now," Jim laughed as he grabbed his own glass. "They'd be *soooo* proud."

Eddie squinted his eyes. "Are you sure these fairies—those fairies—are supposed to be green?" he asked no one in particular. "'Cause the ones I'm seeing—they look kind of—blue."

Tony downed his drink and turned towards Eddie. "They're not blue—they're cerulean. They're *definitely* cerulean."

"Mine look purple," Pete whispered in a raspy voice. "With orange wings."

"All I'm seeing is black," Alan moaned. He stumbled over to the couch in the far corner of the suite. "I think I'm gonna have a lie down."

"Be my guest," Gerry said. He closed his eyes to block out the colored spots that were dancing before his face, then opened his lids to a squint. He watched his friends nod off, one by one. Then he reached for an empty bottle and brought it to his lips.

"I'll just finish off...*hic*...the dregs," he informed the unconscious assembly, "unless one of you...*hic*...objects."

He threw back his head and let a few drops of absinthe trickle down his throat, then attempted to rest the bottle back on the table. It rolled over the edge and fell to the floor with a shattering crash.

He shrugged, leaned back in his chair, and picked up the novel. "Better round up some laudanum, Arthur...*hic*...Huntington," he whispered to the opened page as the printed letters started blurring in and out of focus. "'Cause here I come!"

Chapter Fourteen

Gerry opened his eyes slowly. His head was throbbing, and his stomach felt queasy, but as he surveyed his new surroundings, a palpable sensation of joy started welling within him. He looked to his right and left to make certain his bandmates and Alan had successfully completed the journey with him. Then he stood up and started examining the large, rectangular room in which he now found himself.

A trio of tall windows, each framed by a set of floor-length, red velvet curtains, was set into one of the long walls. A six-armed chandelier hung from the high, arched ceiling. Soft rays of sunlight filtered into the room through the wavy glass in the window panes. They bounced off the crystals dangling from the chandelier and landed as rainbows on the parquet floor.

A massive oil painting of a fox hunt, mounted in a singularly ostentatious gilded frame, hung from the wall opposite the windows. Exquisitely crafted tables and chairs were scattered throughout the room, their mahogany woodwork polished to a gleaming shine.

Gerry soaked in the lavish décor with an appreciative smile, then turned his attention back to his unconscious friends. Tony's long limbs were folded into an uncomfortable-looking, high-backed chair; his right leg was hanging over one of the arm rests. Pete and Eddie were sitting on the floor a few yards away from Tony, their backs propped against a silk-covered wall and their acoustic guitars strapped over their shoulders. Alan was curled up in a fetal position on a small divan to the side of Eddie, snoring loudly. And Jim was sprawled across an elegantly loomed carpet, his head tilted up towards the crown molding that encircled the ceiling.

Gerry took a step towards Eddie. The floorboards creaked beneath him. He stopped in his tracks for a second, then noticed a table at Pete's side that was laden with the remains of a meal. He grabbed an apple off a porcelain plate and bit into it with a loud crunch.

Pete opened his eyes at the noise, then blanched. "Bugger," he cursed under his breath. He stood up from the floor and turned around in a circle. "Am I dreaming?"

"Nope," Gerry assured him. "You just traveled inside the book with me. Welcome to the nineteenth century." He bent down and tapped Eddie's shoulder, then turned towards Tony and Jim and shook them awake.

"Core blimey," Tony murmured as he ran his hands over the silky surface of the upholstered chair. He stood up and walked over to the lunch table. He brought a half-filled tea cup and a small piece of cheese to his nose and sniffed them both. "This is real food!" he exclaimed. "I can practically taste it!"

"Go ahead and eat it," Gerry replied. "It won't hurt you." He took a step towards Tony, grabbed the cheese out of his hand and inspected it more closely. "I take that back. This might. I'd recommended the beef instead." He picked up a small hunk of meat and took a bite. "A bit salty for my taste, but what the hell—nobody had ice boxes yet, so they had to make do."

"Where the hell are we?" Jim asked, his eyes wide with amazement.

"Assuming that I sprinkled the right page of the book, I'd say we're in London, somewhere near Mayfair," Gerry answered. "This building belongs to Lord Lowborough, but he lets his dearest friends use it whenever they're in town and need a place to crash for a night or two. Or three. Or four."

Tony rested the teacup back in its saucer and threw an anxious look at his drummer. "What are we gonna say to his Lordship if he finds us?"

"Dunno," Gerry replied. "I haven't thought that through yet. But I'm sure something will come to me."

"We should wake up Alan," Eddie said. "He wouldn't want to miss this." He rested his guitar against the wall, walked over to the small sofa, and nudged his manager's brother. Alan curled himself into a tighter ball and buried his face in a pillow.

Pete slipped his guitar off his shoulder and rested it beside Eddie's.

"Hey, get a load of this!" Jim exclaimed as he lifted a tasseled cloth off a small pianoforte. "I've seen pianos like this before in museums, but I've never been able to touch one. They're always cordoned off by velvet ropes." He sat down on the small bench in front of the instrument and cracked his knuckles. "What do you think? Should I play it?" he asked excitedly.

Gerry thought for a minute, then nodded. "Go ahead. We have to find Arthur Huntington one way or another. If you play something loud enough, then he'll probably hear you and come find *us* instead."

"Something loud, eh?" Jim asked. He brought his fingers to the keyboard and started pounding out the opening chords of Chopin's Polonaise in A-flat major.

He was hardly a few measures into the piece when the door to the room flew open and a tall, thin man stormed in. His thick mane of black curls shook wildly as he walked, and his brown eyes flashed angrily beneath his dark brow.

"Who the hell are you?" the stranger demanded. "What are you doing here? And what in God's name are you wearing?" He marched over to the piano and grabbed the lapel of Jim's psychedelic coat.

Before Jim could answer, Gerry stepped up to the stranger's side and intervened. "Arthur Huntington, I presume," he said, extending his right hand in greeting. "My name is Gerald Albrecht Enis, and my uncle, Lord Douglas Enis of Cornwall, sent me here. I manage this group of traveling minstrels. We just arrived in town for a series of concerts and need a place to spend the night. My uncle suggested that we look you up. He assured me that your reputation as one of London's most gracious hosts is exceeded only by your well-known appetite for entertainments—of all sorts."

Arthur refused to take Gerry's hand. "Your uncle speaks the truth," he replied haughtily. "But this is not my home. I'm a guest here myself." He scanned the room and silently counted the men. "There are so many of you! However did you get into this room without my noticing? I've been sitting in the parlor for the better part of an hour, awaiting an associate's return, and I didn't hear any of you come in!"

"A member of the kitchen staff led us in through a back entrance," Gerry replied with a twinkle in his eye. "I didn't want to presume upon your hospitality and bring my band of minstrels through Lord Lowborough's front door."

Arthur furrowed his brow. "How did you know I was staying here?"

"As I said," Gerry replied smoothly, "Your reputation precedes you. I believe *all* of the most fashionable members of London society—or at least those persons with whom *I* am acquainted—are well aware of the fact that you are staying here in Mayfair while your new bride keeps a lonely watch over Grassdale Manor, your estate in the country."

Arthur cast Gerry a menacing look. He opened his mouth to reply but was interrupted by a voice calling up from the bottom floor of the house.

"Huntington, you old dog, where the devil have you gone?" cried the unseen speaker.

"Is that Grimsby asking for you?" Gerry inquired. "Or Hattersley?"

Arthur's menacing expression melted into a quizzical one. He took a deep breath, then turned towards the door. "I shall deal with you momentarily, Mr. Enis," he called over his shoulder. "But first, I must see what *Grimsby* wants."

He stepped into the open doorway and yelled down the stairwell, "I'm in the upstairs ballroom, attending to a band of rascals and thieves! I've half a mind to let them rob you first before I dismiss them! Wait for me in the parlor, you pusillanimous windbag. I shall be there forthwith!"

Arthur slammed the door behind him as he left the room.

Tony turned towards Gerry. "Lord Douglas Enis of Cornwall? Where the hell did you come up with *that* connection?"

Gerry brushed a speck of lint off his lapel, then threw Tony a knowing smile. "I didn't. Gilbert Markham did. He's the bloke from the first chapter who introduced me to laudanum. But I thought up the ruse of you lot being a band of traveling musicians. Not bad, huh?"

Eddie rolled his eyes. "Well, it wasn't much of a stretch. We *are* a band of traveling musicians."

"Yeah, but we can't play anything that these nineteen-century toffs will like!" Pete pointed out. "I mean, Jim did a great job there with that bit of Mozart, but *I* don't know any songs that old."

Jim frowned at Pete. "That was Chopin. The Polonaise, Opus 53. Don't you know the difference between Chopin and Moz—"

He stopped mid-sentence and his face blanched white. "Oh, bugger! You said this book was set in the 1820s, didn't you, Eddie?"

Eddie nodded.

Jim started to shake. "Christ, Chopin didn't write that piece until 1842! I've just fucked up the whole space-time continuum!"

Gerry sighed theatrically. "Calm down, McCudden. Nobody knows that but you. Nor does anyone care." He turned towards Eddie. "So, my literary friend, think you can come up with some appropriate nineteenth-century song lyrics for us to sing at an audition?"

Eddie thought for a moment, then nodded. "I'll see if I can fake something." He grabbed his guitar, stepped into the far corner of the room, and started strumming a series of chords as he hummed quietly to himself.

Tony rested his hands on Jim's trembling shoulders. "'S'alright, mate," he said reassuringly. "There's no need for you to palpitate. Let's see if there's some brandy in that decanter by the tea things. I suspect that absinthe left you feeling a little peaky. I'll fetch you a drink you're more comfortable with."

Arthur returned to the room just as Tony was reaching for the decanter. "I say, gypsy, you're a bit free with your ways. I don't remember offering you a brandy!"

Tony met his gaze. "It's not for me. It's for our pianist. He's feeling poorly. We just arrived here from quite a distance, and he's still suffering from the effects of—the trip."

Arthur turned towards Jim and examined his face. "Yes, yes, you're quite right. He looks ill indeed, doesn't he? Well, by all means, give the man a brandy. Never let it be said that Arthur Huntington denied a drink to a man who needed one." He cleared his throat and added in a tone of mock reverence: "*Give strong drink unto him that is ready to perish, and wine unto those that be of heavy heart. Let him drink and forget his poverty, and remember his misery no more.*" Then he turned towards Gerry and flashed him a wicked smile. "That's Proverbs, thirty-one, verses six and seven. The only damned passage in the entire Good Book that's worth memorizing."

Gerry laughed appreciatively at Arthur's joke.

Arthur met Gerry's eye, then grabbed his elbow and led him to a pair of chairs near the cluttered lunch table. They both sat down.

"I'm sorry if I appeared a bit boorish just now," Arthur said quietly. "But you took me quite by surprise. However, since you claim to know Grimsby, Hattersley, *and* my wife, I'm going to give you the benefit of the doubt. Now, it just so happens that I've been wracking my brain all afternoon, trying to think of a suitable amusement for some members of the fairer sex whom my friends and I will be entertaining this evening. Your band of minstrels certainly looks like they could fill the part. Let me hear them sing. If I like their repertoire, I'll tell the maids to set up some beds for you and your musicians tonight in one of the spare rooms. If not, I'll toss the lot of you into the gutter."

"Fair enough," Gerry replied with an air of confidence. "Eddie, c'mere! Let's show this nice gentleman what sort of songs we play."

"Eddie?" Arthur repeated in a mocking voice. "Your companion seems a bit old to go by the name 'Eddie'."

Gerry shrugged. "Yes, I know, you're quite right. But we've been mates since we were lads, so I call him Eddie still. It's short for Edgar."

"No, it's not," Eddie said.

Gerry flashed him a scowl. "Just shut up and sing."

Eddie rolled his eyes at Gerry, then stepped forward. He put his left hand to the neck of his guitar and cleared his throat.

"This lyric is by a young writer from Yorkshire who's just published her first collection of poems. The melody is by an American composer named Chu—I'm sorry, named *Charles Berry*." He leaned towards Jim and whispered, "Join in, if you're up to it. Play *Brown-Eyed Handsome Man*."

He straightened himself back up, then leaned towards Jim once more and whispered, "Play it *largo*. Very *largo*."

Eddie began to sing:

LOVE is LIKE the WILD rose BRI-ar.
FRIEND-ship's like the HOL-ly TREE.
The HOL-ly is DARK when the ROSE briar BLOOMS but
WHICH will bloom most CON-stant-LY?
Oh, yeah, well
WHICH will bloom most CON-stant-LY?...

Jim swallowed a large sip of brandy, then put his fingers to the keys and joined Eddie for a slow second verse.

Arthur cut them off before they could attempt a third. "That's absolutely dreadful!" he exclaimed. "Play something faster. Something less *largo*."

Eddie threw a nervous glance at Gerry, then cleared his throat once more. "Okay. This lyric is by Lord Byron, but I've set it to a melody by two very promising composers from Liverpool named John Lennon and Paul McCartney." He took a quick step towards Tony and whispered, "Join me on the harmony if you can. Just sing 'ooh' and 'ahh' if you don't know the words." Then he strummed the familiar introduction to the Beatles' smash hit *I Want to Hold Your Hand* on his guitar and started to sing:

We'll GO-OH-OH, no more a-RO-OH-VING,
So LATE in-TO the NIGHT,
Though HEAR-RR-RTS be still LO-OH-VING,
And MOON-light STILL be BRIGHT…
We'll GO no MORE a-RO-OH-OH-OH-OH-OH-VING
So LATE in-TO the NIGHT…

"Even worse!" Arthur shouted. He stood up from the table and knocked his chair to the floor. "What a horrible sentiment! I like going a-roving, and I won't have the likes of *him* telling me not to!"

Gerry jumped up from his seat and followed Arthur as he marched to the door. "Please, my good sir, don't go! I'll have my lads sing the original lyrics by Messers Lennon and McCartney for you. They fit the music much better."

"I have no interest in hearing any music written by Scousers!" Arthur bellowed. "Nothing good ever came out of Liverpool!"

Gerry rushed in front of the door and blocked Arthur's exit. "Well, how about the original song by Chuck Berr—I mean by Charles Berry? You'll like it. It's all about a man who goes a-roving on a daily basis, and the women who go a-roving with him!"

Arthur eyed Gerry dubiously, then released a small sigh. He crossed his arms in front of his chest and assumed a challenging pose. "As you wish, Mr. Enis. But this is your last chance."

Gerry smiled at him knowingly, then called to his bandmates. "Pete, grab your guitar! Tony, sing lead! Jim, keep the tempo fast—don't even *think* about playing *largo*. And Eddie, you've been demoted to back-up singer. Now—*hit* it, boys!"

Jim caught Tony's eye, then played a quick glissando on the piano. Eddie and Pete followed through with a rollicking strum on their guitars. Then Tony started crooning, in his raunchiest voice:

Arrested on charges of unemployment
He was sittin' in the witness stand—
The judge's wife called up the District Attorney,

Said, "Free that brown-eyed man!
You want your job? You better free that brown-eyed man!

The group worked their way through the next two verses at a rapid beat. Then Jim played a rocking boogie-woogie solo on the keys while Pete plucked out the song's bassline on his guitar's lower E-string. Tony let out a full-throated howl, then jumped right back in, singing the song's fourth verse.

Gerry kept his eyes on Arthur's face as his bandmates played. He watched the corners of Arthur's mouth slowly turn up, then curl into an increasingly wide smile. When Eddie and Pete hit their final chords, Tony called out a loud, "Oh yeah!" and Jim closed off the song with a second glissando.

Arthur's cheeks flushed. He stood silent for a long moment and appeared to be struggling to form a reply. Then he turned towards Gerry and shook his head.

"I take my hat off to you and your minstrels, Mr. Enis," he said at length. "That was the most original piece of music I have ever heard. Wherever did you learn to play like that?"

Gerry smiled back at him smugly. "We just returned from a tour of America. That kind of music is all the rage there these days."

"I'm speechless," Arthur said. He walked back to the lunch table, picked his chair off the floor, and sat back down to face the band. "Tell me a bit more about this Mr. Berry. He certainly has an unconventional approach to songwriting."

"Chuck Berry's a *genius!*" Eddie agreed. "*Brilliant* lyricist!"

"And he's an American, you say?" Arthur continued.

"Yeah, he's from a city called St. Louis, along the Mississippi River," Tony replied. "We just played a show there."

Arthur nodded thoughtfully. "Ah, I have heard of the place. St. Louis used to be a French trading outpost, I believe, before President Jefferson signed that duplicitous treaty with Napoleon that underwrote France's war against England."

"Mm-hmm," Eddie replied. "I think you're right about that."

Arthur threw him a haughty look. "Of *course* I'm right about that!"

Gerry drew in a quick breath, then offered Arthur a complacent smile. "Would you like to hear another song?"

Arthur squirmed uncomfortably in his chair. "Perhaps. As long as that impertinent prat with the penchant for plodding poetry doesn't sing it." He turned to Eddie and scowled. "Stop looking at me like that."

Eddie met his gaze. "Like how, sir?" he replied politely.

"Like you're trying to read me," Arthur scoffed. "You look as if you want to analyze my character and interpret my motivations. It's very rude of you. I'm your better. Don't forget that."

Gerry nodded at Arthur, then turned to his bandmates. "You heard the gentleman, Eddie. Stop being impudent with Mr. Huntington. Now, Tony, I'd like you to sing an American spiritual for our most gracious host. One composed by the Reverend Richard Penniman."

Tony furrowed his brow. "Say what?"

Gerry cast a disparaging look at his lead singer, then folded his hands, as if in prayer. "*Ooh! My Soul,*" he clarified.

"Ah, right," Tony laughed. "One American spiritual by the Reverend Richard Penniman, coming right up. Pity we can't start this number with a drumroll." He winked at Gerry, then turned towards the piano and beat a rapid tattoo on top of the instrument with the palms of his hands while he yelped, "*Ooh, my soul!*" in a high falsetto. Then he started belting out the lyrics to Little Richard's chart-topper while his bandmates joined in playing:

Well, baby, baby, baby, baby, baby!
Don't you know my love is true?
Honey, honey, honey, honey, honey!
I said, 'Get off of that money!'
Love, love, love, love, love—
Ooh! My soul!

Tony sang the next three verses, his voice sailing through the lyrics like a wind-fueled saxophone, then brought the song to a close with an ecstatic whoop.

Arthur rose to his feet and started clapping, then turned towards Gerry and offered him his hand.

"Mr. Enis," he stated, hardly able to contain the excitement in his voice, "your troupe of minstrels is *very* welcome to spend the night at this house! Nothing would please me more than having my guests hear these new American tunes! I'll have the maids set up beds for your band and bring you a meal. Do you require any servants?"

Gerry shook Arthur's hand enthusiastically. "Oh no, we've got Alan over there," he said, throwing a glance at the small couch where Alan Poole lay sleeping. "He'll do whatever we tell him to do."

Pete laughed in agreement. "He's our roadie for this gig," he explained to Arthur.

"Our valet," Eddie countered, elbowing Pete in the ribs.

Tony frowned at his bandmates. "What are you blokes going on about? Alan's our manager's little brother."

Arthur raised a quizzical eyebrow at Gerry. "He's your younger brother, yet you employ him as a lackey?"

Gerry cast a dirty look at Tony, then turned back towards Arthur. "Well, he's not *really* my brother," he explained. "I mean, that is, Alan's kind of like family, but we—he's got a different last name and—"

Arthur smiled at him. "Ah, yes. I understand completely. My father left me a few 'younger brothers' to look after as well. I'm sure even your esteemed uncle Lord Enis must have some natural children scattered about his estates in Cornwall. All gentlemen do. It's good of you to look after the chap."

He clapped Gerry on the back and led him to the far corner of the room, out of the band's earshot. "Now, I don't know how much you require as payment to perform at private parties," he said softly. "Normally, I could offer you a tidy sum, but I've run up some debts of late and my purse is sadly depleted."

"That's all right," Gerry insisted. "When we first started out in the music business, we used to get paid in beer."

Arthur rolled his eyes dismissively. "Well, I'm sure the servants have some ale at their disposal which they could share.

But Lord Lowborough keeps a fine stock of whiskey on hand from his estate in Scotland, as well as some rum from his plantation in Jamaica. I imagine you might find those spirits more to your liking."

Gerry assumed a thoughtful expression while he pretended to consider Arthur's proposal. "Would he, perchance, have any laudanum at the ready as well?"

Arthur cocked his eyebrow in surprise.

"For medicinal purposes, of course," Gerry quickly added. "I'm recovering from a bit of a chest cold." He forced a few coughs as evidence.

Arthur curled his lips into a lascivious smile. "Yes, I'm sure I could find a flask of that for you too, Mr. Enis, if you'd prefer it to whiskey. In fact, I'd be more than happy to *share* some laudanum with you, if your musicians will perform for my guests tonight."

"You've got yourself a deal, Mr. Huntington," Gerry laughed. He turned to face the band and called out with glee, "Hold onto your wigs and keys, boys! We've got ourselves a gig!"

* * *

A thin ray of morning sunlight poked through the gap in the hotel curtains and landed directly on Eddie's face. He opened his eyes to the sun, then immediately squeezed them shut again and turned his head away from the irritating light. He brought his fingers to his throbbing temples in a half-hearted attempt to massage away the dull pain reverberating in his head. Then he slowly, very slowly, opened his eyes once more and surveyed his surroundings.

He was sitting on the floor of the band's common room in the Mount Vernon Hotel in Cincinnati. His head and upper back were propped against the wall at an uncomfortable angle. His Alvarez guitar was strapped over his shoulders. He looked to his right and saw Pete sitting beside him, also leaning against the wall, also holding his guitar. He looked to his left and saw Tony collapsed on a chair, his guitar case still resting unopened at his feet. Alan was curled up on the sofa where he had fallen asleep. Jim was sprawled across the carpet, his head tilted up towards the ceiling.

Eddie stood up slowly and slipped off his guitar, then stepped over Jim's legs and cautiously approached Gerry, who was bent over the round table in the middle of the room, clutching his copy of *The Tenant of Wildfell Hall* and snoring profusely.

Eddie put his hand on Gerry's back and tried to shrug him awake. Gerry made an irritated snuffling sound, then released the book from his hands and repositioned his head over his folded arms. Eddie started walking away from him, then noticed the smashed absinthe bottle at his feet. He walked into the suite's bathroom, grabbed a small rubbish bin, then returned to Gerry's side and started picking shards of glass off the floor.

"That couldn't have been real," said a voice at his feet.

Eddie turned towards the voice and saw Jim staring up at him with a worried expression.

"Please tell me that wasn't real," Jim beseeched him.

Eddie shrugged. "Careful where you put your hands when you stand up. There's broken glass all over the floor."

"Fuck me," came a curse from a few feet away.

Eddie turned towards Tony, who was staring at him with dazed, blood-shot eyes.

"Did that really happen?" Tony asked incredulously.

Eddie shrugged. "Well, if it didn't, then we all somehow managed to share the same illusion." He fetched a few tour programs from an open box by the television set, then returned to Gerry's side and spread them over the floor to cover the remaining slivers of glass.

Jim stood up and approached Eddie. "Should we wake Gerry? Or Pete or Alan?" He turned away from his snoring drummer and looked towards the window. The beam of sunlight shining through the gap in the curtains had grown wider. "Morning has broken. Emmett's gonna want us all up soon so we can catch our plane to Cleveland."

"I say we let them sleep," Eddie replied. "I'm not sure, but I think it's probably best if they come out of the trip naturally. I imagine they'll get up soon. We did."

"Yeah, but we three were just drinking Lord Lowborough's rum and whiskey," Tony reminded him. "That lot was sampling the laudanum. Do you suppose that makes a difference?"

Jim folded his arms in front of his chest and assumed a defiant pose. "It wasn't real laudanum. They just took it in a dream. It shouldn't matter one way or the other."

Pete started groaning and stirring. Jim, Eddie, and Tony turned their gazes towards him.

Pete opened his eyes and stared back at them. "That was *soooo* fucking amazing," he whispered in a raspy voice. He closed his eyes again and smiled. "I wanna go back."

"Not now, Cooper," Tony replied. "The only place you're going today is Cleveland."

"Cleveland?" Pete repeated disinterestedly without opening his eyes. "Is that our next stop?"

"Read the schedule," Jim said. He grabbed another concert program from the box by the television and tossed it at his bassist. "It's on the back cover."

Pete left the program on the floor where it fell. "That's all right. I trust you."

Eddie yawned and stretched, then turned towards the door. "I think I'll go downstairs and try to find some coffee. Anyone else feel like having brekkie?"

Jim and Tony nodded at him.

Eddie called over his shoulder to Pete as he led his friends to the door. "There's some broken glass on the floor by Gerry's feet. Tell him to be careful when he wakes up, okay?"

"Will do," Pete answered. He sat up a little straighter, slipped off his guitar, and rested it against the wall beside Eddie's. Then he plucked the program off the floor and started reading the tour itinerary.

Gerry released one last thundering snore, then bolted upright in his chair. He turned towards Pete and broke into a wide smile. "Didn't I tell you that laudanum was great?"

Pete chuckled, then warned Gerry about the glass slivers on the floor.

Gerry cast a mournful look at the pieces of broken bottle in the bin at his feet. "The absinthe's all gone," he whined. "And I've used up all my magic pills."

Pete dropped the tour program back on the floor, then stood up and approached Gerry. "Do you still have the medicine bottle that doctor in New Orleans gave you?"

Gerry nodded. "Yeah, I threw my speed in it, so it would look like proper meds if anyone found it."

"It's got the prescription written on its label?" Pete continued.

Gerry nodded once more.

Pete smiled. "I know a bloke in Cleveland who could probably refill that prescription of yours. Might cost a bit more than your last doctor charged, but—" He let his voice trail off.

"Money's not an issue," Gerry replied in a calm, steady voice.

"Fetch me that bottle, then," Pete said. "I'll ring him up before we leave Cincinnati, so he can have the pills ready for us when we land in Cleveland."

Gerry smiled back at Pete and started walking to his bedroom.

"Mornin' Ger," Alan called up from the sofa.

"Bullocks!" Pete swore under his breath. "I forgot *he* was there."

"'S'no matter," Gerry assured him. "Alan's one of us."

"He's our fuckin' manager's *brother*," Pete cursed. He turned towards the couch and scowled at Alan. "How long have you been awake?"

"Long enough," Alan answered. He propped himself upright and scowled back at Pete.

"You gonna tell your brother what you just heard?" Pete asked, his words sounding more like a threat than a question.

"Not if you two let me go back with you to visit Arthur Huntington and his mates," Alan replied calmly.

Pete frowned at Alan, then let loose a quick snort of laughter.

Alan met his gaze and smiled back at him.

Gerry chuckled. "Enough with the drama, already, Cooper. Now let me get my bottle so you can ring up your mate." He turned his back on his friends and stepped into his bedroom to fetch his old vial of hallucinogenic medicine.

Chapter Fifteen

Detroit, Michigan

"I don't care if they're sleeping!" Emmett shouted. "Wake them up! Berry Gordy is expecting us!"

"I tried," Jim replied, his voice ragged with frustration. "I shook them and yelled at them and even dumped a glass of water on Gerry's head! But he just made a goofy face and started snoring even louder."

Emmett cursed under his breath, then fell silent for a long moment before looking back at Jim, Tony and Eddie. "Could you tell if they'd been taking anything?" he asked in a hoarse whisper. "Were there any bottles of pills on the table? Or—needles?"

Jim sighed, then offered his manager a reassuring smile. "Don't worry, Emmett. There weren't any needles. I'm sure Alan would never do anything *that* stupid. And Gerry wouldn't let him, even if he was dumb enough to try that himself."

Emmett lifted a hand to his brow and rubbed at his temple. "I don't feel comfortable leaving them. Something might be wrong. But I don't want to cancel our visit to the Motown studio either. It would make us look really bad."

Tony stepped forward and rested his hand on Emmett's shoulder. "Don't cancel. *I* want to go, and so do Jim and Eddie. And I know Gerry wanted to come too. He just forgot about our appointment."

"So he'll have no one but himself to blame when he wakes up and discovers we left without him," Eddie added.

Emmett nodded. "Then I'll send you three," he said in a hesitant voice. "You can offer my apologies to Mr. Gordy. Jam with whatever musicians he's rounded up. Have a little fun. And try to get your picture taken. I'll stay here and make sure Alan, Pete, and Gerry come to no harm."

Jim crossed his arms in front of his chest and frowned. "Those three don't need a minder. They're breathing naturally, and they've got color in their cheeks. I'm sure they're just sleeping off whatever it was they drank last night. You should come to the studio, Emmett. Berry Gordy is expecting you. And after we say hello to everyone and visit for a while, then one of us can slip out early and check on our pissed-up mates. But let's stop worrying about them for now. They'll be fine."

Emmett glanced at his watch. "I suppose you're right. After all the phone calls I made to arrange this meeting, I'd feel like a complete git if I didn't show up and meet Mr. Gordy myself. Let me just check on Alan once more before we leave. Could one of you go tell the limo driver we're running a little late?"

He rushed out of the room. Jim followed at his heels to run to the car.

Tony cast a worried look at Eddie. "I just don't understand what's going on with our Ger. This is so unlike him. Gerry *loves* Motown! He's gonna be *gutted* when he wakes up and discovers he missed this trip!"

Eddie shrugged. "I think he only cares about tripping into that book these days."

"But why? I mean, that place was fun, but it was just a dream. I'd much rather go to a *real* party and drink *real* whiskey and meet *real* girls than go visit some fantasy world."

"Well, *you* would, and so would *I*. But obviously, Gerry is of a different mind."

"You don't suppose he's—" Tony's voice trailed off, and he finished his question in a whisper, "—becoming addicted to that laudanum?"

Eddie dug his hands into his trouser pockets and looked down at his shoes. "I don't see how he could be. I mean, he's not *really* taking it, so his body can't form an addiction."

"But it's a kind of opium, isn't it?"

"Yes, but Gerry's only taking imaginary doses."

Tony ran his fingers through his tousled mane of thick, brown hair. "How do you suppose he's tripping back into the book, anyway? He used up all the pills from that doctor in New Orleans *and* all the absinthe from your grandparents' farm."

"I don't know," Eddie said. "And I'd rather not guess. But I have a funny feeling that Pete has something to do with it."

Emmett returned to the room with a smile on his face. "Alan seems to be stirring a little. I left a note by his side with the phone number of Mr. Gordy's secretary and a message to give us a ring if any problems arise."

"Great!" Tony exclaimed, his face flush with relief. "Then let's get going. I can't wait to see Hitsville, U.S.A.!"

* * *

Pete stepped through the wide doorway of Lord Lowborough's ornately furnished library and took a seat at a small table between two well-dressed gentlemen.

"Deal me in!" he exclaimed with a grand flourish.

"You need money if you want to play," replied Walter Hargrave, the foppish-looking man to his left. He cut the cards and started shuffling the deck. "No more gambling on credit."

"And no more offering a new song for collateral," added Ralph Hattersley, the more sensibly dressed second man. "I like those dirty ditties you lads perform as much as the next man, but if I'm going to play Whist, I want to come away with some pound notes in my purse. Not just a new tune in my head."

"I've got cash," Pete stated proudly. He pulled a thick wad of bank notes out of the pocket of his paisley-patterned coat.

Ralph and Walter's eyes grew wide as they watched Pete count out the money.

Gerry glanced up from the side table where he was chatting with Arthur Huntington and threw Pete a dirty look. "Christ, Cooper, how the hell did you get your hands on that dosh?"

"Won it from Grimsby," Pete replied with a laugh. "Playing 'Twenty-One'."

Gerry smiled and quickly regained his composure. "Well, my good man," he remarked. "I suppose that's fair enough. But I hope you didn't take advantage of the poor chap."

"A fool and his money don't deserve each other's company," Arthur stated matter-of-factly. "And there is no bigger fool in our company than Grimsby. If Mr. Cooper has mastered the art of robbing old Grimsby blind, then he deserves to sit at the card table with the rest of us."

"I quite agree," Ralph concurred with a twinkle in his eye. "And I would never turn a man with ill-gotten gains away from my Whist game. You're in, Mr. Cooper. But we'll need a fourth. Arthur or Gerald, would either of you care to join us?"

"Not just now," Arthur replied. "Gerald and I were just about to take a stroll to the apothecary's to fetch some more laudanum. We seem to have used up our supply."

"Well, off with you then," Walter said gruffly. "And make sure you buy enough for *all* of us this time."

"Perhaps Gerald's younger brother could be our fourth," Ralph suggested. The men at the card table turned their gazes to the upholstered settee in the corner of the library. Alan was once again passed out across its cushions.

"Can you rouse him?" Arthur asked as Gerry walked towards the sofa.

Gerry shook Alan gently. Alan briefly opened his eyes and smiled, then rolled his head away and started snoring.

"I believe my dear brother has reached his limit for the day," Gerry said with a chuckle.

"But *I* haven't!" Pete barked. "So off with you then! Fetch us some more laudanum!"

"I dare say, you put up with a lot of cheek from these musicians you employ," Arthur chided Gerry. "You allow them to speak to you as if they were your equals!"

"It helps to keep a good rapport with the band," Gerry replied with a lopsided shrug. "That way, the lads don't mind so much when I send them off to perform at venues with less than choice accommodations."

"Less than choice, Gerald? You told me you sent Anthony, James, and Edgar to play a concert for the Right Honorable

Robbie Robertson, the recently returned royal envoy to Ontario," Arthur replied, rolling his 'R's' for theatrical effect.

"Quite right," Gerry agreed without missing a beat. "Sir Robbie picked up a taste for American music when he was living in Canada, so I knew he would like to hear my boys play. But the parties he throws aren't nearly as posh as the ones *you* gents are accustomed to."

"Piss on the pish-posh," Walter said with a sneer. "We London gentlemen know how to entertain ourselves better than any royal envoy to a backwater colony across the Atlantic."

"Indeed we do," Arthur agreed. "And on that note, Gerald and I shall leave you to purchase more provisions for our mutual entertainment."

"But who will be our fourth hand?" Ralph retorted. "Alan's indisposed, Lord Lowborough is out of town, and Grimsby has run out of cash!"

"Where is Grimsby, anyway?" Walter asked.

"He left the building after I took his last pound note," Pete replied. "Claimed he was going to throw himself off a bridge into the Thames."

"That's what he always says," Arthur laughed. "What he means is he's going to throw himself on the mercy of his dear mama and ask for another advance against his future inheritance."

"Well, in that case," Pete said to the men at the card table, "perhaps I could teach you two a game I learned when I was touring America. It's called 'Texas Hold'em'." He picked up the deck and started dealing out the cards for a hand of poker.

Arthur led Gerry out of the room and down the stairs. "Wait for me in the foyer for a moment, my dear Gerald, while I fetch my purse."

Gerry nodded and turned towards the marble statue of a nearly naked Roman goddess that stood beside the front door. He started admiring the sculpture's perfectly shaped breasts, then felt his head being drenched with a splash of cold water.

"What the hell?" he cursed as he ran his fingers through his damp hair. He squinted at the statue and saw the face of his pianist Jim staring back at him.

"Christ!" he swore under his breath. "The pills are wearing off!"

Arthur returned to the foyer and noticed Gerry's sodden state. "Good lord, Gerald! What happened to you?"

"I, umm," Gerry fumbled. "I poked my head outside to see if I needed a brolly. And I got caught by a blast of rain."

Arthur narrowed his eyes. "A brolly?"

"Yeah," Gerry replied. He pointed to an urn by the front door filled with collapsed umbrellas.

"Ah. You meant a Hanway," Arthur corrected him. He stole a glance out the nearest window and chuckled. "It's just drizzling, old boy. You must have been hit by some water a charwoman was chucking out an upstairs window. No worries. I'll have one of the maids fetch you a flannel so you can dry yourself. And I'll send a servant into town to run our errand for us. I can't have you going out like that!"

"Much obliged," Gerry replied. He dug his hands into the pockets of his grey coat and fingered his golden snuffbox. He suddenly remembered that Frederick Lawrence had spoken Arthur's name when he threw the snuffbox at the fireplace in Gilbert's home.

Gerry wrinkled his brow and tried to imagine how Frederick Lawrence knew Arthur. He considered showing the jeweled case to his new friend and asking him point blank, then decided it might be better to broach the topic more discretely.

"So tell me, Arthur," Gerry began. "Have you heard from your wife lately?"

"All too frequently," Arthur scoffed. "She writes me every day, wanting to know when I shall return to Grassdale."

Gerry ran his fingers through his damp hair once more. "And when *will* you rejoin her?"

"No time soon," Arthur chuckled. "Not while there is still fun to be had in London!" He clapped Gerry on the back. "Now tell *me*, my newest and dearest friend, do *you* have a woman waiting for you back home on your uncle's estate in Cornwall?"

"Nah," Gerry laughed. "I have no romantic entanglements at the moment. I courted a lass briefly on my trip to America, but I don't imagine I'll be seeing her again any time soon."

"I should think not," Arthur agreed before leaving Gerry once more to fetch some servants.

Gerry returned his gaze to the statue. This time the face of the Roman goddess looked like his manager Emmett Poole's.

Pete Cooper came barreling down the steps.

"Something's happening!" he exclaimed. "Alan just vanished! I tried to convince the toffs upstairs that he slipped away to use a chamber-pot, but I don't think they believed me."

"The pills are wearing off," Gerry said nervously. "I'm starting to feel a little woozy myself. Quick, grab me a calling card from that basket by the door. I'll write a note to Arthur and tell him we had to leave suddenly."

"What are you going to write with?" Pete asked in a dither. "There's no pens in this house, only inkwells!"

A maid serendipitously approached Gerry and offered him a soft square of muslin for drying his hair.

"Thanks a lot, love," Gerry said as he reached for the door handle. "But I've gotta go. I just now remembered that my uncle came into town this morning, and he expects me for tea. He hates it when I'm late. Be a doll and make my excuses to Mr. Huntington for me, would you?"

He grabbed Pete by the elbow and pushed him through the door into the mist of a foggy London afternoon. Then the fog cleared, and he found himself sitting beside Pete and Alan in a comfortably furnished hotel room in Detroit, Michigan.

* * *

Gerry stared blankly out the window of the chartered plane as Eddie rambled on about his visit to the Motown studio.

"Smokey Robinson was there," Eddie gushed. "He jammed with Tony for a bit while Jim played piano. Then Benny Benjamin and Pistol Allen stopped by. They asked about you."

Gerry turned his face away from the window. "What did you tell them?"

"That you were indisposed."

Gerry sighed. "And they were cool with that?"

"They laughed, but yeah, they were cool," Eddie replied. "Benny hinted that he'd been indisposed for much of the past week himself, but he didn't elaborate."

"Hhmm," Gerry mumbled. He looked back out the window as the plane started making its descent. "What's this sea called again?" he asked in a flat voice.

"Lake Michigan."

"Looks big for a lake."

"It *is* big," Eddie replied. "That's why it's called a Great Lake."

"Everything in America is so big," Gerry whined. "I miss England. I wish I was back in London right now."

"Today's London or yesterday's?" Eddie asked.

Gerry looked back at his friend but offered no reply.

"Don't spend so much time visiting Arthur tonight," Eddie whispered. "You've got to get up bright and early tomorrow. We're doing a radio interview on the WLS morning show."

Gerry rolled his eyes. "Morning radio? Who the hell listens to that?"

"Lots of people," Eddie said. "It's one of the highest-rated time slots of the day. Emmett wants us to reach as many record buyers as we can."

"Hhmm," Gerry mumbled again. "How's our newest album been doing lately, anyway?"

"It peaked at number nine on the Billboard chart. I think it's sitting at about sixteen or seventeen this week."

"Right," Gerry said half-heartedly. "Well, that's not bad."

"Our last LP stayed in the top ten for a month-and-a-half," Eddie reminded him.

"Well, there are more important things in life than selling records," Gerry replied. He leaned forward and pulled his traveling bag out from beneath the seat in front of him. He took out the leather-bound copy of *The Tenant of Wildfell Hall*, opened it to the page he had earmarked, and skimmed a few paragraphs. Then he closed his eyes again and smiled.

"Some things in life are *much* more important than selling records," he repeated. He rested the book on his lap and closed his eyes as the plane approached the runway of Chicago's Midway Airport.

Chapter Sixteen

Denver, Colorado

"*Please* come to the party," Jim begged Gerry. "Honestly, it just hasn't been the same without you there. It's like there's a big, gaping hole in the fun department!"

Gerry brushed him off. "I've been to more after-show parties than I can count. I'm just taking a little break for a while. What's so wrong with that?" He slipped off his dress shoes and grabbed the set of street clothes he had worn into the Denver Coliseum.

Tony exchanged an anxious glance with Jim, then turned towards Gerry. "You should have seen the girls in the beer hall we visited after our show in Milwaukee. The waitresses were wearing these dirndls cut down to there, and the chicks on the dance floor were wearing mini-skirts cut up to here..."

"And you would have loved the band at the club we visited after our show in Minneapolis," Eddie piped in. "They really rocked! Honestly, they could give us a run for our money on the charts."

Gerry took off his psychedelic coat and frowned at Eddie. "Why the hell would I want to hear some two-bit bar band showing off on the hopes that our manager might sign *them*? I work my arse off up on the stage! Sometimes I just want to relax afterward."

"Alan's coming with us tonight," Jim pointed out.

"At Emmett's insistence," Eddie added.

Gerry slipped off his satin trousers and flung them over a chair. "I don't give a fuck. Drag Pete along too if you want his company. Doesn't matter to me. I can have fun by myself."

"I think Emmett might just do that," Tony said. "He seems quite determined to separate you three."

"Yeah, I noticed when we checked into our hotel," Gerry replied with a sneer. "He put me back with Eddie again, set Pete up in the room by the bouncers, and kept Alan by his side in the Poole brothers' executive suite."

Eddie rolled his eyes. "C'mon, Ger. Even *I'm* going to the party tonight. It's gonna be fun!"

"Just think of all those luscious ski bunnies who'll be there," Tony added. "They're going stir-crazy now that it's off-season and there's no snow on the mountains. They're just dying to practice schussing and sliding and gliding again."

Gerry squared his eyes at his lead singer. "If you're going to attempt a dirty joke, then at least try to make it funny." He threw his stage clothes into a pile for Alan to collect, then slipped into his jeans, polo shirt and loafers.

"Have a good time, mates," he called over his shoulder as he headed to the dressing room door. "One of the ushers is giving me a ride back to the hotel. I don't want to keep him waiting."

Jim, Eddie, and Tony watched in disbelief as Gerry slammed the door shut behind him.

"This can't be happening," Jim said after a few silent seconds had passed. "This is the fourth night in a row that Gerry has skipped out on our after-show party."

"The fifth," Tony corrected him. "He was a no-show in Detroit too."

"And he only stopped by our parties in Cleveland and Toledo to grab some booze from the barkeeps," Eddie reminded them. "Then he went straight back to his hotel room."

"With Pete and Alan," Jim added.

Tony sighed. "Where are those two now, anyway?"

"Last I saw, they were hanging out with the new roadies behind the stage," Eddie replied. "I got the distinct impression that they didn't want to be disturbed."

"Then let's ditch 'em," Jim said. "When they're ready to come to the party, they can hail their own cab."

"Maybe we should start sending out feelers for a new bassist," Eddie added. "Again."

"Fine with me," Tony said with a sly smile. "But not tonight. I've got other plans for the evening. I'm gonna be auditioning some new groupies!"

"Let's see how many pass the test," Jim laughed. The three men changed out of their stage clothes, then jogged out of the arena to their waiting limousine.

* * *

Gerry's eyes fluttered open. Everything around him was dark. He felt a quick tug of panic, but then he noticed a pale stream of light pouring into the dark room in which he had awoken. He stood up from the floor, put his head to the crack in the doorway, and let his eyes adjust to the light. He saw Arthur Huntington sitting in a straight-backed chair in the far corner of the next room, his head bent low over a writing desk.

Gerry sighed in relief, then slipped out of the windowless closet in which he had emerged and approached the desk.

"So, Mr. Huntington, we meet again!" Gerry bellowed by way of a greeting.

Arthur startled momentarily, then broke into a welcoming smile. "Mr. Enis, my dear fellow, you surprised me," he replied. He rested his dip pen on the desk and pushed aside his blank sheet of stationery. "I didn't hear you coming down the hallway."

"I crept up the stairs like a cat," Gerry whispered, scrunching up his hands to mime claws. "The house seemed so deathly quiet when I entered that I was afraid everyone was still sleeping off the effects of last night's revelry. I didn't want to disturb anybody."

"Good thinking, as always," Arthur replied with a nod. "You wouldn't want to cross paths with Grimsby the morning after he's drunk himself blind. He doesn't make for very pleasant company under such circumstances." He furrowed his brow and tapped his fingers against the desktop. "Then again, Grimsby's not very pleasant company when he's in his cups either, and he was tight as a boiled owl last night. Ralph and Walter were both sizzled as well."

Gerry chuckled. "But *you* seem to be wide awake. All bright-eyed and bushy-tailed."

"Well, I wouldn't describe my disposition quite like *that*," Arthur scoffed. "To tell you the truth, I'm in rather a foul mood."

Gerry glanced at the desktop and noticed a small stack of letters addressed to Arthur from his wife Helen. "Bad news from home?"

"No," Arthur replied. "Nothing bad is happening in Grassdale. In fact, nothing at all is happening in Grassdale. Nothing *ever* happens in Grassdale. That's why I prefer to spend my time in London. But Helen claims to miss me."

"And do you miss her?" Gerry asked.

Arthur sighed and looked away. "I miss the woman I fell in love with," he confessed in a sad voice. "Helen used to be—that is—oh, dear Lord, Gerald, I fear I made a most grievous mistake when I married her."

"How so?" Gerry asked, pulling up a chair beside the desk.

Arthur stared into space for a few seconds. "Oh, I don't suppose it matters that much," he admitted after his pensive moment had passed. "I gather that most men regret the tie that binds once they feel its knot squeezing tightly around their necks. I had just rather hoped—when I first met Helen, I believed—I thought she was a different sort of woman than she actually is."

"Care to elaborate?" Gerry asked. When Arthur failed to reply, he reached across the desk and picked up a decanter of brandy. "Tell you what, old friend, why don't you have a sip of this first? When a cat catches my tongue, I often find that liquor will loosen it."

Arthur smiled more warmly this time and nodded. "Thank you, kind sir. I think I might just need a restorative libation. More than I care to admit."

"Can't make it through the morning without a stiff one, eh?" Gerry joked as he poured himself a small snifter of brandy as well. "I hear you, man. I know exactly how you feel."

Arthur sipped his drink, then placed his glass down gently on top of the desk. "Now, on that point, I beg to differ, Gerald.

You are not married, so you can have no idea how I feel." He fell silent for almost a full minute.

Gerry cleared his throat and made another attempt to draw out his friend. "So, what's been eating you, mate? Problems with the missus?"

Arthur made a puzzled face at Gerry, then laughed. "Indeed. Your peculiar turn of phrase seems to describe my circumstances precisely. It feels like my wife is trying to eat me up alive."

"That might not be such a bad thing," Gerry teased. "Depending, of course, on where she aims her mouth."

Arthur gazed dumbly at Gerry while he tried to make sense of his words, then shook his head. "I can only guess at your meaning, Gerald, but if you are suggesting that my Helen is capable of engaging in marital relations of an unconventional nature, then I must put you to rights. I discovered on my wedding night that Helen was quite a disappointment in that respect."

"Sorry to hear it," Gerry replied. "But, you never know—things might get better. I imagine she was probably very innocent when she first came to your bed. You just need to teach her a thing or two."

"I've tried," Arthur said, reaching for his glass once more. He downed his drink and immediately refilled it. "When I first made Helen's acquaintance, I thought she was different from the other young ladies of her class whom I had met. She had a bit of fire about her. Her uncle and aunt kept trying to hand her off to an astoundingly boring old man who possessed a large fortune, but Helen would have none of it. I admired her strength of spirit. I thought to myself, 'Now *here's* a girl who isn't interested in marrying for wealth or status. Here's a girl who's not afraid to speak her mind. Here's a girl who might just want to experience more out of life than conventional society expects of her.' But I was utterly mistaken. She turned out to be the most conventional woman I have ever met. It's as if—as if I married my old parson's daughter, who taught me Sunday School lessons when I was a lad."

Gerry blanched. "Merciful heavens!" he exclaimed. He downed his own brandy and reached for the decanter to refill his glass. "That can't be good."

"You should read some of these letters she sent me," Arthur continued. He pushed a stack of papers towards Gerry. "She quotes the Bible at least once on every page. Good Lord, how did this happen to me?"

Gerry skimmed the top letter and placed it back on the desk. "Well, is it too late to get out of it?" he asked, trying to sound helpful. "I mean, you've only been married to Helen for a few months now. Maybe you could plead your case to a sympathetic judge or priest and ask for an annulment. You know—not a nasty divorce or anything like that. Just a simple, public acknowledgment of the fact that you both rushed into this marriage when you were too young to know what you were doing, and now you both want to make a clean break."

Arthur stared at Gerry for a long moment with a befuddled look, then reached for his glass of brandy. "I don't know what in God's name you're talking about, Gerald. There has been no cause for an annulment. I am not a bigamist. Helen's family gave their full consent to the union. The minister who witnessed our vows was properly ordained."

"But—" Gerry began, but then his eyes fell on a newspaper sitting on the edge of the desk, and he remembered that he was talking to a man from the 1820s, not the 1960s. Realizing that he was standing on unfamiliar ground, he reached for his own glass and gently clinked it against Arthur's. "Oh bugger, don't listen to me. I don't know what the hell I'm talking about. Let's just drink to the good times. Even in the darkest hour, they're never far away."

"Do you really believe that?" Arthur asked after taking another sip of brandy.

"Sure!" Gerry replied. "I've got to believe that. It's what keeps me going."

Arthur arched an eyebrow and poured himself another drink. "And *this*, my dear friend, is what keeps *me* going." He lifted his glass and winked at Gerry. "I don't know how I'd face life without the support of my faithful friend John Barleycorn."

Gerry downed his drink and rested his glass on top of the stack of Helen's letters. "Tell you what, Arthur," he proposed, "why don't you put off writing to your missus until later? We could enjoy a little indulgence or two first. Get you in a happier mood, so you'll be more inclined to write something nice to her. Let's pull out the laudanum."

Arthur stood up from his chair and smiled. "An excellent idea. To tell you the truth, Gerald, I don't even know why I bother writing to Helen in the first place. Her friend Milicent tells her everything that's going on here in Mayfair, and there's little I can add to her report. At least, little I can add that I want Helen to know."

"Milicent—" Gerry mumbled, scratching his sideburn. "I've heard Ralph and Walter mention a woman by that name once or twice."

"Yes," Arthur agreed as he returned to the table with a small blue medicine bottle. "She's Walter's sister and Ralph's fiancée."

"Ah, so another member of our distinguished company is about to set aside his carefree bachelor ways and join the ranks of the unhappily married, just as you have."

"I hope not," Arthur replied. "I married Helen on the mistaken assumption that she would be an entertaining sort of wife and found myself woefully disappointed. But Ralph is attracted to Milicent precisely because she is so innocent. He believes he can keep the wool pulled firmly over her eyes after they exchange their vows and continue to partake in his 'carefree bachelor ways' with minimal impediments."

"Well, that might not be such a bad arrangement," Gerry said, eagerly eying the small bottle of laudanum. "What the girl doesn't know won't hurt her."

"Perhaps you're right," Arthur agreed. "And perhaps Ralph might end up a happier husband than I am. What do you say we drink to his good prospects?" He popped the cork off the laudanum and sipped from it, then handed the bottle to Gerry.

Gerry accepted it greedily. "To Hattersly!" he called out as he raised the blue flask up in a toast. Then he brought it to his mouth and took a swig. The familiar, blissful sensation immediately started coursing through his veins as the opium took effect.

"Now tell me, Arthur," he added with a loopy smile. "Just what sort of stag party have you got planned for our Ralph on the eve of his nuptials?"

"Stag party?" Arthur replied in an inquisitive tone. "I'm sure I don't know what you mean. Is that another American expression you picked up across the pond? Please explain the term to me."

Gerry rested the medicine bottle on the writing desk and focused his gaze at Arthur. He slowly raised his left eyebrow while keeping his right brow in place. "My dear sir, I'd be delighted to do just that!"

* * *

Gerry slipped out of his hotel bedroom and stumbled into the dark sitting area of the suite he was sharing with Eddie. He worked his way through the unfamiliar maze of furniture towards the bathroom, then noticed a light shining through the crack beneath its door. He took a cautious step backward and threw a glance at Eddie's opened bedroom door. The early morning light had just started to peek through the curtains, revealing the shape of a woman on Eddie's mattress. Gerry smiled to himself as he admired her lovely form beneath the crumpled sheets.

Then he heard the toilet flush. He tiptoed quietly back to the bathroom. As soon as Eddie opened the door, Gerry whispered, "Boo!"

Eddie flinched, but quickly recovered his composure.

"Did I scare you?" Gerry asked.

"Your face is enough to scare anyone first thing in the morning," Eddie replied.

Gerry ignored the insult. "So, Mr. Rochester," he stated in a tone of mock-formality. "There seems to be a woman in your bed."

"Yeah, I noticed," Eddie agreed.

"So, tell me about her."

"What's to tell? She's lovely."

"And that's all you have to say about the fair lass?" Gerry teased.

"What else do you want to know? I met her at the party. I asked her to come back to my room, and she said yes." Eddie turned towards his bedroom door. "She seems to be stirring," he whispered. "I wish I could remember her name."

"You goat," Gerry chided him.

"Yeah, you're right," Eddie agreed. He took a step towards his bedroom, then stopped and turned around. "So, how was your evening with Arthur and the lads?"

"Laudanum rocks," Gerry answered with a sweet sigh.

A quiet murmuring emerged from Eddie's bedroom.

"Listen," Eddie whispered. "It was the lark, the herald of the morn. Be still my heart. My lady wakes."

"Eddie?" A soft voice called out from the bedroom.

"Yes, my darling girl," Eddie called over his shoulder. "I just went to the loo. I'll be right there."

Gerry chuckled. "Talk to you later, mate. Seems like the honor of your presence has been requested elsewhere."

Eddie returned his friend's smile and was just about to walk back to his bedroom when he noticed his evening's companion standing in the doorframe. She had slipped his oxford shirt over her shoulders, but hadn't buttoned it. Her long dark tresses cascaded messily over her partially exposed breasts.

"Are you going to introduce me?" she asked as she eyed Gerry.

"Right," Eddie said. "Gerry, this is—Maryanne."

"Mary Beth," she corrected him.

"I knew that," Eddie replied smoothly. "I was just teasing you."

"Mm-hhm," she purred. She took Eddie's hand and pulled him towards her. "Let's go back to bed."

"Who could argue with that?" Eddie said. He threw Gerry a sly smile, then stepped back into his bedroom and shut the door.

"Lucky sod," Gerry murmured under his breath. He stood still for a long moment, staring at Eddie's closed bedroom door.

Maybe I should have gone to that party, after all, he thought with a sudden pang of regret. *There's something to be said for enjoying the genuine pleasures of the flesh.*

But then he remembered the powerful sensation of bliss that the laudanum never failed to deliver.

Nah, he promptly decided. *Nothing beats that.*

He tried to remember why he had come into the sitting room in the first place. He looked around for a few moments. His glance fell upon the bathroom door.

Right, he remembered. *I came in here to use the loo. God, I'm not thinking very clearly these days, am I?*

* * *

Eddie returned to the hotel suite after seeing Mary Beth off in a cab. He found Gerry dressed in a clean set of clothes and sitting at the table in the middle of their shared living room. He was holding a lit cigarette in one hand and a laminated menu card in the other.

"I've taken the liberty of ordering your breakfast," Gerry announced. "I hope you're in the mood for a Western Omelet. It seemed like an appropriate thing to eat, seeing as how the view from our window looks like the backdrop from a John Wayne movie."

"Sounds great," Eddie replied. He walked to the window and admired the spectacular Rocky Mountain vista for a few seconds before joining Gerry at the table. "You're up pretty early," he added as he took a seat. "Is something wrong?"

"Nope. Nothing's wrong," Gerry said. "In fact, things couldn't be better."

"You haven't worn out your welcome at Lord Lowborough's Gentlemen's Club?" Eddie teased.

"Far from it," Gerry insisted. He took a last drag on his cigarette, then crushed it out in a cut glass ashtray and smiled. "I've been invited to a party that Arthur is throwing to celebrate Ralph Hattersley's impending nuptials."

"A nineteenth-century bachelor party?" Eddie laughed.

"Should be fun," Gerry said. "I'm sure you'd be welcome too, if you'd care to tag along. The lads have all been asking for you. Alan, Pete, and I have tried to teach them some new songs, but none of us can sing or play an instrument as well as you, Tony, or Jim can."

"That's not true," Eddie retorted. "You're a damned good drummer."

"'Preciate the compliment," Gerry replied, "but I haven't been able to carry my kit back with me like you did your guitar. Lord Lowborough lent me some drums from the regiment he supports, and I tried rigging them together so I could play along with Pete, but they didn't hold a candle to my Ludwig snares and toms."

Eddie chuckled. "You've piqued my curiosity there. I'd love to see what sort of rhythmic contraption you Mickey-Moused together from that old military gear. But I'll still pass. I've seen enough of Arthur and his friends to last me a lifetime."

A knock on their door announced the arrival of room service. Gerry let the waiter in while Eddie cleared some papers off the table. After they took their first bites of breakfast, Gerry put down his fork.

"I've got a favor to ask of you, Eddie," he said in a hopeful voice. "My cartoon potion is running low. Could I use some of yours when mine's gone?"

Eddie stabbed at his omelet and sighed. "I dunno. I'm inclined to say no. I really don't think it's healthy for you to keep going back there." He looked up at Gerry's pleading eyes, then reached for the coffee pot and poured himself a cup. "But I could change my mind," he added reluctantly. "Ask me again when you actually do run out."

"Okay," Gerry said. He picked up a slice of toast and started buttering it. "I've got enough for a few more trips anyway. Which reminds me, what do you think I should take to Hattersley's party as a gift? I'd love to bring a stag film. That would completely bowl the lads over. But I don't suppose I could manage that."

"I don't suppose you could either," Eddie agreed. "The motion picture projector wasn't invented until sometime in the

151

late 1800s, so you'd have nothing to play the movie on. And even if you carried a machine into the book with you, there wouldn't be any electrical current available to run it."

"Right," Gerry sighed. "So what do you think? Maybe I could bring an issue of *Playboy?* They'd all get a kick out of that!"

Eddie shook his head. "*Playboy* is a news periodical. Its journalistic standards might not be up to snuff with *The Times* of London, but it's still printed with a date. And it runs articles about contemporary culture and ads for products that won't be invented until the 1960s."

"Maybe just the centerfold then?" Gerry proposed. "I could tear it out and have it framed as a gift for Hattersley."

"I don't think photography existed in 1827 either," Eddie replied. "Maybe some primitive daguerreotypes, but not full-color, glossy pictures."

"So what?" Gerry countered. "I don't think the lads will be as interested in the science of the print job as they will be in the glorious splendor of Miss July's breasts."

Eddie laughed. "Well, mount it in an old-fashioned frame then. Go to an antique store before we leave town and see if you can't find one that looks like the right age."

Gerry finished off his coffee and rested his cup in its saucer. He grabbed his packet of cigarettes off the table and slipped it in his shirt pocket. "How much time do we have?"

"I don't know," Eddie answered. "Probably a couple of hours. I don't think our plane leaves for Phoenix until three or four."

"Will you come shopping with me? I don't know anything about antiques."

"Neither do I," Eddie said. "But I'll tag along, at least as far as a book shop. You can buy your copy of *Playboy* while I look for a paperback edition of *Wildfell Hall*. I want to finish reading it. You seem to have pinched my copy."

Gerry smiled and stood up to fetch the *Yellow Pages* from the shelf beneath the rotary phone. "Let's see," he said as he started thumbing through the directory. "How many calls do you think I'll have to place before I can find a bookdealer who can sell us a girlie magazine *and* a debauched Victorian novel?"

Chapter Seventeen

Phoenix, Arizona

Tony threw an irritated look at Gerry. "Should I even bother asking you to join us for drinks?" he said as he shut the door to the band's dimly lit dressing room.

Gerry slipped off his psychedelic jacket and threw it in the pile for Alan to collect. "Dunno. Probably not. Who's all coming?"

"Jim and Alan and me," Tony replied. He unbuttoned his ruffled shirt and turned to his rhythm guitarist. "And possibly Eddie?"

Eddie sat down on a metal folding chair and started untying his shoes. "Count me out," he replied. "I want to go back to the hotel and finish reading the book I bought in Denver."

Gerry focused his gaze at Alan. "You sure you want to hit the Phoenix nightclubs with this lot? I know another party happening tonight that'll probably be a lot more fun."

Alan hung his head low. "Emmett ordered me to stay away from both you *and* Pete this evening," he mumbled.

"Ah, fuck, Alan, how old are you?" Gerry teased.

Alan looked up and squared his shoulders. "I'm old enough to hold my whiskey."

Gerry smirked. "Well, maybe *sometimes*."

Alan's face flushed red, but he held his tongue.

"You're old enough to stand up to your big brother," Pete interjected.

Alan turned towards the band's bassist, then lowered his head once more. "That's easier said than done. Emmett's not just my brother. He's also my boss. *And* he rings up our mum every Sunday and gives her a full report on what I've been up to."

Eddie smirked. "The formidable Grace Poole casts a long shadow."

Pete rested his stage clothes on the table for Alan to sort, then leaned in close to his ear. "Ditch the club as soon as you can and take a cab back to the hotel," he whispered. "I'll be in Room 326 with Mickey and Ken as soon as they finish clearing the stage."

Alan nodded. "Right," he whispered back.

"What are you two mumbling about?" asked Jim.

"Nothing," Pete snapped. "So mind your own damned business. Have fun at the club." He buttoned his wide-collared, rayon shirt and headed to the dressing room door. "I'm gonna see if the roadies need any help packing up our instruments."

"Since when have our roadies needed help packing our instruments?" Tony called after him.

Pete ignored Tony's question and stepped out of the room.

Eddie stood up and slapped Gerry on the back. "Alright then. Let's get a cab back to the hotel. You can re-visit your chapter of *Wildfell Hall* while I read ahead in the book."

"*Now* you're talking sense," Gerry laughed. He waved at Jim, Tony and Alan and shouted, *"Tootles!"* Then he followed Eddie out of the dressing room and into the labyrinth of hallways that led to the exit of the Arizona Veterans Memorial Coliseum.

Jim threw an exasperated look at Tony. "God, this tour is getting weird."

"No kidding," Tony replied. "And I suspect it's going to get even weirder before we're done. How many more gigs have we got lined up, anyway?"

"I have no idea," Jim sighed. "I'm just tagging along for the ride."

Tony chuckled. "Yeah, me too." He turned towards Alan. "Here, let me help you get these coats on hangers so we can head to the club. You look like you could use a drink."

* * *

Gerry rested the framed *Playboy* centerfold on the side of his hotel bed, then turned towards Eddie. "Sure you don't want to join me for the bachelor party? Arthur's gonna invite some 'high-class dancers.' It should be fun to see what passed for burlesque entertainment back in the day. And I'll be bringing along *Miss July* to give Ralph."

Eddie sat up a little straighter against the headboard of the adjoining bed. "Thanks, but no thanks," he replied. He threw a quick glance at the nude portrait by Gerry's side, then looked back at his paperback. "But I'll be spending the evening with Arthur too. I hope to finish reading this bloody book tonight."

"Well, don't spoil the ending for me," Gerry said. "I want to take my time going through all the good chapters." He grabbed the leather-bound novel off his nightstand, sprinkled a few drops of potion on top of a dog-eared page, then lay his head on his pillow and closed his eyes.

"Aren't you forgetting something?" Eddie called to him.

Gerry opened his eyes and frowned at his roommate. "What? I sprinkled the book, and I put on my funny old suit."

"Your magic pill," Eddie reminded him.

"Ah, Christ, you're right," Gerry sighed. He sprang off his mattress and jogged to the bathroom to grab his medicine, then returned to the bed and poured himself a large drink of bourbon. "I don't know where my head is these days. I'm all fuddled."

"Yeah, I've noticed," Eddie agreed. He flipped the page of his paperback and continued reading.

"Think I should sprinkle some cartoon potion on Miss July too?" Gerry asked.

Eddie shrugged. "Beats me. I don't suppose it would hurt, so long as you don't streak the ink on the paper."

"Right," Gerry agreed. He sprinkled a few drops of potion onto the gilt frame, then kicked back his pill with a large gulp of Maker's Mark. "It'll be nice to spend a couple of hours at Lord Lowborough's pad tonight," he added as he set down his glass. "This hotel room's kind of crap."

"Yeah," Eddie agreed without looking up from his book.

Gerry poured himself another drink. "Why do you suppose we keep switching back and forth between four-star hotels and cheap roadside inns on this tour?"

"Dunno," Eddie said distractedly. "I suspect Emmett's trying to stretch the tour budget as far as he can while still letting us splurge on nice digs every once in a while."

"Hhmm," Gerry mumbled. "You're probably right." He downed his second glass of bourbon, then lay back on his bed. "Well, good night," he called out.

"Night," Eddie replied. He read in silence for several minutes until Gerry's snores filled the air. He threw a quick look at his somnolent drummer, then turned back to his book. He flipped a page and finished reading Chapter Twenty-Five, then glanced back at his roommate.

Gerry was smiling in contented bliss. The framed centerfold had vanished from his side.

* * *

Gerry awoke to the morning sun, the smell of breakfast, and the sound of music. He sat up in his bed and saw Eddie sitting at a table in the corner of their room, strumming his Alvarez guitar and singing an unfamiliar song.

Eddie put down his guitar pick and scribbled some words on a sheet of hotel stationery, then looked up at his roommate and smiled. "Did Hattersley like his gift?"

"Loved it," Gerry replied with a yawn. He stood up and scratched himself for a good half-a-minute. Then he smoothed out the collar of his grey coat and approached Eddie.

"Absolutely fuckin' loved it," he added as he grabbed a slice of cold bacon off Eddie's discarded breakfast plate. "'Course, he can't hang it up in his own home where Milicent might see it. So we hid it behind that big painting in Lord Lowborough's ballroom. You know—the one of the fox hunt? It should be safe there."

"Were the lads confused by their first sight of a color photograph?" Eddie added.

"A little," Gerry admitted. "They asked a couple questions about how it was printed, so I made up some story about a new lithography process that had just been invented in America. They fell for it." He took a bite of bacon and washed it down with the dregs of Eddie's orange juice. "But they seemed more confused by Miss July's grooming habits. They'd never seen a girl with hair or makeup quite like hers. Or red-lacquered fingernails. And her straight, white teeth just blew them away."

He finished his strip of bacon and chuckled. "I learned a new phrase too—'cupid's kettledrums.' That's what they used to call ladies' tits back then!"

Eddie laughed. "And how were the dancing girls?"

Gerry grabbed Eddie's last triangle of toast and smiled. "I can answer that question in two words—crotchless knickers!" He broke into a throaty laugh. "I thought the dancers wore them special just for us, but no one else seemed surprised by the holes in the girls' undies, so I suspect that's what women wore back then. God, I love this time period!"

He finished his toast, then pulled a chair up to the table and grabbed the room service menu. "Do you suppose I could still order breakfast? You didn't leave much behind for me."

"I'm sure *le Chef de cuisine* of the Howard Johnson's kitchen would be happy to oblige you," Eddie replied. He clicked the button on his retractable pen a few times, then jotted down another phrase on his lyric sheet.

"So what's up? Are you writing us that new hit song at long last?" Gerry asked.

"I'm trying to," Eddie said without looking up from his paper. "Jim and I started working on a number back in Kansas City, but I wanted to play with the words a bit more."

"What's it about?" Gerry asked as he reached for the phone.

"Meeting girls at parties," Eddie replied with a smirk. "A subject you used to be very interested in, once upon a time."

Gerry ignored Eddie's remark and placed an order with the hotel restaurant. Then he slipped off his grey, wide-collared coat and tossed it on his mattress.

Eddie rested his pen on the table, put down his guitar, and looked squarely at Gerry's face. "I finished reading the book last night," he stated in an eerily calm voice.

Gerry scooted his chair a few inches away from the table. "Don't tell me how it ends. I don't want to know."

Eddie continued staring at Gerry. "I think you ought to at least read a few chapters ahead. Arthur and his friends keep partying, so you might enjoy that aspect of the story. But you'll get the chance to learn more about Arthur's true character."

Gerry scowled at him. "What do you mean? Arthur's a *great* character! He's my favorite character from any book I've ever read in my entire life! He's charming and clever, and he's always up for a laugh. And what's more, he's got a capacity for alcohol consumption that puts even *me* to shame! I admire him deeply."

"You realize that things don't go well between him and Helen, right?" Eddie continued. "I mean, I'm not giving anything away by telling you that. You've read the opening chapters of the novel. You know that she takes their child and goes to live in Gilbert's neck of the woods, and tries to pass herself off as a widow named 'Mrs. Graham'."

Gerry looked away from Eddie's penetrating gaze. "So what are you trying to tell me?" he asked, a note of worry creeping into his voice. "Is Arthur going to die young?"

"Why don't you read the rest of the book and find out for yourself?" Eddie suggested.

Gerry stood up from his chair and unbuttoned his silk waistcoat. "Nah," he said as he pulled a clean shirt out of his suitcase. "If Arthur's gonna die young, then I don't want to read about it. I know that medicine wasn't very good back then. Everyone died of consumption before they hit forty, right? If that's gonna happen to Arthur, then I'll just ignore those chapters."

He switched out his shirt and sat back down at the table. "And why shouldn't I?" he added in a defiant voice. "That's what people always say at funerals, isn't it? That we shouldn't dwell on the sadness of death, but try to remember the joy that our loved ones brought us in life."

Eddie leaned his elbows on the table and rested his chin on top of his folded hands. "Arthur is not going to die of consumption. Or from scarlet fever. Or from typhoid, or a pox, or from any other ghastly, incurable, nineteenth-century malady."

Gerry smiled in relief. "Well, that's good to know."

"Read ahead in the book, Ger," Eddie pleaded. "At least a few more chapters. Find out how Arthur behaves when he's home with Helen and their baby."

"I'm not interested in reading about Arthur and Helen having a row over who's supposed to change the kid's nappies!" Gerry replied testily. "I'd rather stick to the good chapters. And what's wrong with that? A book is kind of like an LP, right? And sometimes there's a crap song on an album that you don't want to hear, so you pick up the needle and place it back on the track that you like, and listen to that number again. There's no difference between doing that and revisiting the same chapter of a novel, like I'm doing now."

A knock on the door interrupted their conversation. Gerry stood up and accepted a plate of food from the bellhop, then sat back down at the table and tucked into his late breakfast. Eddie picked up his guitar and started humming the melody to the song he was working on.

Gerry watched Eddie in silence while he ate, then noticed the far-away look on his friend's face. He put down his fork and offered Eddie an apologetic smile.

"Why don't you sing me what you've got so far?" he said. "Who knows—maybe your song might inspire me to go back to enjoying groupies and parties again for a change."

Chapter Eighteen

Tucson, Arizona

Eddie sprang from his bed at the sound of Gerry's screams. He ran into the hotel corridor and found Emmett struggling to open Gerry's bedroom door with a spare key.

"Christ, which of these damned fobs fits his bloody lock?" Emmett swore as he grabbed the next key on his chain.

Another horrific scream rang out of Gerry's room.

Jim ran into the hall and joined Eddie and Emmett. "What the hell? Did someone break into his room? It sounds like he's being murdered!"

Tony opened his bedroom door a crack and poked his head into the hallway. "Is everything all right?" he called to his bandmates.

Eddie turned to him and shrugged.

Gerry's shrieking voice echoed down the corridor: *"Ab insidiis diáboli, libera nos, Dómine!"*

"Holy fuck!" Jim cursed. "Now it sounds like an exorcism!"

"Well, our Ger *is* Catholic," Tony called down to him. "Maybe we should ring for a priest?"

"He's more of a lapsed Catholic," Eddie called back.

Tony nodded in agreement and slipped back inside his room.

Emmett found the right key at last and pushed Gerry's door open. He ran into the bedroom with Eddie and Jim close at his heels. He grabbed his drummer's shoulders and shouted, "Wake up, Gerry!" over and over as he shook him furiously.

Gerry flailed his arms and smacked Emmett hard across his face. "You're a devil!" he screamed. "A fiend at my elbow!"

"Ah, shit," Eddie cursed. He lowered his head in embarrassment and planted his face in his hands. "I know what he's dreaming about."

"Fine!" Emmett yelled as he rubbed his sore cheek. "Then *you* can wake him up!"

Tony slipped through Gerry's open door, wrapped in a blanket. "Michelle here keeps a Holy Card in her wallet that her auntie gave her!" he shouted over the ruckus. "Might that help?"

A small blond woman poked her head out from a fold in Tony's blanket. "It's of Saint Michael the Archangel!" she exclaimed, her voice barely audible over Gerry's moans. "He battled Lucifer in the Bible! And I have a St. Christopher medal in my car that I can fetch too!"

Jim threw an exasperated look at Tony. "Take her back to bed! Eddie's got this under control!"

"Glad to hear it!" Tony shouted back to him. He wrapped his blanket more tightly around Michelle and himself and shuffled out of the room.

"Nooooo!" Gerry shrieked. "Don't touch me!"

Eddie looked to Emmett for guidance. "Think we should throw some water on him?"

"It'd be safer than trying to shake him awake," Emmett replied, still rubbing his cheek.

"I'll get some," Jim volunteered. He ran into Gerry's bathroom and filled a plastic ice bucket with cold water from the tap, then returned to the bedside. "Stand back!" he warned his manager and songwriting partner.

As soon as Eddie and Emmett stepped out of the way, Jim doused Gerry with the water.

Gerry bolted upright in his bed and shouted, "Fuck!" Water dripped from his hair onto his cheeks and streamed down his nose. He opened his eyes wide and scowled at his friends, then released a long, sad moan and collapsed back on his mattress.

"Are you alright, Ger?" Emmett asked in a calm, steady voice.

Gerry panted for a long moment, then sat back up and wiped his damp face with the sleeve of his grey coat. "Yeah, sure, I'm fine," he whispered hoarsely. "Never been better."

"You scared the living daylights out of us!" Jim exclaimed.

"And you slugged Emmett," Eddie added.

Gerry turned towards his manager and frowned. "Oops. Sorry about that, Chief."

Emmett offered him a forgiving smile. "That's alright, son. You didn't know what you were doing."

Jim returned to the bathroom and filled a water glass, then walked back to Gerry's side. "Here, drink this," he said as he handed him the water.

Gerry accepted the drink and gulped it down greedily.

"You want to tell us about your nightmare?" Emmett said gently.

Gerry held his manager's gaze for several seconds, then looked away. "Nah, you wouldn't believe me."

"Well, of course we wouldn't!" Emmett laughed. "It was just a bad dream. Nightmares aren't supposed to make sense."

Eddie caught Gerry's eye, then turned towards Emmett and Jim. "I'll take it from here," he offered. "You two go back to bed."

Gerry nodded in agreement. "Yeah, I'm fine now. Just let Eddie talk me down."

"Alright then," Emmett replied. "Goodnight, Ger. Try to get some sleep."

He left the room with Jim and closed the door behind them.

Eddie pulled a wooden chair away from a desk and dragged it to the side of Gerry's bed. "So tell me what happened," he said as he took a seat.

Gerry sighed theatrically. "I did what you told me to do. I read ahead in the book."

Eddie furrowed his brow. "Really? Which chapter did you visit?"

"I'm not sure," Gerry admitted, lowering his gaze. "I just opened it to a random page."

"Okay," Eddie said. He threw a glance at Gerry's cluttered nightstand and frowned. "Did you follow your usual routine?"

"Pretty much," Gerry replied. He drew in a deep breath before beginning his explanation. "I changed into my traveling clothes after the concert. Then I took a magic pill and washed it down with a big glass of bourbon. I lay down on my bed and waited for something to happen, but nothing did. So I finished off my bottle of bourbon, and still—*nada!* Then I realized I'd forgotten to sprinkle the bloody book! So I pulled out my bottle of cartoon potion and looked for the novel, but I couldn't find it. I searched through all my suitcases and drawers until I finally found a leather-bound book tucked away inside the nightstand. I grabbed it and opened it to a random page and sprinkled the last of my potion on top of that. But then I realized I'd sprinkled the goddamned Gideon's Bible by mistake! So I stepped into the loo and poured some mouthwash into my potion bottle, thinking maybe it might mix with whatever drops were still clinging to the inside of the glass. Then I came back to my bedroom and found the stupid novel under my top hat. I opened it up and sprinkled a page with the mouthwash potion. Then I lay down and finally fell asleep."

Eddie tried to hide the exasperated look on his face. "Okay. Sounds good. Then what?"

"Well, that's where things start to get weird," Gerry said. His voice began to shake. "I traveled into the book, but I found myself in a room with Helen Huntington. She was reading her Bible. Then she turned into Sister Aloysius, this horrible nun who taught me Sunday school when I was small. You know how people can do that in dreams, right? Then she saw me and grabbed her ruler and was just about to rap my knuckles, when Arthur ran into the room and started screaming at her. She turned into an angel then, and flew into the sky and started dive-bombing him. So he turned into a demon and started shooting blasts of fire at her. *Then* that bloody hobgoblin I met earlier in the fairy ring popped into the room and started poking me with a branding iron. So I screamed. Then Helen and Arthur turned back into themselves. Arthur opened a bottle of laudanum and tried to pour it down my throat, but Helen pushed him away from me. I got right cheesed of at her then and smacked her. Hit her right across the cheek, I did, as she shouted, "*Wake up, Gerry!*" Only she sounded kind of like a man. I think maybe that's when I hit Emmett. Then Arthur turned back into a demon and grabbed the branding iron from the hobgoblin and held it up against me, and my skin started burning off my face. But then someone threw some water on me, and that put out the fire."

"And woke you up, too," Eddie added, trying to sound reassuring.

"Yeah, I guess so," Gerry agreed. He fell back against his pillow and squeezed his eyes shut.

The two men sat in silence for a long moment. Eddie waited for Gerry's breathing to become steady once more, then rested his hand on his friend's shoulder. "I think you should change out of your wet clothes now and put on your pajamas," he said gently.

Gerry nodded and sat back up in his bed. He started loosening the knot in his damp ascot, then put his hand to his cheek to wipe it dry.

Eddie examined Gerry's face but couldn't tell if he had wiped away a tear or just a trickle of water that had dripped down from his wet hair.

"I can stay here, if you'd like," Eddie offered as Gerry changed into his pajamas. "We could watch TV together until you fall back asleep."

"Yeah, okay," Gerry agreed, but then his face fell. "No, we can't. It's the middle of the night. Nothing's on but the bloody test pattern."

"Right," Eddie replied. "Well, I could read to you then."

Gerry turned his pillow over to its dry side and slipped under his covers. "No. I've had enough bloody books for one night." He closed his eyes, then opened them back up and gazed at Eddie with a beseeching look.

"Could you maybe fetch your guitar?" he asked. "When I was small, my Opa used to sing me back to sleep whenever I had nightmares."

Eddie smiled and stood up from his chair. "Don't go anywhere, old friend. I'll be right back."

Chapter Nineteen

San Diego, California

"Oh, c'mon, Eddie!" Gerry pleaded. "Just give me a few drops of your cartoon potion! You know I used up the last of my stash yesterday!"

Eddie tightened his grip on his suitcase and marched out of the sitting room of their shared hotel suite, then threw his bag on top of his mattress.

Gerry followed him into his bedroom. "Just a few drops! That's all I ask! Then I'll slip into my own room and leave you alone for the rest of the night. I promise!"

Eddie rubbed at his sore temples and checked the clock on his bedside table. It was half-past midnight. The band's flight out of Tucson had been delayed by a monsoon, and he was tired. Tired from sitting in an airport terminal for hours on end. Tired of flying from one city to the next all summer long. And tired of listening to Gerry's incessant badgering.

He opened his suitcase and grabbed his pajamas. "No," he stated firmly, refusing to meet Gerry's eyes. "I feel guilty enough for starting you down this path you've been following all summer. I am not going to contribute any further to your laudanum addiction."

"But I'm not addicted!" Gerry protested. He slammed the suitcase shut, just barely missing Eddie's fingers, and plopped himself down on the mattress. "I haven't got the shakes. I'm not breaking into sweats. How can I be addicted to a drug I'm not really taking?"

"But you *think* you're taking it," Eddie countered. "You're psychologically addicted to it, even if you aren't physically.

You've told me yourself that you're always thinking about your next hit. And then if you miss a fix, like you did last night, you get all irritable."

"Bullocks!" Gerry cursed. "I'm not irritable! I just want to have another sweet dream, after that nightmare I had in Tucson."

"Your dreams have become real," Eddie retorted. "You can bring people into them with you. You even brought that framed centerfold into your dream and left it there!"

Gerry shrugged. "So I'm magic. But it's harmless magic, like the fairy godmother's magic in Cinderella that ends at midnight. I always come back to reality, right as rain, as soon as I'm done with my trip."

"Fine," Eddie said dismissively. "Our next stop after this is Los Angeles. You can go to Disneyland and chat up Cinderella. Maybe her fairy godmother can wave her wand over you and send you back into that goddamned book. But *I'm* not gonna help you. Now get off my bed. I'm tired and I want to go to sleep."

"What's gotten into you all of a sudden?" Gerry scoffed. He stood up from the mattress and plopped himself onto an upholstered chair instead. "You were so nice to me last night. And now you're acting like I'm some junkie hitting you up for cash so I can buy more dope."

"That's not far off the mark," Eddie said. He took a deep breath to calm his nerves, then focused his gaze at Gerry and started speaking in a softer voice. "You've used up a whole bottle of animation potion traveling into that goddamned book so you could keep getting high on imaginary laudanum. If I let you have my bottle, you'll use that up too. And *then* what will you do? You'll have to find another way to fly. I have a sinking feeling that Pete and Alan have already given up on your dream-opium and are going after the hard-core fix."

Gerry's face blanched. "No," he insisted. "Alan wouldn't do that."

"But Pete might," Eddie countered. "I wouldn't put it past him. And Alan's been following him around like a puppy dog ever since our show in Cleveland."

Gerry considered his response before replying. "Alan *always* follows people around like a puppy dog," he said at length. "He's just happy to have a new friend. The four of us always pick on him for being so young, and lately, we've been pickin' on Pete too. So they're probably just bonding together—the two sad boys who feel like they've been left out of the party."

Eddie frowned. "They're partying, alright. The two of them have gotten very tight with those new roadies we picked up in Philly—sneaking off to places where no one can see what they're up to. And when they *do* come out and join us, they always look either strung-out or hungover. You'd notice too if you spent any time hanging out with the band."

Gerry fell silent once more. While he struggled to formulate a reply, Eddie unbuttoned his oxford shirt and slipped on his pajama top.

"Would you mind leaving now?" Eddie said irritably. "I mean it. I want to go to sleep."

Gerry stood up and walked to the bedroom door while Eddie stepped into his pajama bottoms. Then he turned to face his friend once again.

"Listen, I'm sure things aren't that bad," he said softly. "Alan's not the sharpest tool in the shed, but he's smart enough to not take heroin. And I would never take it either. Really and truly—I can't stand needles. So even if I *did* try it, I'd only snort it, and that's not even addic—"

"Would you *listen* to yourself?" Eddie shouted, cutting him off. "You're talking like a pillock! *Don't take heroin!* Not with a needle and not up your nose! Which, by the way, is just as dangerous as shooting up! That goddamned book has gotten the better of you, Ger. It's taking away what little good sense you had to begin with. How can I make you see that?"

"By going with me," Gerry answered without missing a beat. "Take me to whatever page you want and show me whatever you want me to see."

Eddie hung his head and stared blankly at his feet. "I don't want to go back there. Arthur Huntington's an arsehole. He's a cruel, selfish bastard. I have no desire to ever see him again."

"Arthur is *not* a bastard!" Gerry protested, his temper flaring once more. "You've been reading Helen's diary. Everything printed on those pages is told from *her* point of view. And she's a sanctimonious, hypocritical, Victorian do-gooder. She doesn't know what goes on at Lord Lowborough's house in Mayfair because she's not there. But *I* know, because I've learned how to read between the lines. If you came back with me, Eddie, and spent some time with Arthur, then you'd understand how I feel. I'm *not* just going to visit him because he lets me share his laudanum. I visit him because I genuinely enjoy his company."

Gerry leaned against the doorframe and sighed. "He's just like me," he added in a sad voice. "We're two of a kind. We're rebels at heart, but we have to act respectable to keep up appearances. We're both rich enough to flaunt the rules, but neither one of us can afford to bite the hands that feed us. Arthur has to mind his manners when he's with upper-class toffs who outrank him. And I have to put on a clean face for the big brass at EMI, so they won't lose faith in me or the band. But when we're done playing all those stupid games, we like to let down our hair and play games that are more fun. Arthur is more like me than any other person I've ever met. It's almost as if—as if that goddamned book of yours were written about *me*."

Eddie squared his eyes at Gerry and offered him a sad half-smile. "Then that's all the more reason why you should read ahead a few chapters," he said.

Gerry's face flushed again. "But I *hate* reading! I'm not like you! I was a terrible student at school, and I never read for fun in my spare time." He pulled the leather-bound copy of *The Tenant of Wildfell Hall* out of his jacket pocket, marched back to Eddie's side, and handed it to him. "Pick a page, any page, then go there with me. You can try to teach me the moral of the story while I try to prove to you that Arthur Huntington is not a wanker."

Eddie sighed and rested the book on his nightstand without opening it. "I'll think about it," he agreed reluctantly. "But I don't want to take one of those black-market pills that Pete got you. I don't trust them."

Gerry cracked his knuckles and thought for a long moment, then met Eddie's eye. "So if I found another way for you to enter the book—without taking a pill—*then* you'd go with me?"

Eddie snorted. "What—are you thinking of hopping a train to Tijuana this afternoon and trying to score some peyote?"

Gerry walked back to the chair at Eddie's bedside and collapsed into its cushions as he considered his options. Then he looked up at his friend and smiled.

"Actually, that's not such a bad idea," he said with a twinkle in his eye. "But I had something else in mind. While we were waiting out the storm in the airport, Emmett handed me a copy of yesterday's San Diego newspaper. It had a big article about us and our upcoming concert. But there was another story that caught my eye."

"I saw the paper too," Eddie said. "And if you're thinking about that piece on the hippies from Anza-Borrego who got busted for stockpiling drugs in their commune, then you can just forget about it."

Gerry cocked his left eyebrow and held it aloft. "Did you read the whole story?"

Eddie stared at Gerry's raised eyebrow for several seconds, wondering when he'd mastered that trick, then looked away and shrugged. "No, I just skimmed it. Why?"

"Because it had a happy ending," Gerry replied smugly. "A magic guru came from out of nowhere and saved the day. He taught those poor lost souls how to achieve a higher level of consciousness without the aid of drugs, and how to travel into new worlds of being and nothingness using only the glorious wonders of transcendental meditation."

"Oh, God, help me," Eddie moaned. He reached across his nightstand and turned off his lamp. "Go to bed, Ger. And close my door as you leave."

"All right, then," Gerry replied. He stood up, walked to the door, and turned towards Eddie one last time. "Sweet dreams, old friend," he said, "even if you won't help me dream a sweet dream of my own."

He shut Eddie's door. Then he stepped into the suite's sitting room, pulled the crumpled copy of the *San Diego Evening-Tribune* out of his traveling bag, and re-read the article about the hippie colony from Anza-Borrego before he turned in for the night.

* * *

Eddie stumbled out of his bedroom and found his drummer sitting at a table in the middle of their shared common room. A bright ray of morning sunlight streamed through the window behind Gerry, casting a radiant, golden halo around his mop of uncombed hair.

"It's all been arranged," Gerry announced in a solemn voice.

"I see," Eddie said. "Thanks. It looks delicious." He sat down at the table and poured himself a cup of coffee.

"I'm not talking about brekkie, you pillock," Gerry replied. "While you've been sleeping, I've been busy. I showed that newspaper article to Emmett and explained the whole situation to him."

Eddie swallowed a sip of coffee and frowned. "I'm sure your explanation must have been truly illuminating. Hand me some toast, would you?"

Gerry passed Eddie a plate and continued talking. "Emmett's worried sick about Alan, and he's willing to try anything to help him. He figured if that guru could get those hippies off mescaline, he might be able to set Alan straight as well. So he rang up the reporter from the *Evening-Tribune* and found out where the swami is living. And right now, as we speak, our trusty manager is driving out to the desert to pick him up—along with the journalist who wrote that story and a photographer from the newspaper. Emmett's also arranged for us to have a hotel ballroom for the afternoon, so the guru can lead us all in a little session of transcendental meditation."

Eddie stared at Gerry with a bleary-eyed expression, then reached for a knife. "But I don't want to have my consciousness raised," he replied as he spread some butter over his toast.

"Too bad," Gerry retorted. "Emmett's been talking to some of his friends at EMI, and they told him the Beatles are going to Wales this August to do a course on Indian spirituality. I'm guessing George Harrison's behind the gig—it doesn't sound like one of Ringo's ideas to me. But in any case, Emmett figured it wouldn't hurt if we got *our* pictures taken with a yogi too—maybe even beat the Fabs to the punch for once. Make it seem like *we're* the trendsetters, instead of the other way around. Tony wants us to wear our stage costumes while we pose with this groovy guru. He figures it'll make for a real vibrant photo, and maybe some glossies might pick up the shot and run it in full-color instead of the usual black-and-white. And I gave him my whole-hearted approval. The way I see it, if this swami can transport us into the pages of our book, then you lot can pretend to be my band of traveling minstrels again!"

Eddie bit into his toast and chewed for a long moment before responding. "I could hardly understand a single word you just said," he replied at length. "I must still be dreaming. I think I'll go back to bed." He gulped down the rest of his coffee, then stood up from the table and headed to his bedroom.

"You're not dreaming," Gerry called after him. "You're just bound by the shackles of earthly consciousness, so you can't see the higher meanings of the words I speak. But once the guru gets here, you can start to dream the impossible dream!"

Eddie stepped into his bedroom and slammed the door shut behind him.

Chapter Twenty

Gerry fastened the top button on his psychedelic stage coat, then led his bandmates into the hotel ballroom to join their manager. Emmett introduced them one-by-one to the two journalists from the *Evening-Tribune*. Then he directed everyone's attention to a bone-thin, long-haired, East-Indian man named Harish Maitreya Bhati.

Gerry shook the yogi's hand enthusiastically. Tony, Jim, and Pete exchanged a few pleasantries with him. Eddie rolled his eyes as he offered a brief hello, then walked to the far corner of the ballroom to chat with Emmett's brother Alan. The photographer immediately called him back and asked him to join his friends at the feet of the yogi for a picture.

"Fine," Eddie groused. He returned to the middle of the room and plopped himself down on the beige carpet next to Jim.

The reporter asked each of the Pilots a few questions about their spiritual quest while the photographer clicked away with his camera. Then Emmett scheduled a follow-up interview for the next morning and asked Alan to escort the journalists out of the room.

As soon as Alan returned to the assembly, Gerry and Emmett pulled their honored guest aside. Mr. Bhati nodded politely as they tried to explain their real reasons for summoning him, then smiled a snaggle-toothed grin and assured them in a gentle, sing-song voice that all things were possible through the powers of transcendental meditation.

Emmett flashed Gerry a hopeful—if dubious—look, then excused himself from the gathering, claiming he had to make some phone calls before the evening's concert. Gerry cleared his throat, clasped his hands together, and turned towards his bandmates.

"Thank you for joining us, gents," he said, assuming the polished voice of a smooth-talking radio announcer. "I am so glad you could come on such short notice. Emmett and I have just told Mr. Bhati all about our recent journeys through time, space and literature. And he has most kindly agreed to show us how to meditate our way into a nineteenth-century novel, using only the power of our minds."

Mr. Bhati placed his palms together in a prayerful gesture and cast an earnest look at the five musicians and Alan. "I shall *attempt* to guide you," he clarified. "I will teach you how to release your innermost self into the pulsing rhythm of the universe. In this heightened state of consciousness—or should I say, *trans*-consciousness—you will become open receptacles to the life force that surrounds you. The karmic power that permeates space and time will flow through you. The 'here and now' of your daily existence will melt into the 'what-ifs?' of alternative realities. I shall then attempt to lead you to the exact place and time that your friend Mr. Enis wishes to visit, though I cannot make any guarantees. For us to embark on a successful journey, you *each* must be equally willing to let go of the ties that bind you to this particular place and time. You must *all* believe this voyage is possible."

Tony broke into a laugh. "Well, I'm always up for a holiday. Count me in."

"I'll give it a try too," Jim agreed with a loopy smile. "A few weeks ago, I wouldn't have thought this was possible, but after Gerry led us on that whacked-out trip to the Victorian Gentlemen's Club, I'm starting to believe in magic. I'm open to possibilities."

Pete and Alan nodded and murmured their ascent in hushed tones.

Gerry flashed an angry look at his rhythm guitarist. "Eddie?" he challenged.

"This is bullshit," Eddie replied.

Gerry glowered at him. "Well, maybe so, but since *you* won't pop another pill, and there's no more absinthe to be had, this is our next best option. I'm doing this for *you*, you wanker."

Eddie glared back at him. "Gerry, you know damn well that I don't want to do this. But despite my reservations, I'm willing to travel into the pages of that goddamned book once more if it means I can help you see the error of your ways. I'm doing this for *you*, you pillock." He turned to face the yogi. "You can count me in too."

Gerry flashed an icy grin at Eddie, then turned back towards Mr. Bhati. "Well then, swami, that makes six true believers. So take us away."

Mr. Bhati nodded at him. "First, I would like to see this most extraordinary book."

Gerry pulled the novel out of his coat pocket and handed it to Eddie.

Eddie quickly flipped through the pages and handed the book back to Mr. Bhati. "I've picked a chapter that I think we should visit," he said, pointing to the page.

"Oh, and one more thing," Gerry interjected. "Before we start our trip, we have to sprinkle some magic potion on the book."

He held out his hand to Eddie and raised his right eyebrow at a stiff angle. Eddie pulled his bag of potions out of his coat pocket and handed the yellow flask to Gerry.

A curious expression washed over the yogi's face. "What is the source of this 'magic' potion?"

Gerry smirked. "Eddie bought it at a Voodoo store."

"An *Obeah* shop," Eddie corrected him. "In the French Quarter of New Orleans."

Gerry rolled his eyes. "Whatever."

"So there is bad karma involved in these trips you've been taking," Mr. Bhati surmised. He clucked his tongue in disapproval. "This is a very important detail. I cannot in good conscience take you to a place that might cause you harm."

"I see," Eddie replied in a challenging voice. "In case you aren't able to transport us into the book, you've got yourself a handy excuse now."

Gerry scowled at Eddie, then turned back to the yogi and held up the yellow bottle. "This potion is perfectly harmless. And the man who sold it to Eddie was a real nice bloke—not some scary witchdoctor. He even sold Eddie a love potion! And that's what you and your hippie friends are all about, isn't it, Mr. Bhati? Love? It's all you seem to need these days."

Mr. Bhati smiled and held out his hand. "Please let me see *both* of these potions."

Eddie pulled the rose-colored flask out of his bag and reluctantly gave it to Gerry. Gerry then handed both bottles to their transcendental tour guide.

Mr. Bhati held the potions up to the ceiling light and examined them carefully. A plethora of rainbows refracted through the crystal containers and shimmered across his long white beard. "And just how do these work?"

Gerry cleared his throat and offered a hasty explanation.

"I see," the yogi said, nodding his head thoughtfully and assuming a sage expression. "The person who created these potions must have a very deep understanding of the interlocking powers of the universe."

Eddie snorted. "The person who created them was a quack. There's nothing in these bottles but oil and perfume and rubbing alcohol."

Mr. Bhati held the rose-colored flask back up to the overhead light. He twirled the bottle at an angle so that the rainbows refracted onto Eddie's face. "Then why did you purchase them?"

"As a joke," Eddie insisted. "I was gonna give the yellow bottle to my kid brother as a gag gift. He's been having a hard time at school lately. I thought it might make him smile and—who knows—maybe boost his confidence a bit."

The yogi lowered his eyes and focused his gaze on Eddie. "And the other potion?"

"That's for me," Eddie said, reaching out his hand and grabbing the bottle back.

Mr. Bhati curled his lips into a knowing smile. "Ah, so you *do* believe in the power of these potions."

"No, I don't," Eddie retorted. "It's just that—I mean—I think *some* people are particularly susceptible to the powers of suggestion. And if *they* got hold of this potion, they might use it incorrectly." He threw an accusing look at Gerry.

"Well then, if you truly don't believe in this love potion's powers, perhaps you could give it to me?" Mr. Bhati proposed. "There is a young couple living at my ashram, and I feel a strong karmic pull between them. But they both seem to be avoiding each other. I would like to see if this love potion might break down their barriers of doubt, and help them unlock their mutual destiny."

"There's no magic in any of these bottles," Eddie repeated. He slipped the pink flask back in his pocket and wrapped his fingers around it more tightly.

"Well, then you shouldn't mind giving one of them away," the yogi pointed out.

"I bought it," Eddie protested. "It belongs to *me*."

Mr. Bhati tilted his head to one side and offered Eddie a gentle smile. "I could pay you the same price for the love potion that you paid the shopkeeper in New Orleans. I have a little cash on me at the moment."

Gerry snorted. "You have a *lot* of cash on you. Your services don't come cheap!"

A faint blush rose to the yogi's cheeks. He fell silent for a few seconds, then looked back at Eddie with an earnest expression. "I sense your hesitation. You are impatient to find a mate and are hoping this love potion might speed things up for you."

Eddie dropped his chin and stared blankly at a small stain on the beige carpet. He traced his fingers over the cut-glass pattern on the bottle in his pocket and thought about the discouraging fortune the shopkeeper had predicted for him—that no woman yet born could bring him true love. He sighed.

"Fine," he said in a frustrated voice. He plucked the potion out of his pocket and handed it back to the yogi. "Go ahead and give it to your star-crossed hippie lovers. They seem to have a more immediate need for it than I do."

Mr. Bhati accepted the bottle with a grateful smile and slipped it into the pocket of his white, saffron-trimmed robe. "Thank you, my son. Kamadeva and Rati will surely look favorably upon you for your generous sacrifice and lead you on your own path towards love. Just be patient. Now, why doesn't Mr. Enis read us a scene from the book that he wishes to enter, and I will attempt to lead you brave young men into this strange, new dimension."

"Wait!" Gerry exclaimed. "I have to switch clothes with Alan first!" He ran to the corner of the room and started undressing. Alan handed him a garment bag containing his old-fashioned costume from New Orleans, then slipped on Gerry's psychedelic coat and ruffled shirt.

Gerry dressed hurriedly, then ran back to join his friends at the yogi's feet. "Does my cravat look alright?" he asked Eddie.

"Sure," Eddie said indifferently. "It looks perfect."

"Nah, it's crooked," Tony countered. He stood up and re-knotted Gerry's tie, then sat back down on the floor, leaving room for Alan to squeeze into the circle beside him.

Gerry picked up the worn copy of *The Tenant of Wildfell Hall* and recited the first paragraph from the page that Eddie had selected. He threw a quizzical look at Eddie, then shrugged and sprinkled a few drops of animation potion on top of the yellowed paper. He rested the book at the yogi's feet, then sat down on the floor between Jim and Pete.

Mr. Bhati asked the six young men to fold their legs crosswise and place their hands palms-upward on top of their knees. "Chanting a mantra will help you clear your minds of distraction. I suggest we recite the phrase, *'Ghaas kee havelee ka maidaan'.*"

Alan furrowed his brow. "That's a lot of syllables. What does it mean?"

"Meadow mansion," the yogi replied. He closed his eyes and started to chant.

"What the fuck?" whispered Pete.

"Grassdale Manor," Eddie chuckled. "That's the name of Arthur's home in the country."

"Ah," Gerry sighed. He smiled contentedly. "I've always wanted to visit Arthur's pad. This should be a gas."

"Ghaas kee havelee ka maidaan," intoned Mr. Bhati. *"Ghaas kee havelee ka maidaan…"*

Eddie, Tony, Jim, Pete and Alan bit back smiles as they attempted to chant along.

"Behave yourselves!" Gerry admonished them. "Close your eyes and stop giggling!"

"Ghaas kee havelee ka maidaan!" Mr. Bhati repeated, his voice gaining strength with each syllable. *"Ghaas kee havelee ka maidaan!"*

Gerry frowned at his bandmates as they chanted a cacophonous jumble of sounds, then turned his full attention to the yogi. He picked up the rhythm of the mantra and started reciting the words in a pattern that was easier for his friends to follow. They quickly fell into pace with him. Before long, they had each closed their eyes and were swaying in time to Gerry's beat.

"Ghaas kee havelee ka maidaan!" they repeated, their voices growing stronger with each repetition of the mantra. *"Ghaas kee havelee ka maidaan!"*

The strange words filled the room with a powerful presence. Each man's breath became the words, and the words became each man's breath.

Gerry rocked his body in time to the mantra. His heartbeat fell into pace with the rhythm.

"Ghaas kee havelee ka maidaan!" he repeated, closing his eyes and giving himself over to the refrain. His words echoed off the walls and chanted back to him: *"Ghaas kee havelee ka maidaan!"*

He opened one eye. He saw his breath take shape in front of his mouth, like a cloudy gasp of vapor on a cold winter day. He watched it join forces with the breaths of his bandmates and form a small mist. The mist rose to the ceiling, then started spinning around the room, like a cyclone of sound, growing larger each time it lapped the circle of seven men.

Gerry closed his eye once more and sensed his soul rising out of his body…

Chapter Twenty-One

"Ugghh—" Pete groaned. He stretched out his arms over a sodden patch of earth and grabbed a handful of damp grass.

"Mmm—" Alan sighed in a tone of blissful contentment.

Jim rolled over on the wet ground and frowned at his manager's younger brother. "Did you just say, 'Om'?"

Alan closed his eyes tighter and broke into a beatific smile. "Mmm-hmm."

Eddie propped himself up on his elbows and examined his new surroundings. He and his bandmates were spread across a grassy lawn, dotted with purple violets and pink foxglove. A row of tall pruned hedges cast a shadow over them from the right. Beyond the hedge, he glimpsed the towering rooftop of an old English manor house. A densely vegetated forest lay to his left. At the edge of the woods, the slumbering body of Harish Maitreya Bhati rested beneath a canopy of dangling willow branches.

Tony stood up and wiped a few blades of grass off the sleeves of his psychedelic coat. "Where the bloody hell are we *now?*"

Gerry put his hand to his brow and examined the turrets of the nearby mansion. "If the cartoon potion worked its usual magic, then I'm gonna guess we're lying on a grassy dale just outside of Grassdale Manor. We're at Arthur's pad."

Pete stood up and admired the imposing edifice. "That's one fucking big pad."

Tony sighed. "Someday, *I'm* gonna buy one of these old country estates. There's a crap ton of them on the market now, you know. I've heard John Lennon has his eye on a Georgian manor house near Ascot."

Alan opened his eyes at last and chuckled. "Maybe you could try to out-bid him."

"I'd rather own one in the North," Tony replied without missing a beat. "And who knows—the way England's tax rates keep soaring, soon all the posh toffs will have no choice but to sell off their estates. Then pop stars will be the only Brits left who'll be able to afford them."

Eddie rolled his eyes. "Right, and maybe someday the Queen will knight Mick Jagger and Paul McCartney."

Jim turned towards Gerry. "Well, now that we're here, what are we supposed to do?"

"Find Arthur," Gerry replied. He turned towards the row of hedges and searched for signs of life amidst the shrubbery. "I'm kind of surprised we materialized here in a field and not inside the building. Usually, I show up right where Arthur is in the book. And he's much more likely to be drinking indoors with his mates than strolling around a garden, admiring the daisies."

Pete threw a furtive glance at the slumbering yogi. "Suppose we ought to try to wake up Mr. Bhati?"

Gerry gazed at the willow tree and smiled. "Nah. He looks like he's found his own little private nirvana. Let him enjoy."

"Hey, check out these clothes!" Tony interrupted. He held up a navy-blue coat with matching trousers, a cream-colored shirt, and a long, silk ascot. "I found them behind that bush over there."

He examined the suit's seams and let out an appreciative whistle. "The tailoring on these pieces is extraordinary! It's all hand-stitched. There's not even a hint of machined needlework."

"Well, of course there isn't," Jim scoffed. "Elias Howe didn't invent the first sewing machine until 1846."

Pete furrowed his brow. "Where the hell did you learn *that?*"

"From the Beatles film *Help!*" Jim answered. "Don't you remember? In the credits at the end, the Fabs respectfully dedicated the movie to him."

Tony started walking into the forest. "'Scuse me for a bit, lads. I'm gonna try this on and see if it fits."

Gerry frowned in disapproval as he watched Tony duck behind a tree. "Why's he so modest all of a sudden? We've all shared dressing rooms before."

"I suspect he thinks the person who left those clothes on the ground might still be lurking about," Eddie suggested. He scanned the area for a naked stranger, and instead saw six well-dressed men and women walking towards them through a gap in the hedges.

Jim blanched. "What should we do now?"

"I dunno," Gerry whispered. He put his hand over his brow once more and scanned the assembly. "I don't see Arthur in this lot. But I recognize Walter Hargrave, Ralph Hattersley, and Lord Lowborough."

"Don't forget Grimsby," Alan added. "He's slinking behind the others."

"That looks like Helen in the back of the group," Eddie said. "Gerry and I caught a glimpse of her once in an earlier scene. And the woman she's walking beside is probably Milicent Hattersley. She's Ralph's wife, Walter's sister, and Helen's best friend."

"Where do you suppose Arthur is?" Pete asked.

"I'm right here, you imbecile!" a voice hissed.

Each of the Pilots turned towards the sound. A nude man was standing directly behind them, covering his privates with a large sycamore leaf.

"Where the devil are my clothes?" Arthur cursed. He crouched down and ran his free hand under the small bush where Tony had found the suit.

"Ummhh—" Eddie mumbled, throwing a nervous glance at the party of six that was approaching from the hedge.

Gerry ran in front of the bush to block the newcomers' view of Arthur. "You don't have time to worry about that now, Arthur," he warned his fictional friend. "Helen's coming! Tell you what—I'll create a diversion, so you can sneak back to the hedge through the woods and run into your house that way."

"Thanks, Gerald!" Arthur exclaimed. "I don't know what in blazes you're doing here, but your timing could not have been more fortuitous." He ran back to the forest for cover, then started working his way through the trees towards the row of tall shrubs.

Gerry approached the small walking party. He bowed to Lord Lowborough, then extended his hand in greeting. "Ralph! Walter! What a delight it is to see you again! And Grimsby too, you old sod! I'm passing through these parts on business. My troupe of minstrels is performing at a fête in the neighboring village the day after tomorrow. When Arthur heard we were going to be in the area, he asked us to stop by Grassdale so we could entertain you lot first!"

Ralph Hattersley broke into a broad smile. "How grand, Mr. Enis! I'd love to hear your boys play again. Did you just arrive?"

"Yes, we slipped in the back way, on a road that runs through those woods," Gerry fibbed. "Come hither, lads! Don't hide from the nice gentlemen."

Eddie, Pete, Jim and Alan stepped forward and greeted the assembly. Helen and Milicent started to giggle.

"I dare say, darling," Milicent said to her husband. "These young men look more like gypsies than minstrels. I've never seen such colorful coats!"

Grimsby counted the trespassers and frowned. "Where is your singer, Gerald? I thought there were *four* performers in your band. Or have you re-assigned that task to your brother?"

Gerry threw a nervous glance at the woods. "Anthony is—umm—momentarily disposed. The jostling of the carriage over these winding country roads didn't much agree with him, and he got sick all over his costume. He's resting just now, but he should be with us shortly. After he has a little lie-down and changes into a clean suit, that is."

"Where are your guitars?" Walter asked.

"Our instruments are in our carriage," Gerry lied. "We left it a quarter mile down the road, in the woods. Arthur wanted us to surprise you this evening. But you found us out!"

Helen curtseyed to Gerry and tried to excuse herself so she could make arrangements for the new guests with her household staff. But Gerry engaged her in a drawn-out exchange of pleasantries until he saw Arthur's naked form slip through the gap in the hedge. Only then did he send Helen on her way. Milicent cast a sweet smile at Eddie before turning to accompany her friend back to the house.

Hattersley, Grimsby and Lord Lowborough peppered the Pilots with questions until Gerry cut them off, claiming his musicians needed to bring their gear up to the house. With a dismissive wave, he promised to rejoin the party as soon as they fetched Tony and their carriage.

Lord Lowborough furrowed his brow. "I do hope your friend has come to no harm," he stated in a sonorous voice. "You said he was feeling poorly."

"Oh, I'm sure he's fine," Gerry insisted. "He just needed to get off his feet for a bit."

"Very well," Lowborough replied with a theatrical nod. "Then I shall return to the house. I must find my wife and tell her to expect a special evening of entertainment."

After Arthur's guests left, Pete turned towards Gerry. "So what are we supposed to do now? We didn't bring any guitars with us!"

Gerry shrugged. "I'm sure Arthur has a spinet or harpsichord in one of his drawing rooms that Jim can play. The rest of you lot can just sing along. And I dare say," he added, pulling a face as he turned towards Eddie, "I don't think our lyricist will need to hide behind his guitar this evening. Did you notice how shy little Milicent never took her eyes off our *Edgar?*"

Eddie crossed his arms in front of his chest and frowned. "Don't be getting any salacious notions in your addled brain, *Gerald.* Milicent is a well-brought-up, married woman from the early nineteenth century. So even though her husband is a complete prat, she would never willfully engage the affections of another man."

"She might," Tony interrupted. He straightened the knot in his ascot as he rejoined the assembly, then brushed a few loose blades of grass off the wide lapel of his new navy blue coat. "You shouldn't judge a girl by her time period. I'm sure if you looked beneath these poor birds' layers of reserve, you'd find hearts overflowing with repressed passion. In fact, if you want my honest opinion, I think early nineteenth-century chicks are *hot!*"

Eddie's face fell. "Oh dear Lord, what did you just do?"

"Well, I found a naked lady in the forest when I nipped in to change my clothes," Tony answered. "So what was I *supposed* to do?"

"Was her name, perchance, Anabella?" Eddie continued in an exasperated voice.

"How did you know?" Tony replied with a smile. "Yes, as a matter of fact, it was—Anabella Lowborough. And, damn, for a fictional character, she sure knew how to make me feel like a real man!"

"Leave it to you to find the only slutty woman in this book," Eddie said, rolling his eyes.

"Slut?" Tony challenged him. "How dare you speak that way about my new old lady? I think I might just be in love with her!"

"Arthur Huntington thinks he is too," Eddie replied. "He came out to the woods just now to have a tryst with her. You're wearing his coat."

"Well then, I compliment his taste in both women and suits," Tony said, running his right hand over the left sleeve of his borrowed coat. "They both fit like gloves."

Jim chuckled. "I can't believe you had sex with an imaginary character, you wanker! Can't you keep your trousers zipped for even one bloody chapter?"

"Apparently not," Tony laughed. "Though I should point out that these trousers don't have zippers, just buttons and ties." He patted his groin to make certain he'd fastened his fly properly. Then a look of panic washed over his face. He turned towards Eddie. "You've read the whole book, right? Anabella doesn't have any bastard children in the later chapters, does she?"

Eddie started to laugh. "No worries, mate. No characters from this work of fiction are going to file paternity suits against you."

Tony smiled in relief, then bent down to retie his shoe.

"So now that Tony's back, I say we go inside," Pete proposed. "I could sure use a fix of laudanum."

"I don't imagine they'll be breaking it out until tonight, after the ladies are safely tucked away in their beds," Eddie said.

"So what's the plan then?" Alan asked.

"Yes, Eddie," Gerry said, squaring his gaze at his rhythm guitarist. "Why did you pick *this* chapter for our visit? It seems like we're in a rather awkward part of the story."

"Because I wanted you to see what Arthur is really like," Eddie explained. "I want you to experience his true character."

"And how would *you* describe my true character, Edgar?" asked a familiar voice.

The Pilots turned towards the voice and saw Arthur staring at them. He was wearing a new suit and glaring menacingly at Tony.

"What in blazes are you doing with my clothes, you clodpole?" Arthur sneered.

"Just trying them on for size," Tony replied nonchalantly. "I'd like to show them to my tailor in London so he can make me a copy. But perhaps you could save me some time and just tell me the name of your clothier?"

Arthur eyed Tony warily, then broke into a laugh. "I say, Gerald, your friends are a cheeky lot. I've half a mind to throw them all off my property, but I think it might amuse me more to watch them mingle with my guests. So tell me, what brings you to these parts?"

Gerry approached Arthur and patted his back. "I was just telling Hattersley that we were in the area to play a fête at the local village, and that you'd arranged for us to stop by Grassdale for a brief visit along the way. Your lovely wife Helen has gone back to your home to make arrangements for our dinner."

"Well, then I needn't bother asking you inside, since you've already invited yourself!" Arthur laughed. "But I will be gracious enough to extend you my warmest welcome. Tell me first, though, did you happen to see Lady Lowborough? She asked me to meet her here, so we could—continue a private conversation that we had begun yesterday."

185

"I just saw a woman in a light blue dress," Pete replied, pointing to the gap in the hedge. "She's heading towards the house."

"Damn, what rotten luck," Arthur muttered as he caught a glimpse of Anabella's back. He sighed in disappointment, then he turned towards Gerry again. "Well, what are you waiting for, gentlemen? I require entertainment. Come inside, so you can amuse me and my guests!"

Gerry started following Arthur, but Eddie gestured to the other Pilots to hold their ground. "We have to fetch our instruments first," he called up to Arthur. "We'll be with you shortly."

Arthur looked back at him and scowled. "Indeed, indeed," he said dismissively. "But don't keep me waiting too long. I'm dying to hear some more hymns by the Reverend Richard Penniman. I dare say, ever since that evening when you first performed for me, I've been getting the words to *Tutti-Frutti* stuck in my head at the *most* inopportune times."

Eddie watched the two men cross the field, then turned towards his other friends.

"Well, *that* was stupid, Rochester!" Pete spat out. "We haven't *got* any instruments! What are we supposed to do now?"

"Just let the two of them talk for a bit," Eddie answered calmly. "It's important that Gerry sees how Arthur behaves in front of his wife. He needs to discover what a tosser Arthur really is, so he'll stop wanting to come back and visit him."

"And we're just going to sit here and twiddle our thumbs?" Alan retorted.

"Hell, no!" Tony said. "I can sing for the guests while Jim accompanies me on Arthur's spinet. And while we're inside, I can chat up my dear, sweet Anabella once more."

"Let's just wait here for a few more minutes," Eddie pleaded. "Give Gerry a chance to witness Arthur's boorish behavior while he's lording over his guests."

Tony started to argue but was interrupted by another unexpected visitor.

"Excuse me, my good sirs, but I am looking for Mrs. Huntington," the new man said. "Do you happen to know if she is at home?"

Eddie instantly recognized the speaker as Frederick Lawrence. He hoped that the new guest would not recognize him in return. But then, with a flash of insight, he remembered that his previous encounter with Frederick had actually occurred *later* in the story, and that the Pilots were currently intruding upon an *earlier* scene, which was being described in a flashback. Nevertheless, he took a small step back into the shade of the willow tree before he replied to Frederick's question. "Yes. We just spoke with her. She's gone inside to make dinner arrangements for her guests."

"Thank you," the man said. He hesitated for a moment before adding, "And do you happen to know if *Mr.* Huntington is presently in residence as well?"

"Yes, he is," Tony replied. "We just spoke with him too."

"Dash it all," Frederick cursed under his breath. "I was hoping to catch her in priv—" He stopped midsentence and smiled awkwardly at the Pilots. "Well, thank you again, gentlemen. But I must be going. I have no desire to see the master of the house." He started walking back to his carriage, then stopped abruptly. He turned towards Eddie and eyed him more carefully. "I'm sorry, sir, but have we met before? Your face and your voice seem terribly familiar to me. And yet, I can't recall ever having been introduced to you."

Eddie stepped further into the shade. "I don't think so, sir," he replied. "Perhaps my brightly patterned coat and the brilliant midday sun are playing tricks on your eyes."

Frederick squinted at him, but Eddie's face was obscured by a long, dangling willow branch swaying softly in the breeze.

"Yes, you must be right," Frederick agreed. He turned and started walking away.

"I'm just a foreshadowing!" Eddie laughed as he stepped back into the sunlight. He cast a quick glance at the sleeping yogi and smiled at him indulgently.

Frederick continued walking back to his carriage. Then a voice rang out from across the lawn, calling to him. Frederick looked up. Arthur started hurrying towards him. The two men were soon exchanging heated words. Arthur's friends ran out of the house to witness the argument. While the fictional characters crowded around the two quarreling men, Gerry snuck away from the melee and ran across the grass to join the other Pilots.

"What gives, Eddie?" Gerry asked. "What's Frederick doing here? I didn't read this part of the novel yet. Have he and Helen begun their love affair already?"

Eddie shook his head. "Frederick and Helen have never been lovers. They're brother and sister. He was just trying to comfort her that time we saw them hugging outside Wildfell Hall. He understands that she loves Gilbert, but he also knows she's irrevocably tied to Arthur, so she can't marry anybody else."

Gerry threw Eddie a puzzled look. "Huh? Why not?"

Eddie took a deep breath and started explaining the novel's back story to the band. "Gilbert's friends were right when they guessed that Helen wasn't really a widow—she was still married when she moved into Wildfell Hall, but she had left her husband. And what's more, she had taken his child with her when she ran away—Arthur's first-born male heir. By the laws of her time, Helen had no right to leave. And if Arthur had been able to track her down after she deserted him, he could have taken his son back and made sure she never saw the child again. He could have even thrown her into prison for kidnapping the boy. And then, after she got out, he could have divorced her, so she'd be treated like a social pariah for the rest of her life. Frederick Lawrence arranged the tenancy at Wildfell Hall for his sister after she ran away, so she could live near him, under his protection. He also invented the ruse that she was a widow named Mrs. Graham, so the two of them could keep her marriage to Arthur a secret."

"Well, hell, that's great!" Gerry exclaimed. "I've gotta go back to the beginning of the book now and tell Gilbert the good news! He'll be so happy!"

"So happy about what?" Eddie challenged.

"So happy to hear that Helen and Frederick aren't in love," Gerry replied. "And that Helen really and truly loves *him*, just like he loves her. Now they can be together!"

"No, they can't," Eddie countered. "Helen was still a legally married woman in those first few chapters that you read. Admittedly, she was married to an alcoholic, laudanum-addicted, cruel and selfish douchebag of a husband. But nevertheless, because of her married status, she *can't* get together with Gilbert."

"I don't believe that," Gerry replied. "C'mon, Eddie—where's your sense of romance? Love conquers all. It always does."

"Not in *this* story it doesn't," Eddie insisted. "Don't forget—it isn't 1967 here. It's 1827. Love is *not* all you need. It doesn't matter *how* much Helen cares for Gilbert or how much her brother is willing to help her. Helen is stuck with her tosser of a husband until he dies."

Arthur and Frederick's voices continued to rise, momentarily drowning out the voice of *another* man who was attempting to speak to the Pilots. But after the new visitor tapped Tony on the shoulder, the band's lead singer turned and broke into a wide smile.

"Why, look who's here, mates!" he called out. "Our trusty manager has traveled back through time and literature to rescue us!"

Emmett Poole laughed and stared at his protégés with an expression of wide-eyed wonder. "I can't believe this, Gerry. I honestly can't believe this! You've been telling me the truth all along! That magic potion of yours really *works!*"

After a volley of questions, Emmett explained to the band that he had found them lying unconscious on the floor of the hotel's ballroom and become worried. When he couldn't rouse them, he took one of Gerry's pills with a large glass of wine and sprinkled some more animation potion on top of the book that Mr. Bhati had left open at his feet.

The Pilots' loud conversation finally drew the attention of Arthur Huntington. He broke away from his brother-in-law and inquired about the new guest who had shown up uninvited on his property.

Eddie cleared his throat and pointed to Emmett. "Why, this is Mr.—"

"*Mister*, my arse!" Gerry interrupted. "This is *Lord* Douglas Enis, my uncle!"

Arthur and his friends eyed Emmett suspiciously.

"You are dressed in a most unseemly manner, Lord Enis," Arthur noted as he examined Emmett's brightly patterned polyester shirt, flared plaid slacks, and white tennis shoes.

"He's a Peer of the Realm!" Gerry huffed. "He can wear whatever he damn well pleases!"

"He's no Peer," declared Lord Lowborough. "I happen to know Lord Douglas Enis of Cornwall, and he looks *nothing* like this imposter. This man is a fraud!"

"Don't you go calling my uncle a fraud, you two-bit minor character!" Gerry shouted.

Before Lowborough could reply to the insult, Gerry clenched his hand into a fist and smashed it into the Lord's chin with all his strength. With tempers already raised, the punch was all it took to set off a free-for-all. Hattersley dealt Eddie a keen blow to the face in exactly the same spot where Gerry had struck him previously. But this time, Eddie was prepared to retaliate and answered Ralph's punch with a pounding right hook of his own.

Arthur took the opportunity to vent his mounting anger against both Frederick *and* Tony, and assaulted them both. His two victims caught each other's eyes, then teamed up and turned the tables on their assailant. Tony grabbed Arthur's arms and twisted them behind his back, allowing Frederick to land a few good blows to his detested brother-in-law's face and chest. Lord Lowborough began swinging at Gerry and Emmett to defend his honor—*and* the good name of his dear friend from the House of Lords. And Jim, Pete, and Alan started punching Grimsby and Hargrave just for the hell of it.

As the twentieth-century interlopers gave themselves over to their mounting passions, the blissful sensation of peace that the yogi had instilled in them quickly dissolved. The fight had hardly lasted two minutes when the musicians and Alan found themselves once again back in the hotel ballroom in San Diego. Eddie rubbed his freshly aching cheek and started to chuckle.

"Well, that was fun," Jim laughed. "I can't remember the last time I was in a fist-fight!"

"We're like the Three Musketeers!" Tony chimed in. "All for one, and one for all!"

"But there's six of us," Pete pointed out.

"Seven if you count Emmett," Eddie said. He threw a glance at his unconscious manager. "Though it looks like he hasn't rejoined the land of the living yet."

"Well, obviously the pills have a longer-lasting effect than the meditation does," Tony surmised. "Do you suppose we should try to rouse him?"

"Or the swami over there?" Jim asked, casting a doubtful look at Mr. Bhati.

A blissed-out expression of inner peace radiated from the yogi's face as he continued to sit cross-legged on the carpet, his up-raised palms open to the universe.

"Nah," Gerry decided. "Don't wake the poor sod. He looks so happy. He'll come back around when he's ready."

"But what if Arthur and his friends find him under that willow tree?" Tony asked.

Eddie shrugged. "Well, then they'll just have to deal with a new plot twist."

"But what about Emmett?" Alan asked, his voice tinged with worry. "It takes a while for that medicine to wear off. He could be stuck in that fight for a long time."

"Doubtful," Gerry countered. "I'm gonna guess that Arthur and his mates started freaking out as soon as we six disappeared. They probably just left your brother under the willow tree with our guru."

"Do you suppose Emmett and Mr. Bhati can somehow help each other travel back to the real world?" Jim asked.

"I guess they'll have to," Tony answered. "We have to get ready for tonight's concert. Good thing we're already wearing our stage clothes."

"'Cept you," Jim noted.

Tony looked down and realized he was still dressed in Arthur's navy-blue coat and trousers. He stroked his sleeves and smiled. "Shit, man, how about that? I *love* this suit! I can't wait to show it to my tailor on Savile Row! He's gonna be blown away."

"Well, if Tony's not wearing his psychedelic suit on stage tonight, then I'm not either," Eddie insisted.

Jim, Gerry and Pete exchanged quick looks with each other, then voiced their agreement.

Tony rolled his eyes. "Well, I guess that's it then," he said with a sigh. "From this day forward, the Pilots' matching-suit dress code is officially declared null and void. Wear whatever you want for tonight's show."

Eddie flashed him a smile and started walking out of the ballroom.

Gerry jogged up beside him. "What about Emmett?" he asked as he approached the door.

"I dunno," Eddie sighed. "Maybe Alan can find a way to wake him up before we leave for Balboa Stadium. But for now, I think we should just let him be. After all the stress he's been under lately, it's good to see him looking so rested."

He stepped out of the door and headed to his room to change for the night's performance.

Chapter Twenty-Two

Los Angeles, California —Late July, 1967

"Do you suppose I'm going through withdrawal?" Gerry asked Eddie. He stirred a third spoonful of sugar into his coffee cup and reached across the breakfast table for the jug of cream. "I mean, from the lack of laudanum? I've been feeling a little peaky these past coupla' days."

Eddie rubbed his temples and gazed back at him with a bleary glint. "Dunno, maybe," he mumbled. "Tell me again what you take for hangovers. Is it Vitamin B or C?"

"Vitamin B. Vitamin C is for scurvy."

"Right," Eddie groaned. He pushed aside his breakfast plate, folded his arms over the table, and lay down his head.

Gerry rested his coffee cup in its saucer, then jogged into their shared bathroom and grabbed his bottle of vitamins.

"Here you go, roomie," he said when he returned to the table. He twisted the lid off the vial and pulled out two tablets, then poured a glass of water for Eddie. "These'll help."

"Thanks," Eddie whispered. He tossed the vitamins into his mouth and washed them down with a big gulp of water.

"You were hitting the sauce pretty hard last night," Gerry noted as he sat back down.

"Yeah," Eddie agreed. He finished his glass of water, then rested his head on the table once more. "Second night in a row, too," he mumbled.

Gerry chuckled. "Last night's party at Papa John Phillips' pad was a lot more fun than that snooze-fest Emmett dragged us to the night before. Seriously, why was he making us drink cocktails with record company toffs at that Brentwood mansion? That's really not our scene."

Eddie raised his head a few inches off the table and glared at Gerry. "Because he wants to make sure Capitol Records renews our contract. This tour's not really driving sales for our latest album."

Gerry sighed and reached for his cup. "Yeah, I suppose you're right," he replied with a hint of irritation in his voice. He took a sip of coffee and frowned. "The fans keep shouting out for *Yesterday's Girlfriend* and *Too Much Trouble*. Sometimes when I'm playing those songs, I want to start smashing my drum kit to pieces like Keith Moon does and call it a day."

Eddie curled his lips into a half-smile, then lowered his head and closed his eyes again. "Then what would you do?" he asked quietly.

"I dunno," Gerry admitted. He grabbed his fork, pierced Eddie's uneaten sausage links, and dropped them one-by-one onto his breakfast plate beside his own serving of bacon. "Maybe I'll go back inside the book and hang out with Arthur again. But I'll make sure I only visit the chapters *before* that scene in Grassdale you dragged us into. I'm not sure how I'm gonna face him again after coming to fisticuffs with him and his mates."

Eddie raised his head slowly, poured himself another glass of water, and took a large drink.

Gerry ate his breakfast in silence, then finished his cup of coffee.

"I really do miss him, y'know," Gerry confessed. "I miss Arthur more than I miss the laudanum. I feel like he's a long-lost friend that I've magically reconnected with."

"You seemed happy enough to reconnect with your long-lost, rock-and-roll lifestyle last night," Eddie noted with a dry laugh.

Gerry rested his empty cup in its saucer and smiled. "Yeah, well, it was fun smoking pot again. There was none of that to be had back in Arthur's day. At least as far as I could tell."

He fell silent for a long moment, then his eyes began to twinkle. "Maybe if I brought along a bag of Mary Jane on my next visit, I could give it to Arthur as a peace offering."

Eddie frowned at him.

Gerry lowered his gaze back to the table. "Yeah, you're probably right. Arthur's never lacked substances to abuse. But still, I really do miss him."

He picked up his spoon and started making a swirling pattern with the uneaten crumbs on his breakfast plate. "I think you and I should go back and visit him one last time before we wrap up this tour. Just to say a proper goodbye," he said quietly.

Eddie leaned back in his chair and folded his arms in front of his chest. "What do you mean, 'a proper goodbye'?"

Gerry continued staring at his plate. "Well, you kind of gave away the ending the other day, you know. I got the impression from what you said that Arthur's gonna die young."

Eddie nodded. "Yes, he will."

"But not from cholera or diphtheria, or any other nasty illness like that, you said."

"Mm-hmm," Eddie agreed. He cleared his throat and waited for Gerry to lift his head and look at him before he continued speaking. "Well, I take that back. Arthur might have contracted a touch of TB towards the end of his life. But that's not what did him in. He drank himself to death. Though I suppose the laudanum also contributed to his early demise."

Gerry sat in stone-faced silence for several seconds. Then he took a deep breath and exhaled slowly before asking, "Was he alone when he died? Did his friends all desert him?"

Eddie reached for his water glass. "Hattersley never abandoned him, though the rest of that lot did. But mostly, it was Helen who nursed him through his final days."

Gerry's eyes grew wide with surprise. "Helen?" he exclaimed. "I thought she left him!"

Eddie grimaced, squeezed his eyes shut, and tightened his grip on his glass.

"Sorry," Gerry apologized in a whisper. "Forgot you were hungover. Wanna bum a fag? Having a smoke might help." He pulled a packet of Pall Malls out of his shirt pocket.

195

"No," Eddie mumbled. "I'm trying to give them up." He took another sip of water, then rested his glass back on the table as quietly as he could.

"Helen did leave him," he continued, his voice slowly gaining strength as he summarized the novel's conclusion for Gerry. "She was living on her own at Wildfell Hall in those first few chapters of the book—the ones that you read. But after Gilbert finished reading her diary, she learned that Arthur was dying, so she went back to Grassdale to take care of him. But he was perfectly beastly to her the whole time. That woman was a saint."

Gerry lit a cigarette and took a small puff, then lowered his head and frowned. "So how did Arthur die?" he asked in a whisper. "Did his liver give out on him?"

Eddie lowered his voice as well. "The author didn't provide a precise diagnosis. But mind you, this novel takes place at a time when medicine was still pretty primitive. Arthur's doctor came in a few times towards the end to 'bleed' him with leeches."

Gerry winced and squirmed in his seat. He took another drag on his Pall Mall and released a long stream of smoky breath, then crushed out his barely touched cigarette on his breakfast plate. His hands started shaking.

Eddie held his gaze as he continued summarizing the novel's ending. "Arthur was in terrible pain his last few weeks. He kept slipping in and out of delirium. But shortly before he died, his pain suddenly vanished. He hoped his disease might have passed as well. But his doctor took Helen aside and told her that 'mortification' had set in—whatever that means."

Gerry covered his face with his hands. "That sounds pretty gruesome," he whispered.

Eddie nodded. "This book pulls no punches. I realize that much of the prose has a floral, Victorian sort of feel to it, but it paints a pretty stark picture of Arthur and his demise. The introduction to the paperback edition I bought in Denver mentioned that the author had nursed her alcoholic, laudanum-addicted brother through his final days, so she knew what she was writing about. She didn't spare the reader any details."

Gerry sighed. He drummed his fingers against the table for a long moment, then looked back at Eddie with a hopeful expression. "I want to visit Arthur at his deathbed. Let him know that Hattersley wasn't the only friend he had left."

Eddie smiled at him. "That would be kind of you."

"But come with me, though, would you?" Gerry pleaded. "'Cause I'm gonna need some support. I don't handle death very well. I bawled so hard at my Grandpa Enis' funeral that my cousin had to take me home early. Then when my mum's dad died, my family wouldn't even let me go to the Mass for fear I'd upset my Oma. And Pop-pop and Opa were both old men when they popped their clogs. I think I might take Arthur's death even worse."

Eddie considered the proposal for a long moment before venturing a reply. "But what would I do if I went there? I'd be a bit of a third wheel."

"I dunno," Gerry mumbled, his voice trailing off. Then his eyes lit up. "Wait—you told me you passed yourself off as a preacher that time we traveled into the book and I saw the hobgoblin. Maybe you could do that again—pretend you're there to say Last Rites over Arthur."

"Wouldn't work," Eddie replied. "Helen tries repeatedly to send a clergyman to Arthur's side towards the end, but he'll have none of it. He scoffs at the very notion of God's existence."

"Well, go visit Helen then," Gerry proposed. "She could probably use a shoulder to cry on. And while you're praying with her, I could have a little private chat with Arthur."

"Arthur would still recognize me," Eddie pointed out. "He doesn't know me as well as he knows you, but he *has* seen me before. Twice."

"You said he was fading in and out of delirium towards the end," Gerry reminded him. "He might not be sharp-witted enough to notice."

Eddie leaned forwards and poured himself a cup of black coffee while he considered the possibilities. He took a long drink, then rested his cup in its saucer and met Gerry's eye. "I'd need a proper black suit. That coat-of-many-colors I wore the last two times I went there might pass for a nineteenth-century minstrel's costume, but a man of the cloth wouldn't be caught dead in an outfit like that."

Gerry broke into a smile. "We just played a concert at the Hollywood Bowl. We're in Los Angeles—the land of movie make-believe! We can drop by a film studio before we leave town and dig up something that'll make you look like the most righteous Reverend Rochester."

Eddie grinned and finished his coffee in a large gulp. "We'd have better luck renting a costume from a warehouse that supplies the studios. But I think you're onto something. This idea could work."

"'Course it will," Gerry boasted. He stood up from his chair and threw his cloth napkin on top of his empty breakfast plate. "When have I ever led you astray before?"

Chapter Twenty-Three

San Francisco, early August 1967

"How do I look?" Eddie asked as he fastened the top buttons on his long black overcoat.

"Like a dour and judgmental Victorian minister who preaches the wages of sin," Gerry replied. "You give me the willies!" He turned towards the floor-length mirror of their hotel room and straightened the knot in his cravat. "But I like *my* new suit better'n that one I bought in New Orleans. It makes me look more like the honorable heir to Lord Douglas Enis of Cornwall."

"His heir?" Eddie repeated. "I thought you were just supposed to be his nephew!"

"Well, the plot has thickened of late," Gerry retorted. "I've decided that all of his Lordship's sons died in a freak hunting accident, making me next in line to his fortune."

Eddie laughed. "You should be a novelist yourself."

"Nah," Gerry replied. "I just like making up stories and trying to fool people into believing they're true."

Eddie brushed a speck of lint off his sleeve. "Let's just hope everyone at Grassdale is fooled by *both* of our costumes."

"Right," Gerry agreed. He picked up the leather-bound copy of *The Tenant of Wildfell Hall* and handed it to Eddie. "You find the page. I don't want to look through the last chapters."

Eddie leafed through the novel until he found the passage describing Arthur's death. Then he opened his bottle of animation potion and sprinkled a few drops on top of the book. "Let's do this then," he said. "Give me a drink, and one of those pills from Pete."

Gerry opened his vial of tablets and handed one to Eddie, then filled two tumblers with whiskey. He popped his pill and raised his glass. "To Arthur," he said in a solemn voice.

"To Arthur," Eddie repeated. He clinked Gerry's glass, then popped his pill and washed it down with a large gulp of booze. He immediately started coughing. "How much do you usually have to drink before you start traveling into the book?" he asked once he had cleared his throat.

"More than that," Gerry replied. He poured more alcohol into both of their glasses.

Eddie carried his tumbler to a table in the middle of their room. "I'm gonna cut mine with Coke. I can't drink this much whiskey straight."

Gerry swallowed another large drink. "Well, be quick about it. I don't want to arrive at Arthur's deathbed alone."

"Be cool, man, I'm comin' with you," Eddie groused. He watered down his drink, then curled his lips into a lopsided smile. "It's ironic, don't you think—our taking drugs and alcohol so we can visit a man who's dying of drug and alcohol addiction?"

"Life is full of ironies," Gerry replied. He brought his bottle of whiskey to the table, topped off both of their drinks, then sat down across from his friend. "So, what is everyone else doing this afternoon? Are we missing another one of Emmett's class field trips?"

Eddie swallowed a large gulp of whiskey-and-cola and rested his glass on the table. "Tony's doing an interview with a newspaper reporter. Pete and Alan are checking out Haight-Ashbury. And Jim is giving his new lady love a tour of the City by the Bay."

Gerry put down his glass and furrowed his brow. "What? When did our Jimbo find time to pick up a bird?"

"He met her at Fats Domino's party in New Orleans," Eddie replied. "He's been ringing her up ever since we left Louisiana, and he bought her a ticket to San Francisco so they could spend some time together, now that this goddamned tour is finally winding down."

"Bullocks!" Gerry cursed. "I don't believe it! *No*body finds a girlfriend on a concert tour. Tours are all about one-night stands!"

"Well, apparently, our piano player just found one," Eddie said matter-of-factly.

"Pour me another whiskey!" Gerry demanded. "Let's toast the lovebirds."

Eddie topped off their drinks, then clinked glasses with Gerry once again.

Gerry threw back his glass, then started singing the opening lines to "I Left My Heart in San Francisco."

Eddie raised his glass and sang in reply, "High on a hill, it calls to me!"

Gerry winked at him. "It's Arthur who's calling to us, mate, not Tony Bennett. Remember that."

Eddie nodded. "Right. I wouldn't want the two of us to end up in some posh jazz club in Manhattan, dressed like this. We'd look like fools."

Gerry clinked glasses with him and smiled. "Right you are, Reverend Rochester. Now fill up my glass once more. I can feel the buzz building behind my eyes."

Eddie poured another splash of whiskey into Gerry's tumbler, then finished off his own drink.

A ray of sunlight burst through the window of their hotel room and fell squarely upon both of their faces. They blinked their eyes to block out the bright light, then rested their heads on the table and waited for the now-familiar magic to carry them back to Chapter Forty-Nine of *The Tenant of Wildfell Hall*...

* * *

Gerry opened his eyes to a blanket of darkness. He straightened his shoulders and immediately hit his head against a low ceiling.

"Fuck!" he cursed. "Where the hell are we?" He stretched out his left arm and accidentally slipped it into the sleeve of a woolen coat.

Eddie made a shushing sound. He tried to cover Gerry's mouth with his hand and ended up poking him in the eye. "I think we're inside a wardrobe in Arthur's bedchamber," he whispered. "Listen—"

Both men fell silent. A wobbly but powerful voice was shouting beyond the closet door.

"I am in hell already! This cursed thirst is burning my heart to ashes!"

Gerry smiled. "Yup, that's Arthur," he whispered. "I'd know that voice anywhere."

Eddie opened the door a crack and snuck a peek at the room outside the wardrobe. Arthur was lying on a high, four-poster bed, moaning with theatrical aplomb. He thrashed his arms up and down with such force that he knocked loose a curtain that had been tied to a bedpost. Helen was sitting in a chair by his side, trying to cool his forehead with a damp cloth.

"You're heaping coals of fire on my head, I think!" Arthur shouted at her.

Helen patiently asked if there was anything else she could do for him.

"Yes, I'll give you another opportunity for showing your Christian magnanimity!" he bellowed. "Set my pillow straight—and these confounded bed-clothes!"

Helen stood up and rearranged her husband's pillows and sheets.

"There, now, get me another glass of that slop!" he commanded her.

Helen grabbed the jug on her husband's nightstand, filled a glass with water, and brought it to his lips.

He took a sip from the glass, then pushed her away. "This is delightful, isn't it?" he asked in a menacing tone. "You never hoped for such a glorious opportunity!"

Helen straightened her back and replied in a determined voice, "Now, shall I stay with you? Or will you be more quiet if I go and send the nurse?"

"Oh yes, you're wondrous gentle and obliging," he answered with a cruel laugh. "But you've driven me mad with it all!"

"I'll leave you then," Helen replied. She walked to the door with her head held high and left the bedroom.

"Now's our chance," Eddie whispered to Gerry. "As soon as Arthur falls asleep, let's sneak up to his side."

The two musicians waited in their hideout until they heard Arthur snoring. Then they slipped out of the wardrobe and approached the bed.

Arthur started tossing his head wildly and cursing in his sleep. Then he opened his eyes, saw the two men, and shuddered violently. "Great God in Heaven, what have you done to me?" he exclaimed. "I prayed for an angel to release me from my torment, but you've sent me the devil himself and an undertaker!"

"Hello, old friend," Gerry said softly, offering Arthur a sad smile. "I just happened to be in the neighborhood, so I thought I'd drop by to see how you were doing."

"I'm ill, you fool, can't you see that?" Arthur shouted. He started to sit up, then collapsed against his pillow. "How in blazes did you get into my bedchamber? Who let you in? I'll strangle that wretched servant if ever I discover his name!"

At the sound of her husband's raised voice, Helen returned to the room. She seemed startled by Eddie and Gerry's appearance, but Eddie immediately put her fears to rest.

"We're so sorry if we upset you, Mrs. Huntington," he stated in a gentle but firm tone. "My friend Gerald Enis had a key to your home that your husband lent him some time ago, and he came to Grassdale to return it. We knocked at the front door several times, but apparently—in the confusion surrounding your household's most unfortunate circumstances—none of the servants heard us. So Mr. Enis and I took the liberty of letting ourselves in. I apologize again for taking advantage of your hospitality."

"Who are you?" Helen asked warily.

Eddie cleared his throat and dipped his head in a small bow. "I am the Reverend Edward Rochester, a Methodist minister. My friend Mr. Enis is an old acquaintance of your husband from several years back. They used to socialize on occasion at Lord

Lowborough's house in London. I believe you may have met him once before, in passing."

A brief look of disgust washed over Helen's face as she examined Gerry more carefully, but she quickly composed herself. "Is this true, Arthur?" she asked her husband. "Do you know these gentlemen?"

"I know Gerald," he replied. "But I'm surprised to find him in the company of a Methodist minister. Any man of the cloth would be a most unlikely companion for the gentleman I befriended in London." Arthur glared at Eddie, then curled his lips into a twisted smile. "However, I *do* seem to remember Gerald having a friend who looked very much like you. A poor singing poet who sang poems very poorly. He called himself 'Eddie'."

Eddie clasped his hands together solemnly as if in prayer. "Ah, you must be referring to my twin brother Edgar. It was he who introduced me to Gerald."

"Well, the devil take you, Edward or Edgar, or whatever your name may be!" Arthur shouted. "I will have no clergyman saying prayers over my body! Off with you! Go comfort my wife. She's more in need of your empty promises of condolence than I am."

Eddie turned towards Helen. "I should be honored to pray with Mrs. Huntington while her husband converses with our mutual friend, if it would so please her."

Helen looked up at Eddie with relief in her eyes and offered to take him to her parlor.

"There's a good lad," Arthur sneered as Eddie started walking to the door. "Go see if you can call down some manna from heaven while you're gossiping with Jesus! I'm hungry!"

Eddie tossed Gerry a knowing smile, then turned to Helen as she reached for the doorknob. "Perhaps you could show me your family Bible, Mrs. Huntington. In Mr. Enis' haste to come visit your husband, he did not allow me the opportunity to fetch my prayer book as we left the parsonage."

Gerry waited for the door to close, then sat down in a chair by Arthur's side. "I was so sorry to hear about your illness," he said softly. "I came as soon as I found out."

"And where did you come from, you gypsy?" Arthur scoffed. "The last time I saw you, you vanished into thin air!"

"Ah! You're referring to my previous visit to your estate, I presume," Gerry replied. "The afternoon we fell into fisticuffs?"

"I most certainly am!" Arthur shouted.

Gerry crossed his arms in front of his chest and forced a laugh. "Well, my friend, if you'd been in as many tavern brawls as my little band of minstrels has, then you'd be good at making quick escapes too. I dare say, my boys could teach a carnival conjurer a thing or two about staging a disappearing act." He leaned towards the bed and winked. "We each just snuck into the woods, one by one, while you and your friends were either blinded by the sun or looking the other way. You were throwing punches so wildly that you didn't even notice we were gone until we were safe inside the shelter of the forest."

Arthur glowered at Gerry. But then the smallest hint of a smile crossed his countenance. "I'm not sure that I believe you, Gerald," he began. "And yet—I do seem to remember Grimsby delivering a few solid blows to both Hattersley and me."

He sighed and rested his head more comfortably against his pillow. "Perhaps you're right, my old friend. That whole day has been reduced to a jumble of tosh in my memory. Indeed—I sent my valet out to look for you and your minstrels, but all he could find was a Hindu Brahman sleeping under a willow tree at the edge of the lawn. So I made him drag the body of that man you claimed was Lord Enis to the side of the Indian interloper. After bandaging my knuckles, I returned to the tree to confront them, but they were both gone!"

Gerry laughed heartily. "I think the sun was playing tricks on everyone that day."

Arthur attempted to laugh but was overcome by a fit of coughing instead. After he composed himself, he wiped a drop of spittle from his chin with the sleeve of his nightshirt. "Please excuse me, Gerald," Arthur apologized. "I haven't been up to dick lately."

Gerry noticed that Arthur's saliva was tinged with blood. He closed his eyes and took a deep breath to calm his nerves, then looked back at his friend. "So what does your doctor say?" he asked, his voice shaking.

"Oh, that man knows nothing," Arthur said dismissively. "He always makes a big show of pronouncing his patients on the verge of death. Then when they recover, he basks in the glory of having rendered their cure and charges double his fee."

Gerry nodded. "So you're not at death's door then?"

"Far from it," Arthur insisted. "In fact, for about a day now, I've been feeling much better. The pains that have been plaguing me have all disappeared. If it weren't for this damned sense of lightheadedness that continues to taunt me, I'd pronounce myself restored to complete health."

"I'm very glad to hear it," Gerry said. He straightened his back and offered Arthur another kind smile. "Perhaps when you've regained your strength, you can come down to London and we can rendezvous once more at Lord Lowborough's house in Mayfair."

Arthur sighed. "Well, I wouldn't count on *that*. I've had a bit of a falling out with his lordship. He seems to be under the impression that his wife's friendship with me was becoming detrimental to her—or should I say to *his*—reputation. That bald-faced, shallow hypocrite! He cares for nothing but how society sees him! Any hint of scandal that might keep his obsequious inferiors from falling at his feet is enough to make him cut off all ties with his oldest friends."

Gerry felt a sudden rush of affection for Arthur—delighted to see that even in the face of death, his old friend had not lost his rebellious spirit. He scooted his chair closer to the bed. "So tell me," he whispered. "Did Lowborough ever find that nude portrait we hid in his ballroom?"

Arthur chuckled. "No, thank God! While he was berating me for besmirching his name and taking advantage of his generosity, Hattersley snuck upstairs and removed the picture. But Ralph didn't feel comfortable hanging it in his own home, as his lily-livered wife is so easily mortified. So he gave it to me for safe-keeping. It's in my wardrobe over there." Arthur pointed to the large wooden cabinet in which Gerry and Eddie had been hiding earlier.

Gerry stood up from his chair, retrieved the picture, and brought it to Arthur's side. "Damn, this woman is hot," he noted as he held the centerfold aloft for his friend to admire.

"An odd choice of words," Arthur replied. "I would have said luscious. Or perhaps even lascivious. But of course, you always *did* have an unusual turn of phrase."

"I picked up a lot of American expressions on my tour of the States," Gerry agreed. He returned the picture to the wardrobe, then sat back down at Arthur's side. "I've heard that you and your missus aren't getting on very well these days."

Arthur scowled. "How could I possibly be expected to relish the company of that sanctimonious harridan? Honestly, Gerald, I can hardly even recall what it was that attracted me to her in the first place. Perhaps she was more pleasant when she was younger, though memories fail me."

Gerry shrugged. "She has a lovely face," he pointed out.

"Yes, you're right," Arthur agreed with a sad sigh. "But Helen is not, nor has she ever been—if I may borrow your colloquialism—'hot'."

"Hhmm," Gerry mumbled. "Pity that."

"Quite right," Arthur replied. "Like so much else in my cursed existence, my marriage is indeed pitiable."

"Arthur!" Gerry scolded. "Don't let me hear you speak like that—wallowing in self-pity like that spineless jellyfish Grimsby! You're too much of a man to let yourself sink to his level!"

Arthur smiled and grasped Gerry's hand. "Thank you, my friend. That was kind of you to say. I'm not certain if I agree with you, but it's good to know that at least one person of my acquaintance still thinks highly of me."

He turned his head on his pillow and started to nod off. But then another spasm of coughing overcame him. He opened his rheumy eyes and gazed at Gerry imploringly. "I say, good man, could you spare me your handkerchief? I seem to be in need of one."

Gerry reached into the pocket of his rented coat and pulled out a rumpled Kleenex. He straightened out the square of soft paper and offered it to his friend.

Arthur wiped his mouth with the tissue, then held it a few inches away from his eyes and inspected it. "What wondrous items you have at your disposal, Gerald! I have never seen anything like this before."

"It's a brand new product that a paper-mill near Manchester is selling," Gerry fibbed. "The mill owner claims it's more sanitary than handkerchiefs. After you use a sheet, you simply throw it away, so you won't pass along any of your germs or viruses."

Arthur arched his left eyebrow. "Viruses? What in God's name are viruses?"

Gerry took the bloodied Kleenex away from Arthur and rested it on the nightstand. "Never you mind about that," he said soothingly. "Just try to rest. You look a bit peaky."

Arthur clasped Gerry's hand once more and lay in silence for a few moments, then started to cough again.

Gerry reached into the other pocket of his coat to search for a second Kleenex. He found his jeweled snuffbox instead. He pulled it out and admired it for a long moment, then offered it to Arthur.

"I think this might belong to you," he said. "I found it when I was crashing a party in the neighborhood where your wife was staying a while back. The gentleman who threw it to the ground mentioned your name as he tossed it aside."

Arthur took the snuffbox in his free hand and examined it. "I gave this to my brother-in-law, Frederick Lawrence, on my wedding day," he said, his voice beginning to break. "I had no family in London, so I asked him to stand as my witness. I offered him this as a token of my gratitude."

His bloodshot eyes filled briefly with tears. He sniffed back a sob, then handed the snuffbox to Gerry once more. "You keep it, Gerald. You've been more of a brother to me than that worthless lout ever was."

"But it's so valuable," Gerry protested. "I had a jeweler appraise it. I shouldn't—that is, you shouldn't—you should give this to your son. Keep it in your family."

Arthur cupped Gerry's fingers over the snuffbox and closed his hand into a fist. "No, I insist. You keep it, Gerald. And remember me." He pulled his hands away from Gerry and lay back down against his pillow. He closed his eyes and soon fell asleep once more.

Gerry sat in silence for several minutes, watching his friend's chest rise and fall with an arrhythmic, labored breathing. But then Arthur's body began to tremble. A small moan escaped from his lips. What little color was left in his face began to pale, and he started turning a ghostly shade of white.

Gerry's face blanched as well. He leapt from his chair and ran to the door. "Help!" he cried into the hallway. "Eddie! Helen! Somebody! Come here! Arthur's not looking so good!"

Three servants immediately ran into the room and gathered around the bed. "I'll fetch the doctor!" one exclaimed. He started running to the door.

Eddie nearly collided with the servant as he led Helen into the bedroom. Helen let go of Eddie's hand and threw herself over her husband's body.

"No!" she screamed. "No! Dear Jesus, save him!"

Eddie cast a nervous glance at Gerry, then walked over to Helen's side. He rested his hand on her shoulder and spoke in a calm, soothing voice. "Your husband is in God's hands now, Mrs. Huntington. Do not give yourself over to despair. Our Heavenly Father is merciful. His Son, our Lord Savior, Jesus Christ, insisted upon that tenet throughout his Gospels."

He gently nudged Helen off her husband's body, then took her hands in his. Looking directly into her eyes, he began reciting, "The Lord is my shepherd. I shall not want…"

Helen and one of the servants picked up the psalm and started praying along with him. After they recited a few lines together, Eddie released Helen's hands and approached the silent maid.

"Fetch the pastor from the local church," he instructed her. "I shall stay with Mrs. Huntington until he arrives. But arrangements must be made for Mr. Huntington's internment."

The servant nodded and dashed out of the room.

Eddie turned towards Gerry. His crest-fallen face looked almost as pale as Arthur's.

Eddie leaned closer to his friend and whispered, "I'll be with you as soon as I can. But I need to stay with Helen until the doctor or the real preacher gets here. I can't blow our cover."

Gerry nodded and continued to stare blankly at Arthur's lifeless body.

Eddie threw a glance at the door, then turned back towards Gerry. "I think there's someone else here who might be able to comfort you," he suggested. He draped his arm over Gerry's shoulder and led him out of the bedroom.

Standing unattended in the grand hallway and looking as nervous as a trapped mouse was Arthur's small son. Eddie crouched down to the child's level and shook his hand.

"You are the master of this estate now, young man," he said gently. "You have a long road ahead of you. This gentleman was a friend of your father. Perhaps the two of you might like to share a few memories of your dad and help each other through this most difficult time."

Eddie stood up and clapped Gerry on the back, then returned to Helen's side.

Young Arthur scrunched up his brow and gave Gerry a dubious look. "Are you one of the wicked men that my mama warned me about?"

The child's audacity immediately shook Gerry out of his stupor. *He's his father's son, alright,* Gerry thought with an unexpected wave of affection. He crouched down to meet the boy's eye. "No," he replied. "I'm no more of a wicked man than your dad was, though we both occasionally indulged in wicked habits."

He lowered his gaze and spied a small tin soldier lying on the floor. "Did you drop that?" he asked the boy.

"Oh, yes," young Arthur said. He stepped away from Gerry and picked up the toy. "Papa gave me a set of tin soldiers when I was small. I was too young to play with them properly then. But now I've learned all about wars and battles, and I like to line them up and make them fight."

Gerry raised his left eyebrow. "Do you want to be a soldier when you grow up?"

The child threw him an imperious look. "Of course not! I'm a gentleman. I shall be an officer, not a soldier!"

Gerry smiled and asked the boy if he could see the rest of his tin regiment. Young Arthur nodded and led him to his room.

Gerry politely admired the child's toys, then noticed one of the wood-ringed, rope-laced drums that he had played at Lord Lowborough's house in Mayfair. "And what's this?" he asked.

"Papa gave me that as well," the boy replied. "And this too." He reached behind a chair and pulled out a child-sized guitar. "I'd like to learn how to play it, but nobody knows how to teach me." He looked up at Gerry with an earnest expression. "Could you?"

Gerry shook his head. "Sorry, lad, I can't play guitar. Just drums."

The child frowned. "Were you a drummer boy in the Army when you were younger?"

"Something like that," Gerry replied. He sat down on a small chair in the middle of the room and examined the guitar. "Your dad really liked music," he added in a sad voice.

"Yes, he used to sing me funny songs when I was little," the boy replied. "After Mama took me away, I asked her to sing them for me, but she didn't know the words."

Gerry's eyes sparkled, and his lips curled into an impish smile. "And what songs might those be?"

The boy answered by singing the chorus to *Be-Bop-a-Lu-La*.

Gerry chuckled. He stretched out his legs and kicked an Indian rubber ball that lay by his feet across the floor. Then he asked Arthur's son to sing him another song.

The child thought for a moment, then started chanting the nonsensical verses of *Who Put the Bomp?* Gerry chuckled and started singing along in his deep, throaty voice. The boy burst into peals of laughter as Gerry began wiggling and yelling, "Boogity, boogity, boogity shoo!"

"That's my favorite song!" the boy exclaimed.

Gerry nodded proudly. "I taught it to your old man."

"Really?" A thoughtful look came into young Arthur's eyes. "Tell me, sir, do you happen to know the words to *Louie, Louie?*

Every time Papa sings that song for me, he mumbles the lyrics, and I can't understand them at all."

Gerry shook his head. "Sorry, lad. That's how the song is supposed to go."

The child offered Gerry a hopeful smile. "Perhaps when Papa gets better, you can come for a longer visit and sing all of those songs for me along with him!"

Gerry's face fell. The boy obviously had not understood Eddie's remark about his being the new master of the estate. He squared his eyes at the child and offered him his hand.

"No, son. Your papa's not going to get better," he said softly. "He can't. Not anymore."

The child blanched and drew in a deep breath. "Will he go to Jesus?" he asked, his voice trembling. "I've heard him argue with Mama many times. Mama tried to make him pray, but Papa said he didn't want to go to heaven."

Gerry slunk back in his chair and closed his eyes for a brief moment. "That's in God's hands now," he replied in as calm a voice as he could muster. "Neither your mama nor your papa can make that decision. Only God can."

"I hope he's with the angels," the boy whispered.

"Yeah, me too," Gerry agreed.

He opened his eyes and examined the small child standing in front of him—a tiny replica of the man whose friendship he had so cherished this past summer. The boy had the same mop of unruly black curls. The same pointed chin and dark brow. He looked to be on the verge of tears.

"Do you have a teddy bear or something?" Gerry asked, breaking the painful silence that had settled between them. "It might help if you held one, you know."

The boy wiped his eyes with the back of his hand and asked, "What's a teddy bear?"

Gerry sighed and fumbled for words. "You know—um, er—a stuffed toy bear that's meant for cuddling. Named after Teddy Roosevelt, I think."

Young Arthur's lip started trembling. "Who's Teddy Roosevelt?"

Gerry's shoulders slumped. He offered the child a weak smile. "Just some bloke with a funny mustache," he whispered. "Here, come sit on my lap."

The boy dutifully climbed on top of him.

"Now, put your arms around my neck," Gerry directed him.

The boy complied with his request.

Gerry cleared his throat and started singing in a hoarse, raspy voice:

Run your fingers through my hair
And cuddle me real tight.
Oh let me be, oh let me be—
Your teddy bear.

Arthur's son cuddled in closer against Gerry's chest, and both of them began to cry.

* * *

Gerry awoke before Eddie did. He lifted his head towards the window and saw a glorious pink and orange sunset streaked across the San Francisco sky. He stood up from the table where he had been sleeping and rubbed a painful crick out of his neck, then started turning on all of the lamps in the hotel room to keep the encroaching darkness at bay.

Eddie started to stir. He lifted his head and gazed at Gerry.

"I'm sorry," he whispered.

Gerry nodded at him and sat down on the edge of his bed.

"I'm sorry I couldn't be with you after he died," Eddie continued. "But I couldn't get away from—"

Gerry cut him off. "S'alright," he said gruffly. "Helen needed you too. And I think it was probably better for me to spend some time with the kid."

Eddie nodded. He stood up from his chair and started walking towards the bathroom. Then he turned and faced his friend once more. "Just leave your costume on the table after you undress. I'll take care of shipping everything back to Los Angeles. I know you've got a lot on your mind."

"Right," Gerry said without looking up.

Eddie stepped into the bathroom and closed the door behind him.

Gerry sat in gloomy silence for a long moment. Then he summoned his courage, stood up from the bed, and took off his coat. He rested it on top of the table and started untying his cravat.

Then a thought raced into his head. He grabbed his coat, slipped his hand inside the front pocket, and pulled out Arthur's snuffbox.

He held it up to the lamplight. The gems sparkled back at him in a cascade of dancing colors. He brought the snuffbox to his face and rubbed it against his whiskery cheek.

"Goodbye, old friend," he whispered to the jeweled case. "And thank you for the gift. This will help me remember you, and remember to take care of myself too. 'Cause I don't wanna die before I get old."

Chapter Twenty-Four

Seattle, Washington

Eddie held two neckties in front of his striped oxford shirt and examined his reflection in the bathroom mirror. "Which one do you think I should I wear tonight?" he called out to Gerry.

Gerry stepped into the bathroom, stood behind Eddie, and frowned. "Are you mental? Tonight's the last show of our tour! Wear something special! Go out with a bang!"

Eddie furrowed his brow, then followed Gerry into their shared bedroom. "Like what? That bloody psychedelic frock coat and ruffled shirt again?"

Gerry unzipped his garment bag, pulled out the grey suit he had bought in New Orleans, and rested it on top of his mattress. "I dunno," he replied as he examined a stain in his coat's wide lapel. "Maybe that bright blue jacket you wore on the *Ed Sullivan Show* back in June?"

"Alan lost it in Texas, remember?" Eddie reminded him. "Along with your trousers."

"Oh, right," Gerry mumbled. He walked to the closet on the side of their room and pulled out an iron and collapsible board. "I wish I'd packed this suit better. It's all wrinkled."

Eddie slipped his paisley-patterned tie under his shirt collar and threw his rejected necktie on top of his bed. "You're gonna wear *that* on stage tonight?" he asked pointedly.

"Of course I am," Gerry replied. "It kind of symbolizes the tour, don't you think?" He set up the ironing board beside a low chest of drawers and plugged in the iron.

Eddie frowned at him. "You should have Alan do that for you. It's his job to look after our stage clothes."

"I'm capable of ironing my own bloody suit!" Gerry barked. He stretched the sleeve of his coat over the top of the board and tested the iron, then lowered his head and his voice. "Alan's not speaking to me just now. All he wants to do is hang out with Pete and those two fucked-up roadies."

"Right," Eddie sighed. He sat down on the edge of his mattress and twisted his necktie into a Windsor knot. "It'll be good when this tour's over, and Emmett can finally separate them."

Gerry looked over his shoulder at Eddie. "Alan's old enough to choose his own friends."

"Yeah, but those two tossers from Philly won't be coming back with us to London," Eddie reminded him. "And I've heard a rumor that Pete might be getting the sack too, as soon as we finish up tonight."

Gerry shrugged and turned back to his ironing. "Guess I'm not surprised. He never really fit in with the band."

"Actually, I'm not catching the flight back to London either," Eddie added. "I'm going to spend some time with my grandparents in Ohio. And maybe look up some old friends too."

Gerry finished ironing the coat's right sleeve, then started working on its left. "Check out Lightning Louie's cellar while you're there. I might have missed a bottle or two of absinthe."

Eddie chuckled and tied the laces on his shoes.

Gerry ran the point of his iron over the sleeve's folded cuff, then cursed. "Bullocks! I nicked a button!"

Eddie stood up and looked over Gerry's shoulder. "Shouldn't matter. It's just decorative. No one's going to notice."

"*I'll notice,*" Gerry groused. He slammed the iron down on the board, then picked up his coat and examined the chipped circle of tortoiseshell.

"Maybe I shouldn't have returned those suits we rented in Hollywood," Eddie said. "That costume fit you better than this one does."

"Yeah, but this is the coat that carries the memories," Gerry replied. He sat down on the edge of his bed and sighed. "This is what I was wearing when I first met Arthur *and* Gilbert."

Eddie chuckled. "I thought you were wearing pajamas the first time you traveled into the book."

Gerry lowered his head, then started to laugh. "You're right. Maybe I should just wear my jammies on stage tonight. Think Emmett would mind?"

"Yeah, I think he would," Eddie replied.

Gerry rested his grey coat on his lap, then looked back at Eddie. "I suppose I should give you back your bloody book now."

Eddie sat down on his own bed and smiled at him. "*And* my bottle of animation potion."

Gerry made a face at him. "Well, I dunno about that. I was thinking maybe after we get back to England, we might want to travel into the pages of *Treasure Island*. Try being pirates for a change, instead of Pilots."

"Make sure you bring along your Vitamin C tablets," Eddie replied. "I wouldn't want you catching scurvy while you're at sea."

"Hah-hah," Gerry scoffed. He tossed his wrinkled coat on his mattress, then looked up at Eddie with an earnest expression. "So tell me the rest of the story. Do Gilbert and Helen get married once Arthur's out of the picture?"

"Yes. And they live happily ever after," Eddie assured him. "They have a few children of their own and raise them alongside little Arthur."

"Hhmm," Gerry mumbled. "And what about the Mayfair gang—Arthur's old mates?"

"Mixed results," Eddie replied. "Lord Lowborough divorces Anabella after she leaves him for some European count. But then her lover loses interest in her, so she becomes a high-priced continental courtesan."

"Don't tell Tony!" Gerry laughed. "He'll be heartbroken. What about Hargrave?"

"He proposes to a rich widow, but she dumps him on the eve of their wedding. So then he settles for a not-quite-so-rich spinster, who regrets marrying him almost immediately."

"I'm not at all surprised," Gerry replied. "And Grimsby?"

Eddie grinned. "Let me find you the passage." He stood up, fetched his paperback copy of the novel from his suitcase, and rifled through the pages. "Here we go—listen to this." He cleared his throat and started reading aloud:

If you are at all interested in the fate of that low scoundrel, Grimsby, I can only tell you that he went from bad to worse, sinking from bathos to bathos of vice and villainy, consorting only with the worst members of his club and the lowest dregs of society—happily for the rest of the world—and at last met his end in a drunken brawl from the hands, it is said, of some brother-scoundrel he had cheated at play.

Gerry broke into a full-bellied laugh. "Well, that figures. I should have guessed as much. And how about Hattersley? Did he fall to pieces too?"

"No," Eddie said. "Arthur's death affected him profoundly. He retired to his manor home with Milicent, threw himself into raising horses, and became a well-known breeder."

Gerry nodded. "Well, good on him. He always did seem to have a little more sense than the rest of that lot, you know."

Eddie closed the book and threw Gerry a smile. "I'll have to trust you on that. Now you tell *me*—whatever happened to that mysterious character Gerald, who lied about his relationship with Lord Douglas Enis of Cornwall to gain admittance to Arthur's private drinking club?"

"Dunno," Gerry said. He stood up from his bed. "The final chapters of his story have yet to be written. As a matter of fact, I think his story has only just begun."

He scrutinized the chipped button on his coat sleeve once more, then shrugged. "Oh, what the hell. You're right. No one's gonna notice this nick." He removed his silk shirt and ascot from the garment bag and rested them on the mattress beside his grey trousers, then opened his suitcase and pulled out the leather-bound copy of *The Tenant of Wildfell Hall* that Eddie had purchased in New Orleans.

"You know what, Eddie?" Gerry continued. "I think this book has a magic all of its own. I really didn't need that cartoon potion *or* the trippy pills to travel into it."

Eddie gazed at his roommate with a curious expression. "Is that so? Do you think it was enchanted or cursed?"

"Neither," Gerry replied. "I think it was blessed—by Saints Monica and Matthias."

Eddie started to laugh. "Help me out here, Ger. I'm not Catholic."

"They're the patron saints of alcoholics," Gerry explained. "My nans used to pray novenas to them all the time." He lowered his head and stared at his feet. "Both of my granddads were boozers, you know."

"No, I didn't know that," Eddie said in a gentle voice.

"Yeah, they were on and off the wagon all of their lives. They were lots of fun when they weren't hitting the sauce too hard, but when they were in their cups—" His voice trailed off.

"I'm sorry," Eddie said. "You never told me that before."

Gerry looked up and shrugged. "No one in my family talks about it much. But I mentioned it to Arthur once. Then he told me *his* dad could drink *him* under the table."

Eddie folded his arms in front of his chest and nodded. "Now *that's* an impressive feat."

"Well, maybe 'impressive' isn't the best word," Gerry replied. He rested the old book on top of his mattress and started changing into his silk shirt. "I've been thinking about some other things too lately, you know? Seeing you with your granny and granddad in Ohio made me realize how much I miss my grandparents. Pop-pop and Opa are both dead now, but my two nans are still alive. So I might—you know—I mean, sometimes—I'm thinking maybe I should go visit them a little bit more after I get back to England. While I still can."

Eddie nodded. "Sharing a little tea and crumpets with your nans sounds like a fine thing to do."

Gerry finished buttoning his shirt and reached for his ascot. "Yeah, well, just on Sunday afternoons, mind you," he insisted. "I'm not gonna go to Mass with them on Sunday mornings."

"I wouldn't expect you to," Eddie laughed.

"And that still leaves six days a week to drink something stronger than tea," Gerry noted.

Eddie frowned at him.

Gerry frowned back. "I'm not talking about laudanum. I'm through with quaffing that crap. I just mean booze."

"Christ, Gerry, didn't you get the moral of this story?" Eddie retorted. "Haven't you learned *anything* from this crazy summer?"

"'Course I have," Gerry said with a sly grin. He raised his right eyebrow in a high arch while keeping his left brow securely in place over his eye. "I learned how to do this cool eyebrow trick. Arthur showed me the secret. It's all in your cheek muscles."

Eddie rolled his eyes. "And that's it then?"

"No," Gerry went on. "I've learned not to ask *you* for advice the next time I'm laid up with a cold. I've had enough book-reading to last me a lifetime." He picked up the leather-bound, water-stained copy of *The Tenant of Wildfell Hall* and lobbed it at Eddie.

The book flew past Eddie's hands and hit the wall with a loud thud. Its torn binding split open upon impact and sent hundreds of pages flying higgledy-piggledy across the floor of the hotel room.

"Oops," Gerry mumbled under his breath. "Sorry about that."

Eddie crouched down and started gathering the loose sheets of paper into a pile.

"Maybe you could take it to a bookbinder and have it repaired?" Gerry proposed. "I'll pay his fee."

Eddie dumped the pages into a rubbish bin, then looked back at his friend. "That's alright. This one's on me. Now change your bloody trousers already! We've got a show to put on!"

Chapter Twenty-Five

New Orleans, Louisiana — Late-August 1967

A small chorus of bells chimed as Eddie opened the door to Madame Francesca's Emporium of Charms. "Hello?" he called into the shop. "Is anybody here?"

"Hold your horses, I'll be with you in a minute!" replied an impatient-sounding female voice from the back room.

Eddie stepped into the store and inspected the merchandise while he waited for the shopkeeper to join him. He threw a quick glance at the corner of the showroom where Signor Paglio had read his fortune two months ago. The long fringed curtains that hung from the high ceiling had been tied shut with a braided rope, blocking his view of Giuseppe's crystal ball.

"May I help you?"

Eddie turned towards the voice. A beautiful Black woman was standing behind the long mahogany counter. Her head was wrapped in an aqua-colored turban. A pink and silver scarf was draped around her shoulders and clasped over her breast with a jeweled brooch. Her lips were painted a bright shade of red, and her eyes were lined with kohl.

Eddie walked up to her and smiled. "I hope so," he replied. "I've come to ask about some potions that I purchased here earlier this summer."

"I don't remember you," she said. "You must have come when I was on vacation. Who sold you those potions—Jo-Jo or Billy Bob?"

"Jo-Jo, I believe," Eddie answered with a smile. "Though he called himself Signor Giuseppe."

The woman snorted. "Well, whatever's good for business," She extended her hand in greeting. Several thin gold bracelets slipped down her arm and collected in a tangle at her wrist. "I'm Madame Francesca."

"It's nice to meet you," Eddie replied, shaking her hand and setting her bracelets jangling with a pleasant tinkling sound. "My name is Eddie Rochester. And I was quite impressed with the potions I purchased here a few months ago."

"Really?" she asked. "And which potions might those be?"

"I bought three—a money potion, a love potion, and an animation potion, though I've only used the animation potion."

She furrowed her brow. "And did it bring something to life?"

"Yes," Eddie said. "I mean, sort of. My friend and I sprinkled it on a book, and the story became alive. We were able to step inside the pages of the novel."

"Is that so?" she replied, sounding very skeptical. "That's quite remarkable."

"Well, isn't that what's supposed to happen?" he asked.

"Dunno," she said. "I never thought to use it that way. It's supposed to make inanimate objects come to life. You know, like a doll or toy. If you mold an animal out of clay and sprinkle some of the potion over it, it might just move."

"And it works when you do *that*?" Eddie replied, sounding even more skeptical than she had been at his response.

"Well, my grandma always swore that it did," Madame Francesca said. "She even taught me how to demonstrate its power—she'd fold a piece of paper into the shape of a bird, then sprinkle a few drops on the creases, and the bird's wings would start to move."

Eddie chuckled. "I suspect the folds in the paper contracted or expanded when they got wet, and gave the illusion that the wings were flapping."

"Yeah, that's what I always supposed too," she agreed. "Though it was a pretty impressive trick. I've never been able to perform it as well as she could."

"So your grandmother used to run this shop before you did?" Eddie surmised.

The woman nodded. "She taught me everything she knew. And I follow her instructions to the tee whenever I make up new batches of potion. Though mine don't generally work as well as the ones she made. Maybe you purchased one of hers—we still have a few in stock. They're the ones in the antique bottles."

Eddie pulled his flask of animation potion out of his pocket and presented it to her. She held it up to the window to examine it in the light before handing it back. "Yup, that's one of hers. You can tell by the imperfections in the glass. The color's not as even as it is in the newer bottles. How much did Jo-Jo charge you?"

Eddie told her how much he had paid for the three bottles.

She threw back her head and laughed, then offered Eddie a kind smile. "Well, Jo-Jo's got a good head for business, that's for sure!" she said once she was able to compose herself. "But don't feel bad, Mr. Rochester. At least you've got yourself some pretty bottles that you can display on a shelf. Some antique dealers come into my shop just to buy my grandma's old flasks. They're real collectors' items."

Eddie drummed his fingers irritably against the countertop. "You seem to be implying that your potions don't really work."

"Oh, they work," she insisted, meeting his gaze and holding it. "Or at least they can. It's all in how you use them. First you have to truly believe in their power. Then you have to use them in the proper spirit. That's what unlocks their magic."

Eddie rolled his eyes. "Well, my friend Gerry certainly believed in this potion's power. He became obsessed with it."

Madame Francesca picked up Eddie's bottle once more and held it back to the light. "How'd he use it?"

He explained the ritual that Gerry always employed to travel into the novel.

She rested the potion back on the counter and rubbed her jeweled brooch thoughtfully. "So you two were always asleep when you journeyed there?"

"Well, more or less. Unconscious, anyway."

"So the potion just directed your dreams."

"No!" Eddie insisted. "In fact, we even brought some objects back and forth between the book and the real world." He told her about the snuffbox, the nude portrait, and Tony's suit.

She furrowed her brow once more. "And were those objects in the actual text of the novel?"

"Well no," Eddie admitted. "But we visited some extra scenes from the book. Parts of the story that the author didn't include in her manuscript. And the objects were in *those* passages."

Madame Francesca cast him a dubious look. "I see," she said, though her voice suggested otherwise. "Tell me, can you think of any other explanation for how those objects came in or out of your possession?"

Eddie considered her question for a long moment, then shrugged his shoulders. "I've wasted too many hours this past summer worrying about that. After a while, I just decided to accept the appearances and disappearances as harmless curiosities."

Madame Francesca curled her lips into a knowing smile. "Well then, it seems to me that you and your friend used this potion in the proper spirit. Books are meant to stimulate your curiosity. They transport you into new worlds where you can learn about people and places you'd never encounter in your usual daily life. This potion made that book of yours become alive to you and your friend on a deeper level than if you had just sat down and turned its pages."

Eddie picked up his bottle and inspected it once more. "I meant to give this to my little brother, to help him with his schoolwork. But I'm a little hesitant to do that now. I think it might be a bit too dangerous for a kid to use."

"Then let me sell you a good-luck charm instead," she suggested. "Your brother could keep it in his pocket whenever he takes a test. The magic won't be as powerful, but it might be a more appropriate gift for a boy. Certainly more traditional."

Eddie nodded. She opened up a hinged, wooden box filled with gold and silver charms. He selected a small trinket shaped like a hawk. "The mascot of my brother's school is an eagle, but this looks pretty close," he said as he reached for his wallet. Then he stopped.

"Those other potions I bought from you," he said hesitantly, "how do they work?"

"Same rules apply," she said. "You just have to use them in the spirit in which they were intended to be used. That money-making potion, for example—it has to be used wisely. If you throw all your savings in some lame-brain, get-rich-quick scheme, then forget about it. No magic potion is going to help you succeed at that. But if you take a small amount of cash out of your bank account and make some thoughtful decisions about how to invest it, weighing all the risks carefully, and then light a candle and sprinkle it with a few drops of potion from that emerald-colored flask—well then, it *might* just be your ticket to financial independence!"

Eddie chuckled. "If I invested my money in the way you're describing, then I'd probably be successful anyway."

"Maybe yes, maybe no," she agreed. "But like I said, you have to have faith for the potions to work. Try to summon up the same sense of conviction that your friend had when he used that animation potion to guide him into the book. Then the powers inside the bottles will be unlocked."

Eddie reached for his wallet again and looked down at the floor. "I'll take another one of those love potions too," he said, keeping his eyes fixed pointedly on his shoes.

Madam Francesca folded her arms back in front of her chest. "Did you use up your first one already?" she asked.

"No," he replied, still not meeting her eyes. "I gave it away."

"Why?" she continued.

He hesitated for a moment, then told her how he had given his bottle to the yogi.

She lowered her arms and tapped her fingers against the counter in a rapid staccato beat. "And did you know this couple—these two hippie lovebirds?"

"No, I never met them," he admitted. He looked back up at her. "But Mr. Bhati felt they just needed something to put a spark to their relationship. He offered me money for my bottle."

"And you took it?"

"No, I just gave it to him. It didn't seem right to take money for it, since—I mean—that would kind of imply that—" His voice trailed off.

"That you believed it was a real magic potion that actually worked?" she suggested.

"Yeah," Eddie agreed with a faint laugh.

"And is that true?" she continued, her voice sharp with challenge.

"I dunno," Eddie mumbled. "I mean—well—when I first bought it, I thought it was just a harmless joke. That it wouldn't hurt to try it. But, well—"

"But after your friend had such success with the animation potion—" she began.

"Then I started to think it might work too," he confessed. "Or, at least, I hoped that it might." He looked back down at the floor. "I haven't exactly had the best of luck finding a serious girlfriend."

Madame Francesca rested her hand on top of his and smiled. "I don't think I need to sell you another bottle," she said gently. "It seems to me that you used yours in the spirit in which it was intended to be used. Love isn't just about finding a pretty girl and kissing her. Love is about sacrifice. Love is about caring for another person more than you care for yourself. You gave away that potion to help two strangers whom you thought might need it, even though you wanted it for yourself. I can't think of a better way to unlock its powers."

"So what does that mean?" Eddie said. He slipped his hand out from under hers and tucked it into his trouser pocket. "That I'll find a girlfriend now?"

"Oh, I don't know. I can't predict the future. That's Jo-Jo's job. I just make the potions." She leaned forward and held Eddie's gaze. "But you know, just between you and me, I don't believe in this Obeah power the same way that my grandma did. I'm a Christian, and I read my Bible every night before I go to sleep. And my favorite passage is that one from St. Paul. You know, the one about love."

Eddie bit his lip and nodded. "The letter to the Corinthians."

Her eyes sparkled as she began reciting the verses: "*If I have the gift of prophecy and can fathom all mysteries and all knowledge, and if I have a faith that can move mountains, but have not love, I am nothing. Love is patient, love is kind. It does not put on airs.*"

Eddie smiled weakly. "That's what Mr. Bhati said to me. He told me to be patient."

"Perhaps he was a wiser man than you're willing to give him credit for," she suggested.

"Yeah, maybe he was," Eddie mumbled. He pulled some money out of his wallet and paid for the charm.

Madame Francesca took his cash, wrapped the silver hawk in a sheet of tissue paper, and handed it to him.

"Be patient," she repeated as Eddie turned to walk away. "Love will come to you someday, Mr. Rochester. Just be patient."

fin

A Note to the Reader

Thank you for reading my novel! This is the third book in my "Rock and Roll Brontë Series," and it was by far the most fun for me to write.

I created the character Gerry Enis for my first novel *Mr. R* (a modern reimaging of *Jane Eyre*) and quickly grew to love him. My initial plan to recast Charlotte Brontë's character "Mr. Rochester" as a rock star hit some snags as I was writing that first book, because I needed to present Eddie as a fairly naïve young man to enable the plot twists I had devised. So I gave my "innocent" Eddie an unabashedly rebellious foil in his drummer Gerry. And I gave Gerry the same last name as my unabashedly rebellious high school friend Kim, who always chafed at the restrictions the Ursuline nuns tried to inflict upon us when we were teenagers.

After I finished writing *Mr. R,* I started plotting out sequels in which I could cast the rest of Eddie's bandmates. The group's pianist Jim got the starring role in my second book *Restless Spirits* (an alternate take on *Wuthering Heights* and *Agnes Grey*). But I knew only Gerry could handle the rigors of *The Tenant of Wildfell Hall*—Anne Brontë's scathing exposé of the evils of alcohol and drug abuse.

Yet I couldn't just have Gerry step into the shoes of Anne Brontë's villainous character Arthur Huntington. That would mean either making Gerry cruel and killing him off (heaven forbid!) or making Arthur loveable and rescuing him from the jaws of death (which would destroy the whole impact of Anne Brontë's powerful cautionary tale). So I thought about ways to have Gerry and Arthur simply meet up for drinks, and came up with the notion of making my novel a hallucinatory road trip, as befitting my literary rock stars.

I tried to humanize the monstrous Arthur Huntington in my book by making him a kindred spirit to Gerry. Arthur was a natural-born "rock and roll" rebel who exuded "bad boy" charm, but had the misfortune of being born a century-and-a-half before the advent of rock and roll. I also suggest towards the end of my novel that Arthur (like Gerry) came by his addictions naturally (both men are descended from alcoholics). Alcoholism is a disease that runs in families, and I believe it is important to be mindful of this.

But I nevertheless tried to show the inevitable destruction that "bad boys" leave in their wake—Arthur makes his wife Helen's life a living hell; Gerry introduces his manager's kid brother Alan to opiates, and starts him down a slippery slope that will lead to heroin addiction in the pages of *Mr. R.*

I also made sure I presented Arthur's obvious faults. Eddie (unlike Gerry) reads the entire text of *Wildfell Hall* during the course of this book, and he never stops reminding his gullible drummer that Arthur is a cruel and selfish man. Moreover, Eddie picks up on the tragic plight of Arthur's wife Helen. Anne Brontë's novel is as much a testament to female suffering and an urgent feminist plea to improve the lot of women as it is a treatise on the dangers of addiction. I didn't include the text of Eddie's conversation with Helen at the end of my book (I focused instead on Gerry's meetings with Arthur and his son). But I'd like to think that Eddie commended Helen on her remarkable strength, and was able to somehow convince her that in the future, women would gain access to better protections under the law.

I wrote the first draft of this book in 2008. I worked on my final revisions during the Covid-19 pandemic of 2020-21. Revisiting my original story—with its prolific traveling and well-attended concerts—was a bittersweet reminder of the freedoms I once took for granted and have since had to set aside. The "band on the run" aspect of this novel now seems almost as mythical as its trippy, pill-popping, time-traveling premise!

Wildfell Summer is many things. It's a contemporary reimagining of a nineteenth-century novel. It's a flashback to 1967's fabled "Summer of Love." And it's an exploration of the lure (and dangers) of drug addiction. But it's primarily a book about friendship.

Gerry and Eddie's friendship forms the cornerstone of this novel. Indeed, as I re-read my original manuscript, I couldn't help but laugh to think that I had reshaped a female-centric, Victorian morality tale into a male-bonding/boys-only road trip! The two rock stars' friendship stretches into the pages of *Mr. R*, where Eddie will continue to help Gerry grapple with his drinking problem. When I daydream about these characters' futures, I like to think that Gerry will eventually get off the sauce. But addictions are hard to break. I'm glad that Gerry always had Eddie in his corner to help him. Arthur had Helen, but I think he might have found greater solace in a male friend (like Gerry) who better understood what he was going through. Yet this was not the case; in *The Tenant of Wildfell Hall*, Arthur dies a miserable, unredeemed man.

But Reader—I don't want to end this letter on a sad note! I had a lot of fun writing this book, and I hope you had fun reading it. I meant this novel to be silly, though I hope it still manages to impart a strong message about the dangers of drug and alcohol abuse.

If you liked this book, please consider reading the other novels in my series: *Mr R – A Rock and Roll Romance* (which includes a lot more background on Gerry's band the Pilots) and *Restless Spirits* (a ghost story which is more of a stand-alone book). Right now, I'm revising the fourth volume in my series. It stars the Pilots' lead singer Tony Wright and was inspired by a novel fragment that Charlotte Brontë left unfinished at her death. I hope to publish it soon.

Until then, I wish you all peace and love,

Tracy Neis

End Notes

I'd like to thank my beta readers who reviewed earlier drafts of this book and offered me their insights: Megan Roxberry; Patricia Courtney; M.J. Buist; Denise Longrie; Mercy Hume; Warren Brown; Paula Roth; Father Jack Wessling; and Mike, Emily, Karen, Laura and Maria Neis.

Special thanks are also due to:

Nicola Friar (author of *The Brontë Babe Blog*) for encouraging me to tell Gerry's story,

My daughter Karen Neis for the beautiful illustrations she created for this book, and

My daughter Laura Neis for lending me her technical expertise in self-publishing (and for preparing and drinking absinthe with me!).

* * *

The following works of literature are quoted in this book:

The Holy Bible: Proverbs 31: 6-7, Psalm 23, and 1 Corinthians 13: 2, 4.

Love and Friendship, by Emily Brontë (published posthumously in 1850)

Romeo and Juliet, by William Shakespeare (written circa 1591-5, first published in 1597)

So We'll Go No More A-Roving, by George Gordon, Lord Byron (written in 1817, published posthumously in 1830)

The Tempest, by William Shakespeare (written circa 1610-11, first published in 1623)

The Tenant of Wildfell Hall, by Anne Brontë (published in 1848)

The following songs are quoted or paraphrased in this book:

A Day in the Life, Strawberry Fields Forever, and *All You Need is Love,* by John Lennon and Paul McCartney (1967)
Brown Eyed Handsome Man, by Chuck Berry (1956)
Kansas City, by Jerry Leiber and Mike Stoller (1952)
I Left my Heart in San Francisco, by George Cory and Douglas Cross (1953)
(Let me be your) Teddy Bear, by Kal Mann and Bernie Lowe (1957)
Mr. Bassman, by Johnny Cymbal (1963)
My Generation, by Peter Townshend (1965)
Ooh! My Soul, by Richard Penniman (1958)
Purple Haze, by Jimi Hendrix (1967)
Who Put the Bomp? by Barry Mann and Gerry Goffin (1961)

Book One in the *Rock and Roll Brontë Series*:

Mr. R – A Rock and Roll Romance

Mad love. Love gone wrong.

A second chance at love. Love gone wrong again.

Rock star Eddie Rochester thought he'd met his soulmate in the passionate Roberta Mason, who inspired him to write a best-selling album of love songs. But Roberta's beauty masked a dark secret that would haunt Eddie for years to come.

Jenny Ayr, the free-spirited daughter of hippies, seemed an unlikely muse to rekindle Eddie's passion for life. But as Eddie fell more deeply in love with the innocent Jenny, his own dark secret threatened to keep him from finding true happiness at last.

This rock-and-roll remix of *Jane Eyre* retells one of England's most famous tales with a British-invasion-era twist, combining classic rock with classic literature to create an unforgettable mash-up of a love story that will make your heart sing!

Book Two in the *Rock and Roll Brontë Series*:

Restless Spirits

Bad luck happens in threes.

Or so it would seem for British Invasion era keyboardist Jim McCudden. First his car conks out on him in a desolate patch of Northern Ohio farmland. Then he suffers a crippling injury while seeking shelter in a seemingly abandoned cottage. But Jim's troubles really begin when he meets the cottage's proprietors — an ethereal hippie chick named Cathy and her bad-tempered ex-boyfriend Cliff.

Meanwhile, across the pond, English piano teacher Maggie Grayson finds herself hosting more visitors than she can handle when she opens her home to three uninvited guests—Jim's two children and the disembodied spirit of a garrulous governess named Agnes.

This rock-and-roll romp through *Wuthering Heights* and *Agnes Grey* brings together the plots and characters from Emily and Anne Brontë's classic novels in a toe-tapping ghost story that will set your heart racing and your spirit soaring.

Coming Soon:

Nowhere Girl

A night of passion with the man of her dreams...

...leaves Emma Smith feeling like a heroine from one of her favorite romance novels. But in the months that follow her impetuous tryst, Emma slowly realizes that her pop star lover was not quite the hero she imagined him to be.

* * *

Librarian Barbara Chalfont receives a most unexpected Christmas gift when a friend brings her an abandoned child to care for over the holidays. Barbara's suitor Will dedicates himself to tracking down the girl's missing father, but soon discovers that...

...the truth of her past remains just out of reach.

Nowhere Girl weaves two seemingly disparate stories into a single tale that bridges continents and decades. Inspired by a novel fragment Charlotte Brontë left unfinished at her death, this story takes the reader through a series of near misses and missed chances while exploring how the things we want the most are sometimes just hiding in plain sight.

About the Author

Since earning her degree in English from the University of Notre Dame, Tracy Neis has written for numerous publications, including *Cincinnati Magazine, Goldmine,* and *Beatlefan*. She is the author of the Rock and Roll Brontë series of novels—*Mr. R: A Rock and Roll Romance, Restless Spirits* and *Wildfell Summer*—and the young adult collective biography *Extraordinary African-American Poets* (Enslow). She also publishes Beatles-themed fan fiction on her blog, cremetangerine.video.blog, and under the name CremeTangerine on fanfiction.net and archiveofourown.org. A proud Ohio native, Tracy currently lives in Southern California with her husband and four daughters.

Made in the USA
Columbia, SC
29 May 2021